P9-ELX-033

GIRLS WITHOUT TEARS

Also available by T. L. Finlay
(Writing as Traci Finlay)

The Falling of Stars
The Rules of Burken

GIRLS WITHOUT TEARS

A NOVEL

T. L. FINLAY

NEW YORK

This is a work of fiction. All of the names, characters, organizations, places, and events portrayed in this novel are either products of the author's imagination or are used fictitiously. Any resemblance to real or actual events, locales, or persons, living or dead, is entirely coincidental.

Copyright © 2022 by Traci Finlay

All rights reserved.

Published in the United States by Crooked Lane Books, an imprint of The Quick Brown Fox & Company LLC.

Crooked Lane Books and its logo are trademarks of The Quick Brown Fox & Company LLC.

Library of Congress Catalog-in-Publication data available upon request.

ISBN (hardcover): 978-1-63910-080-4
ISBN (ebook): 978-1-63910-081-1

Cover design by Melanie Sun

Printed in the United States.

www.crookedlanebooks.com

Crooked Lane Books
34 West 27th St., 10th Floor
New York, NY 10001

First Edition: August 2022

10 9 8 7 6 5 4 3 2 1

For Tarryn

CHAPTER

1

BLOOD IS EVERYWHERE. Splattered on the countertops, the tile flooring, like a horror movie. It streams into the kitchen sink, flowing down dishes and puddling in a glob of congealed duck fat. I haven't been paying attention, been too consumed in my thoughts. Too busy loading the dishwasher.

I drop the glass back in the sink and scour my hands—right first. Fingers, check. Palm, check. Heart line, sun line, life line—check.

It's my left hand that's the problem. My marriage line—the one a palm reader once said would render me a spinster—is no longer a line, but a deep, jagged valley with a red river flowing off my skin.

I've sliced my hand wide open.

Grabbing a kitchen towel, I sop my blood-soaked hand and wrap it tightly before navigating to Uber and punching in Miami Regional Hospital as my destination.

Four minutes is all I have before Hilda the Uber driver arrives in her silver Toyota Camry. But my curiosity as to *why* my kitchen is now painted in blood is piqued, and I retrieve the dropped glass to inspect it.

A lopsided V disrupts the circular flow of the rim, and I gaze into the sink to behold the matching triangle of glass. I hate these cheap glasses from Home Goods. This is the second one that's broken in the last week.

My phone pings Hilda's impending arrival, and I haven't even informed my boss that I'll be late to work today.

I don't have time for this.

I wrap a second towel around it, securing it with a gallon-sized Ziploc bag and a flimsy rubber band.

Locking the door to my one-bedroom beach condo with one hand is no easy feat, and I race toward the elevator to avoid a low rating from Hilda. I am nothing if not a courteous rider.

The elevator doors slide open in the lobby, and Vladimir, the maintenance worker, is pushing a cart of groceries with an older lady next to him. "Noa! How are—why your hand is bagged?" he asks in a thick accent.

"I'll explain later!" I jog through the white marble lobby and past the security desk. The security guard—a ninety-year-old man with an electrolarynx and a Napoleon complex—is fast asleep at his station. I'm sure he's exhausted from his three AM announcement over the building's intercom—assuring the tenants that this is a test, this is only a test—and causing all two thousand of us to shoot straight up in bed with our hearts pounding and ears ringing.

Upon exiting the revolving doors, I pan across the entrance for a silver Camry and spot it at the bottom of the driveway, partially hidden behind some newly planted palm trees. "Good afternoon, Hilda," I say as I slip into the back seat.

Hilda is a young girl, college age maybe, and she smiles at me in her rearview mirror. "Noa, right? You're headed to Miami Regional Hospital?" She turns around and starts when she sees my bandaged hand. "Oh, no! What happened to you? You sure you don't need an ambulance?"

I cradle my hand as she merges back into traffic on A1A. "I'm okay. I cut myself on a broken glass."

Hilda looks at me in the rearview mirror like I'm a hitchhiker who just wielded a gun. "Doesn't that hurt? I know cuts like that bleed a lot. Thanks for wrapping it, by the way. I'd hate to have blood all over my car."

"You're welcome."

We're silent, and I gaze out the window toward the Atlantic Ocean. Parasailers glide through the atmosphere as tourists scoot along the sidewalks on their Segways and locals jog through the sands of South Beach. The pace of the city will soon shift from this leisurely one to speedy and desperate—thanks to the thunderclouds hovering over the ocean like a massive gray ghost. It won't haunt us for long; storms in Miami are more of a nuisance, lasting ten minutes before the sun returns and erases them from our memories. Hilda says something, but I can't hear it over the thumping bass of a Bugatti behind us.

"I'm sorry, what was that?" I yell.

She rolls down her window to flick him off and purposely slams on her brakes. He lays on his horn and she darts down a side street, passing a bright pink boutique hotel and a parking garage. "Morons in this town. All of them. Miami is full of morons. I asked you why you're not screaming in pain. I'm getting the heebie-jeebies right now, and you're acting so calm."

I chuckle and think to myself, *Here we go* . . . "Oh, yeah. That. No, I'm not in pain. I don't feel pain."

I shrug when I catch her eye in the rearview mirror again.

"What are you, Wonder Woman?"

No, I tell her, I'm not Wonder Woman. And I launch into the tale of Noa Romwell and Her Congenital Insensitivity to Pain with Anhidrosis—or for short, CIPA. It's a rare condition, I say, where my body just doesn't feel pain. Nor does it allow me to sweat.

Hilda shakes her head thoughtfully as if pulling herself from a trance. "You *don't feel pain*? That's . . . amazing. My life would be a lot easier if I didn't feel pain."

This is why I generally don't tell people about my condition. They never understand. I thought Hilda would, though; she has kind, trusting eyes. But kind and trusting doesn't always translate to empathy.

I breathe deeply before responding. "Most people think that, but it's not a good thing." I share with Hilda part two of my story: when I almost died as a toddler because I had an ear infection for two weeks and no one knew. Followed by part three: when I was eleven, I broke my ankle and had no idea. To this day I don't know how I broke it. But because we didn't get it set early, I ended up having to have three surgeries on it.

My mother knew of one other woman with CIPA; she met her when I was a toddler, shortly after my diagnosis, at a hospital in Jacksonville during a case study. Her name was Jenny, and they kept in touch for a few years until we learned that Jenny had passed away from a ruptured appendix—she never felt the foreboding pain of appendicitis. It cost her her life.

I watch Hilda, this new information mulling behind her eyes, and I appreciate the small nod it results in. For a moment, a tiny sense of satisfaction settles in my belly.

But then her eyes turn to me in the rearview mirror again, squinting and inquisitive. "So if you can't feel pain and you can't produce sweat, does that mean you can't cry?"

It was a mistake to trust Hilda. People like Hilda think there's so much about life I don't understand. I think it's the other way around. Pain comes in many shapes and sizes. It disguises itself and penetrates senses outside of physical touch, senses most people don't know exist. I would know. "I do cry. I'm not a robot," I respond. Ironic, the truth behind those words when they're spoken so robotically often.

I don't want to continue this conversation with Hilda, so I take a moment to call my boss. I'm formulating what I should tell her during the handful of rings before I'm sent to her voice mail. "Hi Janna, I have to go to the doctor this morning—kind of an emergency, er, last-minute thing. I'll be at the office as soon as I'm done. Don't worry—I'll be there for our eleven thirty."

I end the call just as Hilda pulls into the hospital grounds and follows the signs for the ER. "I have so many questions. But we're here. Run. Don't walk." The first round of thunder rumbles overhead.

I thank her and step out into the ominous weather, heading through the doors and toward registration.

The blood. It's dripping onto my pants now.

* * *

The seats in the waiting room are plush, upholstered in blue vinyl and connected by a solitary metal pole running along the bottom. I'm seated next to an artificial plant, drinking black coffee from a paper cup. Rain now lashes against the windows in monotonous waves, lightning sporadically illuminating the wind-tossed palm trees. Across from me is a small girl curled up on her father's lap; she's shivering. I wonder if it's because she has a fever or because it's cold in here. I think—I *think*—it might be cold in here. But I never know. I can only guess by the weight of the air in my mouth as I breathe it in.

Gauging the temperature by how it tastes. That's rich! My high school science teacher said that once. I'd have told him that comment hurt me, but no one would believe me. Because, you know, *I can't feel pain* and all.

The girl looks miserable, and I hope the nurse calls her back before me. I know emergency rooms cater to the more severe cases, but regardless of how severe my injuries are, my lack of emotion generally bumps me down a few spots on the priority list. Once, a woman claiming to be passing a kidney stone waited for twenty minutes, curled up in a tense ball with tears running down her cheeks. "There's one person ahead of you," the nurse said after the woman's inquiry. That person was me. But when a concussed child came through the doors and was taken immediately to the back, the woman fell to the floor, screaming in pain. That conjured up an RN collecting her in a wheelchair, and her sobbing stopped the moment she was escorted to the back. I waited another half hour before being called.

It's hard knowing when it's appropriate to judge someone's trauma, since *thou shalt not judge*. But in the

ER, a little judgment from the staff is necessary, I suppose. I often wonder when that amendment can trickle into real-life scenarios, too.

The father is snuggling his daughter, his eyes locked complacently on the TV suspended from an adjacent wall. I follow his gaze to a news reporter standing outside an attorney's office in Coconut Grove, according to the white block letters above the running ticker tape. A mugshot of a dark-haired woman is plastered in the upper left corner of the screen—*Attorney Arrested for Forging Divorce Papers.*

". . . woman was about to remarry when she discovered that her recent divorce was, in fact, not final."

The screen cuts to a woman—the victim, perhaps, or another attorney—but my phone alarm beeps a cheery tune. I glance at the screen. *Restroom break.* My finger swipes the phone silent, and I glance toward the restrooms, calculating the odds of going in and possibly missing them calling my name, or ignoring the alarm and potentially peeing myself in the examination room. I've never felt the uncomfortable ache of a full bladder, and by the time I feel the pressure, it's often too late.

"Excuse me," I say to the father as I stand. "If they call Noa Romwell, will you tell them I'm running into the restroom real quick?"

He nods, and the little girl rolls her head on his chest to look at me with glassy eyes. She's chewing on her lower lip.

Noa, stop chewing on your lips. Stop! It's bleeding now!

I catch myself before voicing my mother's words and move to the restroom. This little girl doesn't need to be told that. She knows when to stop. Her pain level monitors silly things like how hard to chew your lip before the skin breaks. When to stop biting your nails before tearing into the quick. She knows to move her tongue out of the way before clamping her teeth down. All things I had to manually teach myself.

It takes a little longer than usual in the restroom, thanks to my injured hand. But the extensive stream of urine tells me it's a good thing I went now. That could've been embarrassing. When I return from the restroom, the girl and her father are gone. I sit back next to my stale coffee and continue watching the breaking news. Tara Alonso, twenty counts of criminal charges, nine Florida Bar discipline cases, and I'm wondering who decided this constitutes breaking news. Then for the second time during this news segment, my phone interrupts.

It's my father calling. I consider my phone as it dances and jingles in my lap. He never calls. We aren't estranged, but we aren't entirely close, either. Thankfully, the door to the corridor opens and a pair of scrubs stands in the doorway. "Noa? Romwell?"

I silence my phone and beeline toward the nurse.

* * *

I've just pulled into the parking garage of my office now, complete with Dermabond, a stack of discharge papers, and a prescription for Extra Strength Tylenol that I crumpled up and threw in the back seat the moment I stepped into my car. I stopped telling ER doctors about my CIPA ten years ago when I was eighteen; they either don't believe that I can't feel pain, or they want to run a series of random tests to satisfy their own curiosity—but the only thing that ends up satisfied is my high deductible.

It's closing in on eleven AM, and I'm intensely aware of a meeting in thirty minutes. My company, Thompson-Miller Corporation, just signed a multi-million-dollar contract with the U.S. Department of Transportation to be the official public relations firm for the road construction project on the Florida Turnpike in south Miami-Dade district six, which includes northern connections to the 878 highway heading east toward U.S. 1 and a westbound extension for Kendall residents to commute daily to downtown Miami. This project will take four years, and we will be the medium between the public and the eleven contractors who will make it happen.

My boss is designating a single public information officer for this project. This person is responsible for overseeing the subcontractors and enforcing equal employment opportunities as well as facilitating public meetings with companies and motorists affected by the construction, writing press releases and handling the media, monitoring safety hazards and implementing protection regulations, all with a smile and an enormous paycheck—double what I'm making now. And I'm a shoo-in.

I can't stop smiling. This morning's incident would normally cause a micro-type of spiral, where the reminder of my condition would crawl into my head and nestle like a parasite, effectively ruining my day. On the contrary, I'm about to walk into work now feeling as optimistic as ever.

I'm striding toward the elevator when my phone vibrates in my purse, and I stop to pull it out. My father is calling again. I'd missed a second call from him while the doctor was gluing my hand; this makes three. I'm tempted to frown, as my father has never even called me three times in a year, let alone in one morning, but I can't jinx this optimism. Whatever his news is can wait—and can serve to rival the news of my promotion when I return his calls later.

And so, because the third time's the charm (I need all the luck I can get right now), I raise a Dermabond-laden hand and hit decline.

CHAPTER

2

As an only child growing up, I entertained an imaginary friend. Her name was Millie, and she was my big sister. I pretended that we looked alike and dressed alike, only she was a bit taller because she was a year older.

Millie was my conscience of sorts. I always listened to her, because Millie was wise. She was the one who taught me how to react to others' pain.

I was in first grade when I watched a girl fall from the monkey bars. I remember the loud crack her body made when she hit the ground. To me, it was louder than her screams that followed.

The second thing I remember is the odd bend in her arm when she rolled over. The incongruous bow in her forearm reminded me of the coral snake my dad found in our backyard after it had just swallowed a palm rat.

But most importantly, I noticed everyone's reactions: the boy who screamed, "Oh my gosh!" and ran away, the girls who cried and covered their eyes, and the teachers who tried to hide their panic by telling everyone else to "remain calm."

I watched the chaos quietly as I stood over the crying girl, drinking it all in like I was some sort of tragedy critic. Until a playground attendant grabbed my shoulders and spun me around. "Did you push her off the monkey bars?" she asked harshly.

Shocked, I simply shook my head.

She asked if I was lying, then angled me toward the building and said, "Well then, don't just stand there! Go get the principal! Run!"

I sprinted through the halls, my mind baffled because she blamed me. Why me?

"Because you didn't act like everyone else. You just stood there like you didn't care," Millie whispered to me.

By the time I was back at the monkey bars with the principal, I was sobbing uncontrollably. I felt ashamed for not helping sooner, for not understanding her pain. Millie taught me that day about sympathy.

I also learned that people react vicariously to pain. So throughout the years, I've taught myself to wince when someone falls, to gasp if someone bangs their head, to say "Ouch! Are you okay?" to the kid who falls off a bike. The judgmental stares have dissipated.

Then I started doing it for myself, when those same judgments started manifesting through people who witnessed my CIPA firsthand. I'd flinch when a doctor poked and prodded at my skin, shake my hand while inhaling through gritted teeth when I'd catch my finger in a door, and swear when I'd stub my toe.

Sometimes I feel like my whole life is a game of charades. But there's nothing I can do about it. Pretending is what I do, lest I be judged.

I don't remember how old I was when I let Millie fade away. I'm not sure why I conjured her up as a child, whether from debilitating loneliness or a wild imagination. But I owe my game face all to her.

I'm wearing that face, I realize, as I stand outside my boss's office at 11:29. It's the moment of truth. I've worked at Thompson-Miller for six years and am the epitome of working one's way up the ladder. I work directly for Janna Miller, the co-owner who runs central and southern Florida while Madison Thompson works out of Tallahassee and oversees the northern districts into the panhandle.

Prior to stepping into Janna's office, I tug on the crotch of my trousers and brush off my blazer. I feel the plasticky Dermabond when my hand forms a fist. I'm wondering how much of my ER trip I should reveal to Janna when I feel a hand squeeze my shoulder.

"Good luck" is whispered in my ear, and I turn to see Shelby Seville brisking down the hall, smiling at me over her shoulder. She seems genuine enough. She's also applied for the position, but she's only been working here two years and does mainly administrative work.

"Thanks," I whisper back—mostly for obligatory condolences. I turn back to the door and focus on my breathing.

My knuckles rap three quick times before I enter, and Janna is seated at her desk in front of a wall of windows showcasing the business district of Brickell in downtown Miami.

"Noa! You're here!" she gushes as she stands and greets me with the standard cheek kiss. "Have a seat. Everything went well at the doctor's office?"

I lower into a chair as she moves back behind her desk and retrieves a manila folder. "Oh! Yes, I'm fine, thank you. Just cut my hand, but it ends up it wasn't as bad as it looked." I flash my injured hand nonchalantly before falling silent, my back rigid and the hems of my pants quivering with nerves. Janna is the only person in Miami who knows about my condition, and that's because I had to disclose it to her when filling out insurance forms. She tends to forget about it, which is fine with me, and I feel like it's slipped her mind even now, because she doesn't bring it up.

"I know we've been discussing this opportunity for a while . . ." Janna puts her glasses on and pushes a rogue strand of gray hair behind her ear as she surveys the contents of the folder. "You know what I think of you, Noa. You've been an outstanding employee. Your performance reviews have exceeded expectations for the last six years. You've implemented an optimal communication strategy between federal and municipal agencies, and you've formed strong, professional relationships with some of the biggest engineering and construction companies in Florida."

"Thank you," I say when she pauses.

Her eyes drop back down to the folder. "I would give you this position in a heartbeat. However . . ."

Both my jaw and my stomach drop.

"Madison and the shareholders disagree."

"But why?" My voice shakes on those two simple words.

"This particular project is very . . . how do I say this . . . intense. It involves at least twenty hours a week on site, which you know is very dangerous. To be present at a construction site with angry motorists, comprehensive machinery, and accidents waiting to happen—not to mention the hours spent in the hot sun—they're not sure you're cut out for this with, you know, your . . .

condition." One corner of her mouth melts toward a frown.

I'm shocked that Madison Thompson, whom I've met once, even knows this information—let alone remembers it more effectively than my own boss. "I—but you know accidents can happen to anyone. I'm no more prone to an accident than the next person, and it's actually a bonus because even if it's hot or uncomfortable out there, I won't even feel it! Ha! I can just keep on working!" I thrust my hands out like an infomercial model, telling myself this is not really happening.

Janna smiles sadly and closes her eyes. "I know you would continue plowing through even if your head fell off. But, Noa . . . they're thinking of the liability. Even with your neon vest and your construction hat, imagine if you simply stumbled on some broken asphalt and sprained a wrist—you might not know for days! It's . . . our attorneys mentioned—"

"You think I would sue you?"

Her hands come up defensively. "No. I don't think that. I fought for you, Noa. I wanted you to have this position just as much as you did. But there are other criteria . . . Madison and the shareholders think it's best to keep you away from potential hazards."

I slouch in the most unprofessional manner. "So if someone else goes out there and gets hurt, it's okay? Is this even legal? Isn't this discrimination?" My voice is escalating, I know.

"You need to let me finish. We have a counteroffer for you."

I raise an eyebrow. "What is it?"

Janna sighs and rubs her forehead with an index finger. "I want you involved on this project. I want you to coordinate all the meetings and document EEO time logs, draft all the press releases, and handle all the office work that generally goes to the PIO." She flips her wrist like she'd just abolished world hunger. "And you can work from home, if you want. For the next four years. Ten percent pay increase. How's that sound?"

I blink. "So basically I'm a receptionist? I'm doing the public information officer's bitch work? For half the pay of the public information officer?"

She drops her head and exhales loudly through her nose. "Noa . . . The stockholders denied your application. I don't know what you want me to say. I'm sorry."

My hands grate against my face, and I drag them down until my skin is stretched and I look like Edvard Munch's *The Scream*. "Who's getting the position?"

She hesitates. "Off the record? Shelby Seville."

It takes everything I am not to jump up and scream. "She's only been here two years. Hasn't even done any PIO work," I say to the floor. "She's the goddamn event planner."

"What if I rally for you and Shelby to do it together? Huh? How's that sound? You both can be PIOs for this project. I'll request a twenty percent pay increase, and I'll get you a corporate credit card. Maybe even a company car. What do you think?"

Twenty percent as opposed to double the salary is laughable. A credit card and a car are pointless if I'm working from home. She's grasping at straws, and this conversation is over. I stand and finagle with my long, brunette ponytail. "That sounds great, Janna. Thanks."

She's quiet as I walk out the door.

* * *

Let's meet for dinner, beautiful.

I met Hector at the South Beach Food and Wine Festival last month in February, and a text from him is the only thing that could get me to smile today. I relish this smile, shutting my eyes and rolling my head back. *Where do you want to go?* I respond.

Ch'i in Brickell City Centre.

Asian fusion cuisine. I could go for that. A glance at the wall clock in my office reveals it's 4:53. Almost the end of this horrible day. *See you in twenty minutes*, I type back.

I arrive ten minutes late. Hector is seated near the bar, a bottle of Mi Sueño cabernet and an appetizer of mushroom ceviche in front of him. I sit opposite him and pour myself a liberal glass of wine.

He chuckles. "Good to see you too. Bad day?" Then he pushes the ceviche toward me.

"Hi, Hector. I'm sorry. But good call on the bad day." I push the dish back and take a generous sip of wine.

His fingers glide along the table like he wants to hold my hand, but he doesn't. "What's going on?"

Hector is a lawyer, specializing in workers compensation and general liability defense. I narrow my eyes at him. "What are the laws about discrimination in the workplace?"

At that moment, the server approaches, and I order a sweet and sour pork chop and Hector the Peking duck. "And may I have a gin and tonic, too? Hendricks, please?" I ask.

The server nods and retreats, and Hector eyes me while snacking on mushroom ceviche. "Easy, there. Liquor and wine together, laws about discrimination . . . What's happened, Noa?"

I reach for my wine but then pull my hand back. He doesn't know about CIPA, so the truth isn't an option. "There's this coworker of mine . . . she's got a health condition. She was passed over for a promotion because of it. It was given to someone with less experience." I glance at him to see if he caught the lie.

He widens his eyes and pooches out his bottom lip while twirling his wineglass. "Well, there are a lot of things to factor into this equation. They're not—"

"Actually, never mind. I don't really like the girl anyway." Without thinking, I take a large gulp of wine and wipe my mouth with the back of my hand.

He rubs his chin contemplatively in typical lawyer fashion. Hector is handsome. Tall and Cuban, lean but not too muscular, sculpted black hair and fingers callused only from typing on a keyboard, maybe strumming a guitar on weekends. His face is clean shaven; I wonder—how would he look with a beard? I can't imagine it.

Hector's voice startles me from my thoughts. "So what's going on with you? If I'd wanted to know about your coworker, I would've asked *her* to lunch." He winks behind his wineglass.

I smile at him, flirting, and flip my wrist in a manner that says *nothing*. It's then that his gaze stops on my hand, his eyebrows furrowing. "What's on your palm?"

"Oh, I had an accident this morning," I say as he grips my wrist and examines the glue-covered slice. "Stupid broken glass in the sink. I'm fine, though. ER fixed me right up."

His semi-calloused finger rubs across the binding before he releases my hand. "That looks incredibly painful."

"Trust me, it was." I shake my hand like I've seen them do on television.

He points his chin toward my wineglass and the gin and tonic the server just set in front of me. "Is that why all the alcohol?"

"Yes." I bite my lip until my teeth are no longer squishing into soft flesh—time to stop.

We engage in small talk until our food arrives, and our pleasant conversation continues while we eat. Roy Orbison echoes throughout the nearly empty restaurant, and I pretend to blow on my food every now and then for aesthetic purposes. The server returns with the check, and I insist we split it. Hector obliges but insists on treating me to coffee this weekend. I smile and tell him I'd love that.

His hand rests on my lower back as we head to the escalators that will deliver us back into the bustling world. We're about to approach the awkward moment where we part ways, and I'm wondering if he'll kiss me.

In the month we've been talking, we've only kissed once—the night we met. Too much wine blotted out any caution between us, and the night ended in a sloppy, middle school make-out session and an exchange of phone numbers. We've gone out plenty of times since then—five at least—and we've held hands, hugged, and he's caressed my jaw. I want to kiss him, but I refuse to make the first move.

The escalator deposits us on the ground floor, and I turn to face him fully. "I'm looking forward to coffee this weekend, kind sir."

He smiles warmly, and his hand goes to my hair. "I can't wait, either. Bye, beautiful." Then he kisses my cheek and walks away.

My phone makes two noises as he retreats. One being a text from my father asking if I'll please call him, and the other being my alarm alerting me to go to the bathroom.

* * *

I'm home now, and it's immature, I know, but despite the pleasant dinner I just shared with Hector, I can't stop pouting. I feel like a child all over again, who was forbidden to have fun outside. Only "fun outside" is the adult equivalent of "receiving a well-deserved promotion."

In high school, I wasn't allowed to play sports. Too risky with CIPA, the doctors said. But I itched to run on a soccer field, scoot across a squeaky gym floor while bouncing a basketball or bumping a volleyball. So I begged my parents to let me try out for cheerleading. I promised no stunts—I'll just stand there and thrust my pompoms toward the sky and cheer from the sidelines like any red-blooded American girl.

Then my mother, a conservative Christian, argued that the skirts were too short. A Christian young lady had no business parading around and tempting the boys. A stumbling block. My father, a prideful agnostic by contrast, scoffed and told her to grow up. This wasn't *Little House on the Prairie*, he'd said. It was times like this I actually liked my father. But she brought up another subject which they agreed upon.

The heat, she said. There's humidity in South Florida, and your body doesn't produce sweat. You'll overheat and collapse. At that, I cried. I promised to drink water, not to overexert myself. Please, I begged, just let me stand on the sidelines and pretend to be a normal teenager.

They finally relented, and in the end I was allotted a pity spot on the cheerleading squad. Ten years later,

Janna is *fighting* for me to *share the position with Shelby*. An adult-onset pity spot.

The moon is full. It's shining through my floor-to-ceiling windows, accompanied by the reflections rippling brightly off the soft, black waves, making the ocean look like a piano playing Beethoven's *Moonlight Sonata*. I consider opening the patio door onto my ninth-floor balcony to hear the ocean, but I remember that a storm recently passed and the humidity is probably high. And even though my body wouldn't react to the heat, my air ducts would get moldy and my wall art would corrode.

I sip on lavender tea and kick out the recliner on my sofa. "Netflix," I say into the voice command on the TV controller. As my TV is weighing my spoken command, the current channel is broadcasting a missing person—a child in Everglades City, Florida.

I cancel the loading Netflix and turn up the volume.

The reporter stands in an area I know like the back of my hand: the school I went to for thirteen years. My heart races. She's rambling on about how this child—a six-year-old girl—left school yesterday afternoon and hasn't been seen since.

I can't believe this. In all my years in that tiny town, no one ever even looked at anyone cross-eyed. Crime doesn't happen there. I wonder who the girl is, if she's a child of someone I know. *Say a name!*

My phone rings, and once again, it's my father. Before I'm able to answer, the reporter confirms my fears.

. . . the name of Skye Flynn. The daughter of Zack and Taylor Flynn.

CHAPTER

3

Zack Flynn. My first love. Middle school crush, high school sweetheart. The love of my life. My first kiss; taker of my virginity.

But we were doomed from the start.

Everglades City is the town where we grew up, a dot on the map near the west end of the Florida Everglades.

It's surprisingly touristy, considering the population is steady at four hundred. Since our little city is the last pit stop for travelers from Naples heading to Miami before embarking upon the primitive Everglades, it disguises itself as a charming, historical muse, attracting passersby and leaving a pleasant taste in their mouths. "What an adorable little town!" they say as they continue on to the larger cities. But those who stick around see through the façade. Because while its intentions are good, underneath it all, it's a dangerous land, looking out only for itself. If Everglades City were a person, it would be a sociopath. And its dwellers—the enablers.

Zack and I met the summer between our seventh and eighth grade years, when his parents bought out an airboat touring company. Ever the planner and progressor, my mother waltzed down the street to Zack's family's house the day they moved in—complete with a bouquet of flowers, a homemade key lime pie, and me complacently in her wake. "I heard you're the new owners of Alligator Airboats," she said to his mother. "I'm Marley Romwell, and this is my daughter, Noa. We run Bramble Rose B&B down the street. Want to offer discounts to each other's clients?"

And that was the day our families partnered companies and I met and gave my heart to Zack.

Tall, dark hair and eyes, and oh, was he shy. His mom—Maggie, her name was—said, "Zack, take Noa down to the boathouse and show her the airboats." And she winked.

My mother bristled at that. But alas, it was her idea to visit the Flynn family, her plan to force me into their home. And according to the Scriptures, we reap what we sow.

I was nervous, following the quiet boy with his hands shoved in his pockets and his hair hanging in his eyes. Being thirteen, of course I tripped—more than once. And finally he said, "Oh, look—you're bleeding. Are you okay? What happened?"

I followed his pointing finger and worry-creased eyes down to my feet. Blood trickled from a splinter protruding out of my sandaled toe.

Before I could respond, Zack swooped me off the ground and carried me to the boathouse, one arm around my shoulders and one behind my knees. I clenched my jaw the entire way.

He deposited me onto a picnic table, plucked the impaling shard from my skin, and scurried to retrieve a first aid kit from a lean-to. I watched amusedly.

"This might sting a little, okay?" He was on his knees in front of me and glanced up into my eyes, monitoring my reaction.

I simply smiled and nodded.

Then he gingerly dabbed an alcohol-soaked gauze pad against my flesh, anticipating a reply that never came.

That's also the day Zack learned about congenital insensitivity to pain.

Despite our attempts at having a Jack-and-Diane relationship throughout our teenage years, the elements were against us. Everglades City had traps—living, breathing pitfalls for anyone trying to thrive in such a primitive land. It was survival of the fittest, regardless of progressive America, because nature doesn't care about cell phones and internet and teenagers in love. And it proved that to us the night we gave each other our virginity.

We were sixteen and snuck out for a midnight canoe ride in one of his parents' rental canoes.

With Zack in the front and me in the back, we paddled south toward the Ten Thousand Islands. The sticky night was loud with nature as we navigated through the dark, narrow mangrove tunnels.

Soon we drifted into the opening of a bird sanctuary, and now egrets, ibises, and roseate spoonbills were our entertainment. Zack laid his paddle on the floor of the canoe and slowly shifted his body around to face me. "I love you," he said suddenly.

Something slithered through the glassy surface of the water a few feet away, and a stork brayed from somewhere nearby. "I love you, Zack."

And so began our first time. Not in the canoe, of course—in the boathouse once we returned. It wasn't the conventional first time; Zack didn't ask me if it hurt. We both knew it didn't. He did ask me, however, if I felt it.

I did. And I liked it. I don't know what sex is supposed to feel like, but I know it made me happy—the dopamine flooding my body was euphoric—and seeing Zack so blissful was enrapturing.

It should have been the perfect, most romantic experience ever. Until Zack sat up right in the middle of it all and pointed in horror at my arm. "Oh, god—Noa! Look at your arm!"

It was purple and swollen, the skin stretched to a shiny bubble. Two large dots oozed with blood and pus. "Now that's weird," I commented.

Zack was already off me and scrambling into his shirt. "It's not weird, you were bitten by a spider! Noa, they're venomous!"

In the end, I was given an antivenin from the hospital and a lecture from my parents. I could've died, they'd said. And they were disappointed in me for sneaking out of the house (of course, we left out the sex part). My mother cried that I was backsliding, until my father told her to shut up and sent me to my room.

Zack was on restriction for a week. *Not only did you sneak out of the house, but you put Noa in danger! You know you can't put her in those positions, Zachary! She's not an average girl!*

I knew his mother didn't mean anything bad by that, but it still bothered me. Would he have gotten in so much trouble if it were someone else? Someone who *could* feel pain? Would he only have been scolded then? I found myself wishing I had actually felt the venomous spider bite.

Things fell quiet after that until a year later, with the arrival of Taylor Spells. Taylor moved to Chokoloskee from Tampa when her father's contracting company began building condominiums in Naples, which happened to be the second week of our senior year. She was a junior, and she took our tiny coastal town by storm. Taylor was beautiful, confident, and rebellious. She hated the town and her parents for making her move there. The one thing she loved in that place was Zack.

For the first time in my life, I cried because the pain was unbearable. Words that never made sense to me were suddenly sparking with recognition behind my eyes—ache, burn, throb, sting—they filled my heart, screamed through my veins, festered in my mind and soul.

"It's just been . . . really hard," he'd said the night he shattered my life. "These last few years—I love you, Noa, but I can't anymore. Always with the fear in my mind that something could be wrong with you and it'd be my fault if you didn't catch it in time. I'm always checking to make sure you're not bleeding, not limping, always having to monitor how hard you're scratching your arm or rubbing your eyes—"

"I never asked you to do those things, Zack!"

"—making sure you're going to the bathroom and eating every few hours."

"Is this about Taylor?"

He said no, but it obviously was. They were dating by Thanksgiving.

Hurricane Taylor destroyed my heart and my senior year.

I went to the University of Miami and never looked back. The day I received my bachelor's in communications was the day he proposed to Taylor, and I told my parents I wouldn't be returning to Everglades City. I moved from the college dorms in Coral Gables to my lofty apartment on South Beach, got a great job working for a public relations company contracted by the Florida Department of Transportation, and posted selfies on the beach to showcase my perfect life.

It's been ten years in the making, but I'm happy. I take clients to lunch at Houston's, get drinks with my coworkers at Prime 112, and take dates to Mary Brickell Village, Lincoln Road, and Wynwood. I'm an independent big-city gal with a career and a social life.

I skip watching Netflix tonight and return my father's call. He doesn't answer, but my mother does.

"Zack's daughter has been kidnapped," is what she says in lieu of a greeting or an explanation of why she's answered his phone.

"I saw. I had a missed call from Dad."

"He's with Zack and the family right now. He left his phone at home, you know him. But I know he wants you to come home, Noa. We both do. We're all—everyone is so scared."

The muscles in my neck tense, hands fisting. "Come home? Why?"

I wait as she blows her nose unabashedly. "We need you. We need all the help we can get."

I hesitate. "But you know nothing has changed. I've never been 'needed' in that town. You know I haven't spoken to Zack Flynn since high school, and now I'm just supposed to show up during the worst time of his life?"

My mother, on the other hand, doesn't hesitate. "That's exactly what you should do. This is bigger than a breakup, Noa. There is a child missing. And it's not just

Zack and Taylor you'd be helping. This is a community in crisis."

"Mom," I say softly before things start to escalate, "this community is also quite dramatic. You know as well as I do how they don't connect with me. I would simply be a distraction. Number two on the list of things to gossip about besides the missing child."

A child is missing, my mother repeats. Six years old. Her name is Skye, and she loves kittens and rollerblading. She has brown hair and beautiful eyes, just like mine. She said if she didn't know any better, she would think Zack had a baby with me and not with Taylor.

CHAPTER

4

MY EXERCISE IS swimming. I stay away from the ocean, considering I could get bitten or stung by a stingray or any number of marine creatures and not know until I was dead. Not to mention the universal fear of sharks—I may not feel pain, but fear is something I'm very familiar with.

After hanging up with my mother, I head to the rooftop pool of my apartment building. The pool deck is floodlit by the large moon. There's a thickness in the salty sea breeze as I breathe it in; it's the humidity. I feel its texture and not so much the temperature of it. Not many residents are here tonight, probably because it's a Thursday. But I greet the smattering of patrons with a nod before breaking the surface of the infinity edge pool with my toe, pretending to test the temperature.

I glance around, trying to gauge the others' reactions. A young couple snuggle together in a chaise lounge, consumed with their phones. An older gentleman with a beer belly and a large gold chain observes me, void of emotion.

And seated at a table is another man with a laptop, talking loudly on a cell phone in Portuguese.

With no help from the onlookers, I determine that the pool must be cold, since I remember hearing pools don't warm up until June, and it's March. But to shrink back now would be a delayed reaction, so I stick my whole foot in and quickly pull it out, shivering. I make sure the wrap I put around my Dermabond is secure, then I take a falsified deep breath and dive in.

I bask being underwater; it allows me to avoid their reactions—the shock the others are undoubtedly experiencing on my behalf. My feet kick and my arms stroke as I glide through the cobalt salt water.

A low whistle greets my ears when I finally surface at the other end. "*Ay, que frío!*" the older man says from his chaise. My instincts were right—the water is cold.

"*Yo sé, pero soy fuerte,*" I respond while flexing my biceps. One can't live in Miami without learning some Spanish.

Back and forth across the pool I swim for around fifteen minutes until the incessant ringing of a cell phone stops me. I plant my feet in the shallow end and gaze across the rooftop in search of the owner of the cackling phone.

I'm shocked to see that it's started sprinkling and I'm completely alone. The couple on their phones, the man in the lounge chair, the guy on his laptop—it's like they were never here. I trudge out of the pool toward my now-silent phone.

After drying my hands on my towel, I curse when I see another missed call from my father. I swipe it open and call him back.

"Noa, hi," he answers on the first ring.

"And the game of phone tag is finally over," I joke.

He ignores it and continues with, "Are you busy?"

I squeeze my dripping hair. "Swimming, actually. What's up?"

"It's crazy here. You heard about Zack's kid?"

"Yes, I—" A loud bang spins me around. Once I realize that the wind tipped the giant aluminum pole of a pool umbrella, I place a hand over my heart and continue. "I heard. Any news?"

"Not a thing. Please come home, Noa. Please. We need you."

To hear my father vulnerable does something to my heart. It's unsettling for a parent to utter words usually spoken by their children. This swapping of roles is nearly as unsettling as the suddenly empty pool deck and the mysteriously fallen umbrella. "But why do you need me? What can I possibly do to fix anything?"

He sighs. "The resources in this town are limited. The search party consists of twenty people. You heard that? Twenty people to search the entire Everglades, which is like half the friggin' state. We're falling apart over here. I know these aren't your favorite people in the world, but they're hurting. No one's thinkin' straight. No one cares about your condition anymore, if that's what you're worried about."

I don't want to see Zack. I almost say it.

"How often do I call you, Noa? Ask for favors? Never. So don't you think this might be important? Or have you forgotten where you came from? This whole thing has really messed with our psyche—your mom's and mine. If anything, you'd be helping us if you came home for a bit."

I lower onto a lounge chair. "I guess I just don't understand what—" There is movement in my peripheral vision. I glance up and am face to face with a small child. A boy, probably four years old.

"One second, Dad." I set my phone on the chair, my father's muffled voice at my hip, as this child and I consider each other. His hair is brown and disheveled, his eyes shiny and nearly black. He's wearing pajamas. "H—hi," I manage.

He says nothing.

Noa, are you there? Is everything okay? my father says from the chair.

"Are you lost?" I ask the child.

His only response is a single blink.

After an eternity or two, there's a commotion near the stairs. I tear my gaze from his solemn face to see a young woman appear in the doorway. "Sebastian? *Dios mío*, Sebastian!" She sprints toward him with Vladimir the maintenance worker in tow, her face contorted in a fit of tears. The boy turns to her and spreads his tiny arms, allowing her to envelop him in a hug and a twirl.

"*Ay, mi hijo!* Don't you ever do that again, do you hear me? You had *Mami* scared to death. *Imagínate si te pasara algo.*"

With an open mouth, I watch this bizarre reunion while Vladimir wipes his brow with a quivering handkerchief. I wait for them to yell at me, to call the cops and accuse me of trying to hurt this child.

Noa, what's going on? Can you hear me? Did I lose you?

Finally, she turns to me. "Thank you. You saved my son. I had no idea where he was. We were doing laundry and he wandered off. He could have fallen *en la piscina!*" She waves her hand toward the pool before placing it back on his soft hair, his head nestled into her neck.

"Or zee rrroof!" Vladimir adds, which only serves to intensify the woman's sobs.

I shake my head. "I—I didn't . . ."

"Noa, you are vonderful. You are superrr hero!" Vladimir says. He winks at me, and I bristle.

"Please, don't call me that."

Noa, is everything okay?

I glance down at my phone.

"Sebastian, say thank you to the lady."

"But I didn't—"

"*Gracias!*"

So he can talk.

Noa! What's going on?

I don't know where to focus. "You're . . . you're welcome?" I mutter as I try wrapping my head around this blur of events.

He nods and bounds off with his mother. I watch their backs as they follow Vladimir toward the doors, and when I'm completely alone again, I look at my phone. DISCONNECTED. I don't call him back. I need this day to end.

* * *

There's no chance of sleep tonight. My body is buzzing, my mind a sparking circuit of wires. Thoughts weave through my head like a fishtail braid—Zack's daughter, the promotion I didn't receive, the little boy on the rooftop.

I grab the melatonin off my nightstand and suck on the chocolate flavored pellets. My priorities have been rocked today, my outlook on life altered. Somewhere, roughly eighty miles from here, Skye Flynn is not in her bed tonight. God knows where she is. And then right here, in my own apartment building, a woman endured the worst moments of her life not knowing where her child was. Then there's me—twenty-eight-year-old Noa, who didn't receive the promotion I wanted. My problems don't even fall to the bottom of that priority list—they fall off the list completely.

I don't have children, but I know the adages—a parent's worst nightmare, and the like. I remember the fear and worry in my parents' eyes whenever I was injured or sick, how they went beyond ordinary human lengths to give their only child the most normal life—the girl whose body failed to warn her when something was wrong inside it. I'm convinced to this day the only reason I'm alive is because my parents broke down the door of the universe and said, "Don't you dare take our daughter away, or you'll have us to reckon with." They put the fear of God into the cosmos. So I can only imagine Zack's and Taylor's world has crumbled and disappeared right along with their little girl. Yet here I am, whining over not wanting to face my ex-boyfriend and the girl who stole him from me.

I think of the look on Sebastian's face, the forlorn stare of a child without protection, exposed to every horrific ailment imaginable. And then the face of the mother—raw, unadulterated horror, whose thoughts were weighing worst-case scenarios and multiplying them by billions.

My phone dings a text from Hector. *You up?*

I call him.

"I guess that answers my question," he jokes.

"Hector, you know I'm from a small town west of here, right?"

"I know. Everglades City," he says triumphantly. "You told me on our first date."

I grin like a schoolgirl. "I did. And you remembered."

He chuckles.

"Anyway, it seems a little girl has gone missing."

"Oh?"

"Yeah. My ex-boyfriend's."

He pauses, and I wish I could see his face. Is he jealous? Trying to hide his jealousy? Knowing Hector, he's genuinely concerned. "What happened?" he asks slowly.

I shake my head. "I don't know much. I obviously don't keep tabs on him. I spoke with my parents, and they said she just never came home from school yesterday. And our town—it's tiny, Hector. Crazy things happen here in Miami all the time, but small-town folks aren't used to this." I shudder. "Anyway, they want me to come home and help look for her."

"What are you thinking?" he finally asks.

It's a vague question, but the meaning behind it is clear. "I don't know," I answer honestly, then launch into the story of Sebastian at the pool.

"Wow," he says. "Do you think it's a sign?"

I pause. "Do you?"

"What's holding you back?" he asks instead.

"He dumped me for her." My palm slaps over my eyes. "Ah, it sounds so childish when I say it out loud." He doesn't reply, so I backtrack. "It's not that, though. I left the small-town vibe for a reason. Things that have nothing to do with them—Zack or Taylor. But I'd like those reasons to stay there." I shouldn't have brought this up. If he asks me those reasons, I'll have to tell him about CIPA. But if I don't tell him, then it looks like I'm still not over Zack.

"So if it were the child of someone besides your ex, would you go?"

My jaw freezes; my eyes blink erratically. "Yikes, good question." I chuckle nervously. "You've really put me in a pickle, Hector. If I say yes, then it sounds like I'm trying to avenge Zack. But if I say no, I sound heartless."

Hector laughs loudly. "Sorry, I have to remind myself that not everything is a courtroom. Your priorities are your priorities. And you don't have to defend them to anyone."

Now we're both quiet. After a moment, he says, "I think you should sleep on it."

We end the call, and I eventually drift off. But throughout the night, I swear I catch glimpses of a little girl on my bedroom balcony. I dream-run to the patio door and throw it open, but each time she's already gone.

It's just my dracaena plant quivering in the sea breeze.

CHAPTER

5

TAMIAMI TRAIL IS an interesting road. It's infamously called *Calle Ocho* in Miami—or simply SW 8th Street—acting as a six-lane host to thousands of houses, businesses, restaurants, traffic, and even Florida International University. But there's a specific point at Krome Avenue where everything west is like a whole other world. There's just . . . nothing. It's the beginning of the Everglades, and what was once 8th Street with its stoplights and buildings and Starbucks and people is now simply a two-lane Tamiami Trail with endless swamplands. Native American reservations and airboat tours are scattered every ten miles, and even more scarce are the small shacks with boarded windows and thatched roofs, complete with a 1970-something pickup truck rotting nearby, or an equally haunted-looking structure that simply says *Restaurant*. No one would ever guess it was the same street where a pedestrian bridge collapsed in front of FIU, killing eight people and making nationwide news.

An eighty-mile canal runs along the entire north side of Tamiami Trail all the way to Naples, protecting the wildlife from passersby, or vice versa. It's spooky making the trek home, even in the daylight. Nighttime is absolutely terrifying, since one can't help but imagine all the alligators, rattlesnakes, and dead bodies hidden in the marshes, but driving during the day makes me feel like a tiny speck of dust in an infinite universe.

I wait until I've passed the Miccosukee casinos to call Janna and tell her I'm taking today off and I'll be back Monday. She doesn't ask questions; I'm sure she's giving me space after yesterday's rejection. When I hang up with her, I voice text Hector. *Good morning and happy Friday! I have good news and bad news. Pick your poison.*

He responds a few minutes later. *Good morning, beautiful. Let's hear the bad news first.*

"Hey, Siri. Send Hector a text message." *The bad news is I have to cancel on our coffee date this weekend.*

He sends a sad emoji.

But the good news is I'm going home to Everglades City. I'll be back Monday.

Within seconds, my ringtone manifests through the car speakers.

"You're going to help find the girl?" he asks when I answer.

I tell him yes, that the encounter with Sebastian indeed felt like a sign. "Also, your question—if the child were someone else's? It sort of changed my perspective on the whole thing, made me feel like I was being selfish. Do you think I'm doing the right thing?"

He doesn't hesitate. "You're doing what you feel is right, so yes. Don't be so hard on yourself, Noa. You're only human."

Human. That's all I am. It's all I've ever wanted to be. Not a superhero, not Wonder Woman, not a fragile bubble or a freak of nature—just human. "That's pretty much the best thing you could've said right now."

He laughs—at the absurdity, no doubt. "You're dealing with a lot, Noa. The missing child, a demanding job—which is apparently discriminating against your friend—then there's something I think you're hiding from me . . ."

At first, I think he's referring to my *friend* at work and that he knows it's me who didn't get the promotion. But that's just a sub-lie in the huge genus of lies I've fed him—that I'm a person who feels pain and takes it for granted just like everyone else.

I exhale a blubbery sigh. I'm not ready to tell him.

"Drive safely. I've got to run. Gotta prep for a deposition today. I won't bug you while you're with your family. But shoot me a text if you think about it, if you want to chat or just to let me know you're okay," he says.

I feel myself smiling. "Bye, Hector."

I slip my phone into the cupholder and listen to an audiobook for the remaining hour through the vast, earthy Everglades. It's inevitable that I'm going to see Zack. And Taylor, for that matter—a thought that makes me grip the steering wheel. But I tell myself I'm okay with that—it's been ten years. I love my life; it's a life others envy. I'd be miserable if I were stuck in that tiny town, married to Zack with lots of children, dealing with the same people I've known my entire life and running an airboat touring company. Taylor can have that life. I can be civil. After all, six-year-old Skye Flynn is an innocent, sweet child, and that's what this is about.

I finally turn off onto CR 29 heading south toward my hometown. I've been home a handful of times since I left for college—five Christmases, to be exact, as we alternate the holiday between there and Miami (and those in Everglades City are spent carefully avoiding the rest of the community). Otherwise, when my mom asks me to visit, I suggest a couple of nights in the Keys, or a quick, $99 weekend cruise to Bimini instead—which they love. There are too many haunting memories of this place, and not just of Zack. I was never just "the girl who couldn't feel pain." Because it's a small town with a small mentality, people decided to make their own definitions of CIPA.

It wasn't always extreme, like the playground assistant who labeled me a psychopath after confusing my lack of empathy with a lack of emotion. More commonly, people thought I was completely numb. Can you feel this? they'd ask while poking me in the arm. Yes, I'm not immune to touch, I'd respond. Do you ever get sad? Yes, I'm sad right now, actually. This whole conversation is making me sad.

As with any condition, CIPA affects its inheritors differently. There is a man in Australia with CIPA who can't taste things, so when he appeared in a popular medical documentary, viewers who knew me thought my experiences were exactly as his—that I must be lying about how good or bad something tastes. Others turned to Google and discovered a little girl in Oregon with congenital analgesia who was able to sweat. Well, she's not me, I'd tell them. Hers is without anhidrosis.

It took work to understand my condition, and most people didn't want to stretch their brains beyond their comfort level. And there was no escaping it because everyone here knows everyone, and I was the girl with the medical condition that everyone needed to watch out for.

No one knows me in Miami, and therefore, they know nothing about me. I can choose what I reveal and to whom. Miami is empowering, where Everglades City was stifling—I was always defined.

I never called my father back to tell him I was coming; surprising them seemed like a good idea until now, as I'm cruising by the lighthouse of Everglades Isle—the front door to my small hometown. Not much has changed in the last ten years, I notice as I pass the ice cream parlor, the post office, and the little trinket shops that advertise live bait for sale. Most of the homes are pastel-colored and built on stilts—including the bed and breakfast my parents own. Driving by, no one would know this town is shaken because of a child abduction. It's been almost three full days since Skye's disappearance.

I glance quickly at the high school, tamping down memories of eighth grade when Zack was the new kid in school, and I dragged him around by the hand showing him the auditorium, the gymnasium, the cafeteria, and the library. I remember how the girls stared—all twenty of them in the entire middle school and high school. How my firm grip on his hand clearly communicated my claim to Zack Flynn. For the next four years, at least.

All too soon, I'm turning off the main street and swerving down the avenues to my parents' bed and breakfast home near Chokoloskee Bay, and I pull into the gravel driveway.

Despite the wooden stilts soaring eight feet below, our home looks very colonial with its pale yellow exterior and powder blue plantation shutters. A pair of white rocking chairs adorn the wrap-around porch, and hanging flower baskets dripping with hibiscus and petunias dangle next to wind chimes and an American flag.

The yard is quiet, but my mother's car is in the driveway. It's mid-March, so they probably won't have tenants for the next couple of weeks until spring break. I kill the ignition and grab my purse and overnight bag, heading up the stairs that ascend past the wooden stilts. Immediately, I spot my mother's gallon glass container sitting on the porch, soaking up the hot sun as teabags steep in the broiling waters. A wreath of soft purple hydrangeas hangs from the front door, which I'd figure would clash with the powder blue shutters, but they actually complement them well.

I give three hard knocks to the door and pan across the yard. The white laminate sign that says *Bramble Rose Bed & Breakfast* is gone. The earth seems to tilt a little as I stare at its absence.

The door opens, and my mother's face is the epitome of shock. "Noa!" She's crying, but it seems as though she's been crying for a while, her tears having manifested well before my arrival.

I drop my purse and overnight bag and bask in the comfort of my mother. Moments like this make me wish I could tolerate this town a little more often. Neither of us speaks; she's squeezing me too hard—I can tell by the way it's hard to breathe. I consciously monitor the strength behind my own embrace, lest I end up hurting her.

She finally steps back and looks up at me. She's a little thing, nearly five inches shorter than I am. But she can be as fierce as she is hospitable—and she's the most hospitable person in the world. When I was three months old, she took me to my doctor because I never cried, not even during a horrible diaper rash. The doctor laughed at her, told her to "count her blessings," and handed her a tube of Desitin. It wasn't until I was eighteen months old that

I was actually diagnosed with CIPA, at which point she screamed at my pediatrician and told him she should've sued him back during the diaper rash, all while handing him a tract and telling him he needed Jesus.

Fresh tears glisten in her eyes, a second coat on top of the originals. "You didn't tell us you were coming. Noa, it's been a nightmare around here the last couple of days."

She retrieves my dropped luggage and ushers me into the house, where I'm greeted with the scent of floral candles and freshly baked goods from the kitchen. The New Testament is opened on a table in the foyer with a sign that says Jesus loves me.

My mother has preserved the vintage interior as much as she can—original pine flooring, a stone fireplace in the parlor, and an arched stained glass window on the landing of the staircase. What has been updated are the kitchen and the bathrooms, and my parents spared no expense—rustic modern, my mother calls it. And her 4.9 rating on Tripadvisor says something. Clearly, none of her guests ever stayed long enough for the town to show its true colors.

"Where is the Bramble Rose sign out front?"

I sit at the long, white marble island in the kitchen while my mother extracts a pan of cinnamon rolls from the oven—an action that doesn't surprise me. Baking is a habit of hers when she's nervous or stressed. "I made your father take it down yesterday. There are creeps in this town, Noa, and I'm not playing hostess to anyone until those creeps are behind bars." She fans her oven mitt furiously over the rolls, extending its trajectory toward her face as if trying to dry her tears, as well.

I want to tell her that creeps will always be a risk, and that she could've just slapped on the *Closed For Business* decal they keep for travel and emergencies, but I don't. "Where's Dad?"

"He's at City Hall with Zack and Taylor and the rest of the search committee. Oh! My sun tea!" She drops the oven mitt and bustles to the front door, leaving me alone with the steaming desserts.

Within minutes, I'm dining on cinnamon rolls and sipping sweet sun tea, discussing everything from life in Miami to life in Everglades City. I push my plate away after two rolls. "Best breakfast ever," I comment.

My mother leans against the counter, staring as though she can't believe I'm here. "I'm really proud of you. I know Zack hurt you. It takes a big person to do what you're doing."

I wipe a drop of condensation off my glass. "It's not about Zack. You were right, this is about a little girl. I can't believe this. Nothing like this has ever happened here. Could she have gotten lost? Maybe she fell into a well or something, taking a shortcut home from school—"

She's shaking her head with a defeated look. "The police have searched every inch of land between Zack's home and the school. Spoken with all her friends. They canvassed the entire city in less than twenty-four hours and learned nothing. Someone took her." Tears well in her eyes again. "They had just sold their house too. Were planning to move to Tampa. Zack got a job at a catamaran company, and Taylor got a nursing position in some hospital ER. I can't help but think this is Zack's retribution for stepping out of God's will. The children always suffer because of the parents' sins."

I halt. "Are you saying that God allowed a little girl to be kidnapped in order to punish Zack for something he did as a teenager?"

Her jaw drops—"Of course not, Noa!"—but the angle of her dropped jaw could communicate either surprise at the accusation or surprise at being called out.

I stand and begin placing our dishes in the dishwasher. I love my mother, but I'm unable to listen to her judgmental rants. She's convinced everything bad that happens to anyone is a result of some sin they consciously or unconsciously committed at any point throughout their lives. For example, she claims my CIPA is because she "unequally yoked" with my father. I heard that my entire life—her parable to keep me from straying—but all it taught me was that I am her punishment. We have different worldviews, and we've agreed to disagree on many things, so our relationship is shallow and happy. It's better this way.

"So what's the plan?" I ask.

"Let's go down to City Hall and find out." She places the remaining cinnamon rolls in a plastic container and snaps the lid on with finality. "Your father will be happy to see you." She smiles sadly.

* * *

City Hall—formerly the Old Collier County Courthouse—is a white, neoclassical two-story built in the 1920s, complete with the obligatory four columns in the front. It's situated along a large roundabout, which alienates a cable tower and a tiny building that simply says *Stone Crab Capital of the World*. "This place hasn't changed a bit," I comment.

I'm startled when my mother hoots loudly. "You should've seen it after Irma. Everything was completely underwater."

I don't reply; a puddle of guilt stirs in my stomach. I stayed in Miami during Hurricane Irma. The storm was supposed to hit Miami directly, and my parents begged me to come home. I used the perfectly legitimate excuse that there was no gas in Miami and the traffic was outrageous due to people trying to escape the storm, but in reality, I simply didn't want to come. The beach was in an evacuation zone, so I commuted to a hotel farther inland and hunkered down. But when the storm took a sudden shift and ended up hitting Everglades City head on, I was a wreck for eight hours until I was able to get hold of my mother and make sure they were okay. They'd lost trees and fences, she'd said, but she and my father were perfectly safe—unlike the majority of the town. And that was it. I didn't come help clean up the mess, didn't participate in the rescue missions, didn't assist in rebuilding the town.

My parents wrote it off as innocuous, since "a person with my condition" shouldn't be sloshing through these infested waters anyway, what with the alligators and who knows what sharp objects lurking below. But that doesn't appease my guilt now.

She parks behind City Hall, and I turn off my emotions in sync with the ignition, telling myself this is business, this is life or death, and there's no need to muddle this already horrible situation with my recent guilt and antiquated bitterness.

I feel her eyeing me as we ascend the steps. "You okay?" she asks.

I muster a smile. "I'm fine."

We walk through the door.

Conference tables have been erected in the lobby, playing host to a handful of seated patrons while another handful mingles throughout the hall. I spot my father right away.

He does a double take when he sees me and abandons his party. "Noa? What—come here!" In four giant steps, he envelops me in an awkward embrace.

"Hi, Dad." I focus all my attention on this rare hug and not on who is here, who has noticed me. It's a contradictory moment, the joy of our reunion squelched by the unpleasant situation that caused it.

He finally pulls away and places his hands on my shoulders. He doesn't speak, which isn't unusual for him. Regardless, I am grateful I decided to come home.

That feeling is short lived when a tall, shapely woman with fading blonde hair and a green sheath dress approaches, and I'm swallowed in her arms. "Oh, my goodness, Noa." And she cries for probably the hundredth time today.

"Maggie . . . I'm so sorry about your granddaughter. We're going to find her." I haven't seen Zack's mother in ages. I try remembering the last time I saw her in person—was it really at graduation? She sent me a friend request on Facebook a few years later, but she rarely posts, and I don't seek out the Flynn family on social media anyway.

"Is that why you're here?" she cries. "To help find Skye?"

I nod, but then the air shifts in the room as people part like the Red Sea, and directly ahead are the conference tables. There are two people seated at them, and they catch my eye at the same time. Zack and Taylor.

CHAPTER 6

To be honest, I'd been so preoccupied with the fact I'd be seeing them again that I never stopped to ponder how I'd feel once it happened. And now here I am, beholding the faces whose expressions rival the subjects of a Renaissance painting, and I can't identify my emotions. One thing I do know—this is not fun.

Zack looks the same as he did in high school, only less boyish. He's filled out more, his facial hair no longer clean shaven. A few gray whiskers harmonize among his brown beard, and I'm sure they sprouted within the last couple of days since Skye's disappearance. He stands, his eyes never leaving me, and begins making his way over. I see Taylor still seated in my peripheral vision, but then my view is obstructed.

"Noer?" I hear. "Is it really you?"

I gaze up into the face of Jamie Camden, Zack's best friend—and, by default, my brother-figure—from high school. "Oh, my—Jamie? I haven't been called Noer since—"

High school. I'm unable to say it because Jamie's shoulder is muffling my mouth, and he squeezes me in such a tight hug, my feet lift off the ground. This moment brings a wave of nostalgia, having been called Noer.

It was a foreign exchange student who first called me that, a boy from England—Brady. Tenth grade. Zack and I were branded as a pair with my name first—Noa and Zack. But with Brady's British accent and the vowel at the end of my name, he said "Noer and Zack." Predictably, with six other uncultured boys in our class, the name stuck—even after the "and Zack" was dropped.

For a moment I forget about Zack. I feel like a carefree teenager again, locked in a pleasant hug from an old friend. When he finally breaks our embrace, Zack is standing next to him. They both tower over me, Zack a hair taller than Jamie. Just like when we were kids.

I stand, waiting, while Zack considers me. I'm considering him too. His hands are shoved in his pockets, his tongue licking his lips—not in a seductive manner; it's like he's concentrating intensely on a test question to which he doesn't know the answer.

I don't know how much time passes, but the tangible tension is disrupted when Jamie clears his throat. "Ehhem. Zack, this is Noa. Noa, meet Zack."

Zack and I finally break eye contact and look at Jamie, and the three of us laugh softly, the tension evaporating. Zack initiates the hug; I reciprocate. It doesn't last long enough for me to identify my emotions, much like when I first saw him moments ago, and Jamie doesn't give me a chance to figure them out.

"You—" He shakes a finger at me. "Now you went and made something out of yourself."

I cock my head. "What do you mean?"

"You left this sorry town, moved to Miami, you're rolling in money, living on South Beach! Do you party, like, every night?"

So Jamie has succumbed to the stereotype, the fantasy life Miami projects. Typical, since he was one of the main people who couldn't seem to understand CIPA, always thinking I was numb or insensitive. He once asked me if I could smell things. As if the inability to feel pain rendered my olfactory sense useless. Jamie was one of my best friends, and even though I knew he was joking with his ridiculous comments, some of them still managed to stick.

Regardless, that was a long time ago. And standing here now in front of him, feeling like no time has gone by, I realize how much I've missed him. I haven't gone out of my way to keep in touch—I guess it's because he stayed in the place I've worked so hard to leave behind—and in this moment, I regret it.

So I won't crush his dreamlike résumé of my life he's just described, especially not with Zack here. Instead, I smile pretentiously. "Spying on my Instagram, I see?"

"I'm not spying, Noer. You post the stuff and it comes up on my feed. That's how Instagram works." He's also succumbed to the illusion of Instagram. But technically, he's right. I'm proud of my life. Although I wouldn't say I'm rolling in money; I just have no dependents who suck me dry financially.

"Yeah, I'm not a small-town girl anymore. I'm a big-city gal with a career," I say, faux gallantly.

"You dating anyone?" Jamie asks.

I feel Zack—still silent—staring hard at me. My eyes stay on Jamie. "Yes. A lawyer. His name is Hector." Shame creeps up my throat, nearly strangling. Hector is not my boyfriend. He could be, someday, but I just turned into one of those insecure people who romanticize a budding relationship.

I finally glance at Zack, who is smiling sadly. I remind myself quickly that this isn't a high school reunion, this is not about me. I'm here because his daughter is missing.

I clear my throat. "Enough about me." I dart my eyes between the two of them and finally land on Zack, instigating the initial conversation. "Zack, I'm really sorry about your daughter. I'm praying we find her, bring her home safely."

His facial expression is one I know well. The plummeting curvature of his eyebrows, the downturned lips. It means Zack is taking the blame of the world on his shoulders. He blamed himself the day I stepped on a rusty nail when we were fourteen and discovered it hours later after I left bloody footprints all over his kitchen, when our families took a vacation together to Marco Island and I threw up a pound of crab legs because I didn't know I had the flu, and the only legitimate one—when he broke my heart.

"Thank you, Noa," he says sincerely. "Thank you for helping. For coming all the way here."

I smile and stand on my tiptoes to peer through the valley of their shoulders. "Where's Taylor?"

They both step aside, and there's Taylor still at the table, her head in her hands, weeping. Maggie sits next to her, comforting her as best she can while trying to hold her own emotions at bay. "Oh . . ." I mutter.

Zack gestures toward them. "I'd better . . ."

I nod. "Yes, of course." And he retreats, leaving me alone with Jamie.

"This is . . . wow," I comment.

Jamie pooches his lips and nods. "Yup. Wow."

I take a moment to study Jamie, the changes the years have made on him. Not much—a sharper jawline, thicker skin—but the roguish charm still lingers in his eyes and the dimples in his cheeks. His blond hair hasn't receded one bit, still thick and unmanageable as ever. He has the same mannerisms, his ADHD manifesting through his constantly shifting feet, always rubbing his hands together because he needs to be doing something with them.

Unlike Jamie, I took the time to educate myself on his condition. He was the first person I'd ever met who suffered from ADHD. And by suffered, I mean went undiagnosed. I watched him in class, way back in grade school. No matter what the teachers threatened him with, he just couldn't sit still. Couldn't keep his mouth shut. Couldn't ace a test for the life of him. I knew he tried to behave, and not just because he was genuinely a sweet kid, but because I was familiar with his home life.

Jamie's father didn't take too kindly to the behavior notifications and poor grades he'd bring home. A few times in elementary, I'd walk by Jamie's house on the way to school and hear Mr. Camden's disapproval. It wasn't always yelling; sometimes it was the sound of his belt or his fists. And while I couldn't empathize with the pain Jamie experienced, I empathized with his desire to fit in, to please his parents. We never discussed it; I never told him what I'd heard. He was a happy kid and a loyal friend, and I'm still marveling at how it doesn't feel like ten years have passed.

"Tell me everything," I say.

Jamie sighs and pulls his eyes away from Zack and Taylor. He stares at the ground, his stance fluctuating like a spooked horse. "It's the craziest thing. She was last seen leaving the school. Zack was working down at the docks, Taylor was finishing up her shift at the hospital. She expected Skye to be home by the time she made it back, but she wasn't. By then it was five o'clock. She called Zack, asking if Skye had come to the docks. Obviously, she hadn't."

My mother interrupts, offering Jamie one of her cinnamon rolls on a foam plate. He graciously accepts, and she winks at me before walking away. Jamie takes a large bite and then turns it to me, his eyebrows raised and his jaw masticating.

"No, thank you. I had two at the house." I glance around the hall, noticing that most everyone is enjoying my mother's cinnamon-infused comfort food. I don't remember her pan of rolls being abundant enough to feed this number of people, especially after I'd devoured two, but if anyone can perform a miracle like Jesus with his loaves and fishes, it's my mother.

"Where's Zack's dad?" I ask, panning across the expanse for the fourth time without seeing Logan Flynn.

Jamie takes a moment to swallow. "You don't know?"

"Know what?"

He dips his head while forcing the last bite of sticky dessert down his throat. He could really use some sun tea, but apparently the scope of my mother's miracles doesn't extend to beverages. "Logan and Maggie divorced. Last year."

My hands go to my face. "What?"

Jamie sets his empty plate on a console table and licks icing off his thumb, looking at me like I'm a child who'd just disappointed him. "Noa, how do you not know that? Logan moved to Connecticut. He was having an affair for years."

I'm shocked into silence—the stages of grief a brevity of events flipping through my mind, and I'm stuck at depression. Why did my mother never tell me? "I—I don't know what to say." I was very close with Zack's father while we were dating, and he and Maggie seemed to have a strong marriage. He was a jokester, a hard-working husband and father, and he reached out to me after Zack dumped me for Taylor, telling me how disappointed he was in his son and how I deserved so much better.

"Well, you can start by explaining why you abandoned everyone here," Jamie retorts with a wink.

My shock twists toward him, equally strong. "What?"

Jamie playfully punches my shoulder. "C'mon, Noer. We were best friends. We grew up together, like brother and sister. But once we graduated, you just dipped and ghosted me. No visits, no phone calls . . ."

I cross my arms. "I could say the same thing—about the visits and phone calls, I mean. And you know I couldn't stay here, Jamie. Not with—" I involuntarily glance toward Zack.

He gives me that disappointed look again. "That was ten years ago."

"Right, and ten years ago was when I left. And don't act like I'm the only person who ever left Everglades City. Look, I like Miami. There's nothing for me here." I shoot my arms out to the side, and he relents.

A woman wearing a navy blue pantsuit speaks above the dull murmuring of the hall. "Excuse me, folks. Let's go ahead and reconvene. We've a lot to do." She reminds me of our guidance counselor in high school—the one who pulled me aside after Zack broke up with me and said, *He wants to have children, Noa. With the life expectancy of someone with your condition, he would be too young to be a widower and too old to have to start over and try for a family again.* I shake off the memory—this woman is not her.

"Who's that?" I whisper as the remaining dozen people meander toward the conference tables.

"It's Shelly Howell, the mayor," Jamie returns with an accusatory tone. He points to a slender, aging man next to her. "That's Sheriff Muncie. He's organizing the search party. C'mon."

My eyes land on the man, this Sheriff Muncie, and he's observing me. I realize I'm observing him back and crack a smile. His gaze lingers for a second, then he turns and heads toward the table, my smile unreturned.

"I'm going to grab some coffee," I say to Jamie and brisk over to the coffee pot at the welcoming station to pour myself a paper cup. By the time I approach the table, the mayor lady is standing at one end, everyone facing her. It seems all the chairs are taken.

Zack is seated at the head—opposite the mayor—with Taylor adjacent to his right. The chair directly across from her—also adjacent to Zack—is the only empty one. I grip my coffee and shuffle toward it.

A woman is talking, but it's not the mayor. A mousy senior is ranting from her seat next to the sheriff. "I don't know what kind of mother allows her child to walk home from school."

I nearly drop my coffee, realizing she's aiming this at Taylor. I don't stop to consider any truth behind her words, because that's not the point. Taylor's eyes are red from the rivers she's been crying, her face frozen at this sudden verbal attack. I scrutinize her, the seething woman. I know her. Her son was in our class in high school.

"Mrs. Mason?" I start. "I haven't seen you since eleventh grade. Remember? In the principal's office? When your son groped my butt at a basketball game? Poor Vinny, what's he up to these days? Last I heard he got busted for marijuana. What kind of mother—"

Shelly the mayor interrupts sternly by mentioning that we're all emotional but we're here to find Skye, not to point fingers, and I glare at Mrs. Mason—her eyes and mouth circular in shock—as I lower myself across from Taylor. I probably shouldn't have said that, but being on the receiving end of so much judgment during my years in this town, I'm a little biased toward people who don't mind their own business.

It's not just the Everglades that are dangerous, it's the tongues of those who dwell here—those tiny members that deliver pain even I can feel.

When I finally break my hateful gaze away from Mrs. Mason, my eyes meet Taylor's for the first time in over a decade. She looks exactly the same. Hasn't aged a bit. The only difference is that the mean, condescending look she sported then has morphed into a genuine face filled with fear and pain. And then she does something surprising—she smiles at me and mouths a thank-you.

And I smile back.

At that moment, I set my coffee on the table. A whirl of steam twists upward, and like a reflex, Zack slides my cup toward him as if it were his.

My eyes—along with Taylor's—dart to his face, and my jaw drops when he brings it to his mouth and takes a sip. After another, he slides it back to me and whispers, "It's really hot. Small sips, and blow on it."

I'm looking at him, but I don't know what to say, what to think. Zack just performed a completely unnecessary action—the exact type of action that caused him to end our relationship. I blink and look back at my coffee, and of all the feelings traveling through me at the moment, offended is at the head of the pack.

I glance at Taylor, whose eyes are back on me. I can't tell what she's thinking about this exchange. If I were her, I'd be furious. But then she smiles again. However, it's much weaker than the first.

I move my attention back to the mayor, who has turned it over to Sheriff Muncie. He is covering all the basic search party protocol: establishing City Hall as the command post, expressing the imperativeness of communicating with your partners, the importance of being conscious of traditions and practices while searching Native communities, and schedules for the various shifts. I don't miss the sporadic glances he's shooting at me, and I wonder if it's because he doesn't know who I am or because of my behavior toward Mrs. Mason.

The mayor is pointing at a grid map of the Everglades, specifically at the Big Cypress National Preserve just east of here, and asks for volunteers to scout that area.

Jamie raises his hand.

She scribbles his name on a pad and says, "Okay. Ideally, at least five people would group together, but this is a small community with an even smaller group of volunteers. So two people can search the preserve. Who would like to partner up with Jamie?"

My hand darts up. "I will."

I'm not sure if she knows who I am (besides the woman who just verbally attacked a senior citizen), and her expression gives nothing away. She starts to say something, but Jamie interrupts. "Hey, wait, Noa. Are you sure it's a good idea for you to be traipsing around that part of the Everglades?"

And before I can reply, another woman—I don't even remember her name—concurs. "I agree. Not with your condition."

All one dozen people are staring at me, and my anger is so prominent I have to remind myself I've caused enough drama at a meeting designed to find a lost girl.

This. This is why I left this place. I don't need Zack telling me how to drink coffee, I don't need Jamie harping on my condition, and surely I don't need this stuffy woman dictating what I should and shouldn't do. I want to scream this at all of them, but instead, I surprise everyone—including myself—when I say, "Oh! Oh, that? The CIPA? Yeah, I don't have that anymore."

The sound of palms landing on the table mixes with sputtered gasps, and my parents' faces are the first I see. Both are eyeing me with quizzical looks bordering on comical. "Is that a joke?" my father asks with a twitching grin.

My chair scrapes a noisy tune as I stand. "N—no, I wanted to surprise you, but I didn't think it—with the timing, I didn't think it would be appropriate."

The room is silent, all eyes on me.

"I'm sorry. This is exactly what I didn't want to happen. I said it now because I really want to be useful with this search party. The doctors gave me intensive therapy and injected me with naloxone—" I'm interrupted by my phone buzzing from my pocket, and to avoid the impending stares, I fish it out.

Restroom break.

"Excuse me, I need to take this call." I breeze down the hall with my dormant phone to my ear and sneak into the bathroom, maneuvering into the alarm setting and deleting the alerts that for half of my life have interrupted me every four hours. Because according to what I just said to everyone at that table, I don't have CIPA. So there's no need for a bathroom alarm.

What have I done?

CHAPTER 7

THE ROAR OF my father's laughter rivals that of the kindling burning in the fireplace in their living room, but the loudest noise of all is my mother's glare.

We've returned to their home, the meeting having ended hours ago. From the couch, I gaze into the flickering flames. It's rare to be able to enjoy a cozy fire in South Florida, but it's March, and a cold front has come through for the weekend, probably the last one for the year. It's fifty degrees outside, and the Floridians are basking in it. I don't notice the weather either way, but the fire is pretty.

The source of my father's laughter and my mother's glare: I've confessed everything. "Of course I still have CIPA," I admitted once we were finally alone, away from prying eyes and ears. "They weren't going to let me participate in the search party otherwise. Also, I'm sick of the people here thinking they know what's best for me. You guys know me better than anyone, and neither of you interjected when I offered to partner with Jamie."

My mother asked how I plan on pulling this off. How will I explain when everyone notices me bleeding before I notice it myself, she inquired.

I'll be careful not to bleed, I said. I told her I've been practicing. I gave them my list of masteries: I can wince, flinch, cuss, and yelp. I've managed to identify the types of pressure—the more intense the pressure, the more likely it is that I should be in pain. Twenty-eight years of acting finally is getting its chance to prove itself, I said.

And now, ten minutes later, my father is still laughing.

"Oh, Vaughn! Stop it!" my mother chides.

Degrading was always his preferred parenting tactic, one of the reasons we aren't as close as we should be. Where my mother is austere and religious, my father is lax and irreverent. They're at polar ends of the spectrum, opposing examples of what not to be, and my goal has always been to live somewhere in the middle. Even though his laughter is something I'm used to, it hurts nonetheless.

"You guys have no idea what it's like, having the four hundred people in this town tell me what to do. You see? You see why I never want to come here?"

Now it's like he was never laughing, the shocked look on his face as he stares at me. I see him rolling my words around in his head, debating their color, their texture, weighing his reaction. My father is the type of person to push his boundaries. If you allow him to disrespect you, he will. Case in point—my mother. But he dredges up respect for those who respect themselves. After a moment, he says, "Look, I get it. I don't care what you tell these people. If you want these idiots in this town thinking you've been miraculously healed, well then, bring on the gospel choir."

My mother tosses a throw pillow to the ground. "I don't agree to this! I don't want to lie to our friends and neighbors, Vaughn! Noa, how are you justifying this . . . this lie?"

I consider her question, marveling at her unyielding commitment to her beliefs. "Don't think of it as a lie; think of it more as an experiment. Besides, you don't have to say anything. Tell everyone the truth—that this is the first you're hearing of it too. That you know nothing about it. That's true, isn't it?"

She retrieves the pillow and dusts it off. "I can't believe you're doing this." But I can tell she's acquiescing, the way she's staring into the fire.

"Why are we still talking about this?" My father swats his hand toward the fire. "Search party starts at six AM. I'm hittin' the hay." He stands, and my mother has long given up on reciting the Ten Commandments at him, so she continues gawking at the crackling flames.

I glance at her. Her beliefs are respectable, and some I've even claimed as my own. I appreciate the virtues I learned as a child—sometimes they pop into my head at the most unexpected times—but I know being left alone with her won't end well, so I tell them both good night and head upstairs.

I pass the guest rooms—the Lavender Suite, the Emerald Suite, the Palm Suite—on the way to my old room. I told my mother to feel free to convert it to another guest room, but she refused. *That's your room, Noa. You always have a place to stay here. You're not a guest.*

And yet all I want to be in this town is just that—a guest.

Outside of a new duvet and a fresh set of drapes, nothing's changed in my bedroom. It's the same furniture since high school, the same wall art. Even the picture frames with old friends that I no longer keep in touch with are spread across the dresser. I survey about four of them, and my eyes land on one in the middle. It's Jamie and me at our graduation, along with a girl—I can't remember her name. Jessica, maybe. Or Janessa.

I pick it up and remove the velvet cardboard backing, carefully plucking out the photo hiding behind the displayed one. The one I covered after Hurricane Taylor. It's of Zack and me after a football game our junior year. He's still in his equipment, his hair slick with sweat and his helmet at his side as he grips it by the face mask. I'm next to him in my cheerleading uniform, my arms around his waist. His other arm wraps around my shoulders, his fingers gripping me like he wants to pull me even closer than I already am. And, oh—our smiles. The pristine grins of children in love.

It's a timeless photo; besides the quality, it could've been taken in the '50s or the '70s or the '90s. High school football games—they're classic. The boys play, the girls cheer, and the spectators watch. Parents come out to support their athlete children, and students socialize and flirt with each other. Some things never change.

And some things do.

* * *

I yawn as I step out from the back seat of my parents' car and onto the front lawn of the Flynn residence. A subtle purple haze ascends over the bay, trekking wearily toward the sleepy dark sky. A few stars still twinkle like celestial insomniacs as the colors of dawn blush toward the heavens.

I've seen this house a million times—even at six in the morning—but I never thought I'd be standing out here again. Four other cars are in the driveway, and the three of us silently walk to the front door, where moths perform rain dances around the illuminated porch light.

Maggie opens the door and greets us with silent hugs—mine being the longest. Inside, I purposely pay no attention to what has and hasn't been updated since my last visit. I beeline past the family room where the search party committee has already started gathering and into the kitchen, where Maggie has two boxes of donuts and coffee on the table. Zack and Jamie sit at either end, the feast spread out between them.

"Help yourselves to breakfast," Maggie calls as Jamie pulls out a chair—an invitation for me to join them. I have a vivid flashback of the lunchroom in high school as I lower myself tentatively in the seat.

"Good morning," Jamie says.

"Morning." I smile at him and glace at Zack, who's hunched over the table, his hands folded on the surface. He gives me a slight smile and a pleasant nod. I wonder how much he's changed since high school, how adulthood has battered him or enhanced him. He's a stranger to me now; I've no idea what kind of husband or father he is.

I turn my eyes down to the donuts and grab a plain one. I don't know what to say in light of the reason we're all reunited again, so I pick at the donut and scatter crumbs on the tablecloth. Soft conversation from the family room wafts into the silent kitchen, the three of us its only occupants. I clear my throat and abandon my donut.

"So, Jamie . . . We're going to Big Cypress Preserve? You and I?"

His elbow is planted on the table, his chin resting in his hand as he watches me. "You and me, kid." He rocks my shoulder with a playful punch. "Just like old times.

Remember that field trip in sixth grade? When we went to the Miccosukee Indian Village?"

I stifle a laugh and end up snorting. I very much remember that day—when Jamie and I snuck away from the tour guide as she droned on about her seashell jewelry. We tried stealing an airboat and ended up lost in the swamps. But now isn't the time to stroll down memory lane. Not with Zack and his missing daughter.

"We got in so much trouble," Jamie huffs, then looks at Zack. "It was before you came, and let me tell you. If you were with us, you wouldn't have made it."

Zack gives a courtesy chuckle, and I feel bad that Jamie is poking fun at him at a time like this. "Where's Taylor?" I ask to change the subject.

Zack picks up the remainder of the donut I haven't picked apart and takes a large bite. I ignore the intimacy of it. "She's sleeping. She was out all night with the first shift. Just got home about twenty minutes ago."

I try to imagine being a mother, combing the Everglades during the witching hours looking for my child. It's a scenario I push out of my mind the moment it enters. "How's she doing?"

Zack finishes the donut and pours himself some coffee. He shakes his head. "About as good as you can imagine."

I have no response to that, so I fall silent. I wonder if more people are blaming her besides Mrs. Mason, but I don't dare ask.

Jamie leans forward. "So tell us more about how you've been cured from your superhuman disease. This is huge."

Zack sets his coffee on the table and leans toward me with notable interest.

I shrug as the proverbial curtain rises for my first act—one I've been preparing for since the moment I turned off my bathroom alarm. "It was the craziest thing. About five months ago, I was in for some testing when a new doctor came in and asked if I wanted to be part of a clinical trial. Said they'd pay me four hundred bucks. What did I have to lose? So they injected me with naloxone."

"Isn't that for drug addicts?" Zack asks.

"Yes, but naloxone is an opioid suppressor. I mean, it blocks opioid receptors. And people with CIPA are without Navl.7 channels, so we produce a large number of opioid peptides, which is a natural painkiller. Kill off the painkillers, and . . ."

"You feel pain," Zack concludes. "So one injection does the trick?"

I think frantically, trying to remember the science behind this theory. "No, one injection will last up to five minutes. But add intensive therapy over a period of time . . ." I'm ad-libbing, grasping at anything that sounds like it makes sense.

I've never been injected with naloxone, but I've heard doctors say it on many occasions. They wanted to experiment on me, but my mother would never allow it. I don't even know if it's true, but the conversations are burned inside my brain like a tattoo. *It will only be for a few minutes, the pain*, they'd said. And I can't go wrong with throwing in therapy. Therapy fixes everything.

"So if I kicked you right in the shin, what would you do?" Jamie's eyes twinkle.

"I would—" At that moment, my eye catches a portrait in the dining room of a little girl. It's Skye. I've only seen her most recent school pictures on the news and the *Have you seen me?* ads, and suddenly I'm plunged into a whole new dimension of this hell.

It's a large canvas print hanging over the buffet, iron sconces as its footmen. Skye is the spitting image of Zack—dark brown hair, eyes the color of a fawn—and she's seated on a log in the middle of a meadow. A wreath of flowers adorns her head. She looks like a pixie fairy with a mysterious smile rivaling the Mona Lisa's. She's wearing a green linen dress with a rosebud mouth and cowboy boots. Her hair cascades down one shoulder like a funnel cloud, and suddenly I can't breathe.

I'm spookily reminded of how my mother mentioned she looks more like she came from Zack and me than from Zack and Taylor, and I see it now. Where Taylor is blonde, my hair is wavy and the color of burnt umber—just like Skye's. And even though my irises are blue, her almond-shaped eyes and thick brows mimic mine.

I'm frozen, stuck in this horrific inability to divert my eyes, when Zack places his hand on my arm and I jump, tearing my gaze away from this angel and onto him.

The silent communication between us is palpable. He's blaming himself for Skye's disappearance, thinking if only he were a better father, this wouldn't be happening—even though nothing about this is his fault. And I'm simply absorbing it because I don't know how to respond. My emotions have transcended the hurt I felt when he left me, and those feelings toward him I'd buried are now manifesting in the disappearance of this child, this little girl who has no idea who I am or who I could have been to her father.

I am witnessing Zack's soul—more deeply than I ever did. But the moment dissipates when Maggie enters the kitchen and instructs the three of us to head to the family room.

We're filing out of the kitchen when I hear, "Excuse me, Miss Romwell?" and I look up.

It's Sheriff Muncie, and I notice both Zack and Jamie tensing as they rush into the family room.

"Yes?"

He sticks out a hand. "Sheriff Muncie. I wanted to introduce myself to you yesterday at the meeting. Didn't get a chance."

I slip my hand into his in an awkward shake. "I'm Noa. Nice to meet you officially."

"Likewise, ma'am. From what I understand, you're Marley and Vaughn's daughter? Moved to Miami a few years ago?"

"Yes. Ten years, to be exact."

"You ever met Skye?"

I shake my head and glance in the family room, where Zack and Jamie are hovering near the door. Zack rolls his eyes.

"So what brings you here?" he continues.

I blink. "What you just said. Skye is missing. These guys were my friends forever." I aim my thumb toward Zack and Jamie.

"Uh huh. Uh huh. So you haven't seen them in ten years, but decide to come back now?"

Before I'm able to formulate an answer, a hand grabs my elbow. "She's here for the search party, Sheriff. That's it," Zack says as he tugs me into the family room.

I glance back at Sherriff Muncie. For a man who asks so many questions, the look on his face right now says he has all the answers.

* * *

Within thirty minutes, I'm in the passenger seat of Jamie's truck, and we're headed east on Tamiami Trail toward Big Cypress Preserve. I note the time, calculating that I'll need at least three to four hours before broaching the subject of using the restroom. I wore thick jeans and steel-toed boots, anything to avoid having to pretend to be hurt by scraping my leg on a branch or plunging my foot into a rogue log.

We were provided with various tools to assist in the search—rope, flare gun—and tons of water in our backpacks. Additionally, I brought a karambit knife from Miami, one my father gifted me years ago. It's compact—five inches when opened and claw-shaped. When folded, it's only three inches. It's tiny but lethal.

Jamie rolls the windows down on his truck, his radio a ruckus of country music and oldies. No one in Miami listens to country or oldies, but I bask in the nostalgic chords of my hometown.

We make small talk, catching up on each other's lives outside of Instagram and Facebook for the last decade.

I ask him if he has a girlfriend.

He snickers and slides his hands to the bottom of the steering wheel. "I was engaged. For a year," he says and glances at me.

"Really? To who? Anyone I know?"

His hand goes to his chin, massaging the blond stubble below his dimples. "Jenysis Barlowe, remember her?"

Jenysis! That was the girl in the photo I saw last night. "I do. What happened?"

"She couldn't . . . *handle* me, if you know what I'm saying," he jokes. I divert my eyes. I vaguely remember the rumors in high school about Jamie Camden's erotic sex drive. I'd heard he was an animal (the girls' word, not mine), but I had pushed it out of my head. I was happily dating Zack, and anyway, Jamie was like a brother. The thought of it always disturbed me, much like it does now.

"You're lying. You don't stay engaged to someone for a year and then end it because of . . . that."

He laughs. "No, not *that*. Hey, pervert, get your mind out of the gutter."

Heat creeps up my cheeks. "What then, if not *that*?"

"Nah, nothing. It just didn't work out for us. It's all good, though. So you got interrogated by Muncie this morning, huh?" Jamie says.

I raise a shoulder, grateful for the topic change. "I wouldn't call that an interrogation."

He smirks. "It would've been if Zack didn't pull you away. That man is a joke. I sat at the station for two hours. Zack was there for three. That's five hours lost we could've been looking for Skye, not counting however much time they wasted on Taylor and everyone else."

I think of Sheriff Muncie, my exchange with him earlier, and while he is an older man, it doesn't seem that he's spent many of his years in the police force investigating child abductions. "I'm sure this is all new to him. It's not every day something horrible like this happens in Everglades City."

Jamie scoffs, and we fall silent. My eyes drift to the dry, barren land whizzing by. Palm trees sporadically blot the empty grasslands, green and brown as far as the eye can see. A translucent haze hovers above the earth's surface, casting mirages on the sunbaked asphalt and blurring the severe austerity of the surrounding vegetation. I may not be able to feel heat, but if heat had a color, it would be that of the Everglades.

Soon he navigates down an inconspicuous dirt road, and I perk up. "What is this? I thought we were going to the preserve."

His voice jostles over the potholes, and dust clouds form in our wake. "This is the preserve. It's a back entrance not many people know about. Think about it, Noer. No one is going to hide a kid anywhere near the main entrance of a public national park." He pinches my thigh, and as if by reflex, I jump.

I yelp and swat him on the stomach.

He hollers with glee. "In high school, a pinch like that would've gone unnoticed. Look at you, princess." He tsks at me. "Welcome to the real world."

Initially, I'm proud of myself for my award-winning reaction. But as his words sink in, a bitter flame sparks in my jaw. *Welcome to the real world.* I itch to mention that I never lived in a fantasy land. Instead, I fix my eyes on the narrow trail ahead of us, surrounded by marshes, sawgrass, palms, and cypresses.

"Where is this road taking us?" I finally ask when it feels like we've driven over a mile. "I thought it dropped us in Big Cypress Preserve."

"Oh, it does. My brother and I used to bring our ATVs out here. Trust me, we're at the west end of the preserve. I'm thinking it's best if we start on one end and work our way east instead of starting in the middle and splitting up in opposite directions." He shoots his gaze at me. "You're still a girl, you know. You need protection. From a man like me." He bursts out laughing.

I roll my eyes. "If anything, I need to be *protected* from you. Not *protection* from you."

"You got that right, baby."

I ignore that comment, pondering it. That sounded like flirting. But Jamie? He knows he's like a brother. Before I can analyze it further, he pulls off the trail and puts his truck in park. "You ready?"

* * *

I'd all but forgotten the aura of the Everglades, how every single atom is in a defensive stance. Everything is sharp—from the spiky tips of the palm branches to the dried-out blades of grass. The wind blows, igniting a chorus of off-key whistling across the miles and miles of sawgrass. Major chords clashing with minor chords, haunted harmonies derived from unearthly octaves, relentless. More than once Jamie has winced and covered his ears, and we bask in those moments when the wind stops and the world is once again quiet as a tomb—the only sounds being our sluggish steps and the cawing birds.

We've been plodding through spongy tundra, performing all the protocol we were taught in the meeting yesterday. Calling Skye's name. Keeping our eyes open for anything out of the ordinary—a hair tie, a cardigan, a bracelet. And Jamie has refused to leave my side.

I suggested splitting up to cover a wider path, but he wouldn't hear it. I won't be responsible for another girl gone missing, he said. Besides, this end of the preserve isn't part of the national park, and we could've easily gotten lost in the mangles of trees and brush had we separated. So we stay near the trail—not directly on it, but making sure it's always within sight.

It's been four hours since I've last used the restroom; that's my cue. "Jamie. I have to pee. And I'm getting hungry." I'm sure both are true, but since I can't feel those things, I'm only assuming.

He halts and places his hands on his knees, wiping a bead of sweat from his forehead. I do the same. "The car is a few miles back, Noer. What do you say we take a piss break out here and then head out for lunch?"

I acquiesce and look for the largest, cleanest leaf I can find.

The sun is high in the sky by the time we return to the truck and head back to civilization. "We discovered nothing," I say despairingly.

"Don't worry." Jamie turns onto Tamiami Trail heading west, his eyes peeled for the first thatch-roofed nameless diner. "She's gonna be found. I know it. She's my goddaughter, you know. Did you know that?" His voice has softened, his emotions peeking through his generally playful façade.

I turn toward him and squeeze his wrist. "I'm not surprised at all."

We finally turn into a tiny bungalow in Ochopee. "Where are we?"

"I'm not sure, but I'm sure they have the best fried alligator and frog legs in Florida."

I scoff. "Every restaurant in the Everglades says that."

"Right. Just like every airboat tour claims to be the original." He kills the engine and we head inside.

There are no other diners here besides us. The hostess is an older lady with plenty of spunk who takes us to a table and presents us with sticky menus while heralding that they've got the best frog legs in all of Florida.

The depressing mood lightens when Jamie and I look to one another and burst out laughing, and she simply laughs along. In the end, I order a club sandwich and he orders snapper with jalapeño poppers.

"How hot ya want the peppers?" she asks. "We got mild—them are for the pussies, an' you don't look like no pussy. Then we got medium for the locals, and—oo whee!! We got some that'll put hair on your chest."

Jamie's jaw is working—still reeling from the word pussy coming out of such a tiny old woman, no doubt—and he hands her his menu. "Surprise me."

She returns with a basket of peanuts, and we continue chatting while cracking shells and tossing peanuts into each other's mouths. I catch the most, and we argue over who's winning.

"I'm catching more of them than you are. How is this up for debate?" I say.

"Because I'm making better tosses than you. So that means I'm winning."

"Shut your fat mouth, Jamie Camden. You've always been a sore loser."

He laughs and scoots out of the booth. "I'm gonna hit up the bathroom again before our food arrives."

"Again? We just went in the swamps."

He turns his head toward me as he walks away. "Shut up, Romwell. I gotta take a deuce, okay? Jesus."

When he returns, it's followed by our food. Our server sets our plates in front of us, and I've taken one bite of my sandwich when Jamie swears loud enough to make me jump. "What's the matter?" I ask.

He's fanning his tongue and chugging Diet Coke. "That bitch gave me the hottest peppers, for sure. Sweet Christ on a cracker. My tongue is in hell."

I giggle and eat a french fry.

"Hey, do you remember that time—"

"I won the pepper eating contest, yes. Of course I remember."

We'd gone to the county fair, Zack and I, along with Jamie and whoever he was dating at the time. When a vendor wailed about a pepper eating contest, both Zack and Jamie shoved me toward the tent and yelled, "This girl! She wants to compete!" I'd hesitated at first, until I saw that first prize was a hundred bucks and a fifty-dollar food voucher.

"It's a Carolina Reaper," the vendor had said. "The hottest pepper in the world!"

I ended up competing against five other men in front of an audience of hundreds of spectators. We were seated at a long table with a salad plate in front of us, with one single Carolina Reaper and a glass of milk.

The men's reactions resembled a day care with screaming toddlers. I would have laughed if it weren't so disturbing. I picked mine up and took a single bite. Nothing.

"Whoa, that's enough," Zack said, pushing my hand down when I went for seconds. "You win, babe. Don't overdo it. That thing'll destroy your insides."

He and Jamie laughed and high-fived while I remained stoic as they gifted me my prize.

"My eyes watered just standing next to you," Jamie reminisces.

"Easiest hundred bucks I've ever made."

"Yeah, too bad you can't do that now."

"Yeah. Too bad."

He slides his basket of peppers toward me. "Try one. C'mon, Noer!" he teases.

I laugh. "No, thank you. It's one thing to appreciate the ability to feel pain, and another to purposely inflict it upon myself." I scoot the basket back toward him but only make it halfway when his hand drives it right back.

"Oh, come on! I'll give you a hundred bucks right here if you can do it." He slips his wallet from his pocket and spreads five twenties across the table.

I straighten my shoulders and inflate my chest. I'm seasoned in acting like I'm in pain, but I don't know if I can conjure teary eyes and a runny nose. I can't remember if that happens automatically, but I'm about to find out.

I pick up a pepper and take a dainty bite, chewing for exactly two seconds before sending myself into racking coughs. I make a display of throwing the pepper on the table and scrambling for my drink, wiping my eyes harshly in an effort to make them red, if they're not already.

Jamie doubles over in laughter, clapping with glee.

"I hate you," I tell him between slurps of Diet Coke.

He finally gains control and gathers up his cash. "You lose this one, sister."

I simply smile as we stand to leave. Little does he know—I actually won.

CHAPTER 8

THE NEWS OF Skye's disappearance graces Jamie's radio at least twice while we're in his truck, and each time, I listen raptly. They may have brought it up again, I don't know, because Jamie eventually turns off the radio, leaving us both to our thoughts.

People go missing all the time. For whatever reason. Runaways. Abductions. Deaths. Maybe even alien invasions or time travel. But only special ones get news coverage. I'm still trying to determine the ratio of dynamics to logistics that grants a missing person candidacy for our TVs and news feeds.

About a month ago, I left for work and the traffic was at a dead standstill. There's never *not* a traffic jam in Miami, but this one was abnormally bad, rendering me thirty minutes late. I heard on the radio that they had shut down I-95 south because a body was found on the highway. As if that weren't bizarre enough, Jane Doe had no injuries that would indicate a hit-and-run or even a suicide from jumping off the overpass. No dramatic impact, no head trauma, just one missing shoe. Now isn't that something, I'd thought.

That evening and into the following week, I devoured local websites to solve the mystery of the unharmed, one-shoed corpse. All I'd found was one simple article in the *Miami Herald*. Jane Doe was a prostitute named Sandy. She had allegedly been dumped from a vehicle, already dead. No one knows where her other shoe went. Case closed.

I imagined the reporter who had written the article, slamming the laptop shut once he sent it to the editor and checking that off his list. Now to investigate the real news—*All the rain that has left neighborhoods in the Killian area under six inches of water! Climate change or faulty sewers? Find out next on your local Miami-Dade news station!*

Twilight glitters over the horizon as our search party drags back to Maggie's home. A feast of fried chicken and baked beans awaits us, and my mother has provided Arnold Palmers and chocolate chip cookies, although I don't know when she had time to do that.

Weary bodies move laboriously with exhaustion and despair. We are no closer to finding Skye than we were this morning.

Zack looks especially beat up, I notice, as we file through the front door and head for dinner. Taylor is bustling about in the kitchen, finishing final preparations for the meal. I excuse myself to the guest bathroom to check for any scratches or blood I can croon over before everyone else does. Thankfully, I find nothing.

Upon exiting, I'm heading toward the stack of paper plates when Taylor calls my name. I look up to see a full plate at the empty seat next to hers. She pats at it.

It takes me a moment to realize that Taylor Spells has prepared a plate of food for me.

"Thank you. You didn't have to do this." I sit next to her and gaze at the downtrodden faces mechanically shoveling food in their mouths.

"I wanted to," she replies. "I didn't get a chance to talk to you yesterday. I wanted to say thank you. And not just for defending me against that Mason woman. You've no idea how much it means to me that you're helping us find Skye."

I drop my fork and look at her. Yesterday at City Hall, I thought she still looked like a high schooler. But today I see how the clocks have ticked away at her appearance. Her once full lips are thinned and turned down, a line or two eroded around her eyes. Gratitude is a foreign look for Taylor Spells, one I'm not used to seeing.

She continues. "Noa, I'm sorry about—"

"Don't." I rest my fingertips on her wrist. "It was a long time ago." I turn back to my plate.

"Can we talk? When you've finished?" she asks.

I feel Zack's eyes on us from across the table. I glance up, and he gives me an encouraging nod. How wonderful for him, I think, to have his cake and eat it too—to watch me make friends with the woman he left me for. But guilt shrouds my mentality. What fun is eating cake without your daughter to share it with?

"Of course, Taylor."

* * *

She asks if we can go for a walk, but I tell her my feet hurt from walking all day. They don't, of course, but my body does feel weary and my energy mostly depleted. She doesn't react—it is an average response, after all—and suggests we head out onto the porch instead.

Maggie has a hanging bench swing suspended from the rafters, and Taylor and I settle into it as it rocks gently with our weight. She clears her throat. "Regardless of how long ago it was, I owe you an apology." She leans forward, intensifying our eye contact. "I am so sorry for what I did to you in high school."

It's surreal, this whole situation, and I can't help wondering if it's genuine or riddled with ulterior motives. But regardless of its validity, the closure I've sought for so long is suddenly tangible—dangling between us, shiny and iridescent—mine for the taking. "Thank you, Taylor. That means a lot. Please—let's not talk about that anymore. It's in the past, and I'm doing just fine." I smile.

She smiles too, through her veil of sadness.

"Would it help to talk about it? About Skye?" I ask, initiating the first conversation ever with Taylor Spells.

She leans back on the bench, her posture rigid. "I don't even know what to say. I just don't know how this could happen. You hear of this kind of thing on the news, and the parents always talk about how they never expected it to happen to them. It's so cliché right now, but I really never expected this. Skye . . . she's so perfect. I never even wanted to be a mom, but she was the best baby ever, never cried. I could leave her in her crib for hours. Even now, she's so happy, never gives us an ounce of trouble. She's literally the perfect child."

I give a half smile.

"I became a nurse practitioner early for that reason. I had planned to go to school part time, which I did for the first couple of years. But Skye was practically raising herself. She wanted to go to preschool when she was three, so we took her. Then I was able to complete the accelerated track, and I thought I'd finally be happy.

I thought jump-starting my career would help. It didn't. I was still stuck here in this"—she glances at me—"this godforsaken town. I begged Zack to move us away from here. He finally relented. Everything was working out perfectly. We found a house in Lutz, we both got jobs . . . And then this happens."

I don't know what to say. I remember my mother mentioning her job at the ER, but I had no idea she was a nurse practitioner. And I'd forgotten that they were moving away.

"Everyone is blaming me, Noa. And they're right. I shouldn't have let her walk home alone from school. I'm the worst mother ever. I knew I should never be a mom."

"Stop saying that. You are *not* a bad mom. It's not like she was the only kid ever to walk home from school. Zack, Jamie, and I did it all the time, our entire lives. It's no one's business but yours. Taylor? We're going to find her. I'll make sure of it."

She wipes tears from her eyes. "I know everyone used to call you Wonder Woman, so if anyone can, it's you."

I find it strange that for the first time ever, that name doesn't offend me. Of all the things I've been called in my life thanks to CIPA—dead girl, psycho, Numb Noa—superhero misnomers were the worst. Because superheroes never spent as much time in doctors' offices as I did. But it's different this time. On the surface, this is the first time Taylor has ever acknowledged my condition. So something about this coming from her is saying something. But the context is what stirs my emotions. I will gladly be a superhero if it saves the life of a little girl.

* * *

The hours of sleep weren't nearly enough, and I find myself nodding off the next morning in Jamie's truck. He hits a pothole and it jerks me awake. "My feet are killing me," he says.

"My head hurts," I lie. "How far are we?"

"Couple miles."

I sigh deeply and pray we aren't doing all this for nothing. No one has breathed the possibility of Skye no longer living, although the weight of the elephant on everyone's shoulders speaks for itself.

Taylor looked like a zombie this morning when she returned from the overnight search. She dragged into Maggie's house and collapsed on the floor, tears streaking down her dirty cheeks. I almost ran to her, but it was Zack who collected her off the floor and escorted her home.

Unlike yesterday, Jamie pulls into the main entrance of the Big Cypress Preserve Welcome Center. He parks in the empty lot and we get out and stretch. "We've got everything south of Tamiami Trail, which is the smaller half of the preserve." He turns westbound. "Yesterday we covered that area . . ." He pulls up Google Maps on his phone, and I peek at it over his bicep, noticing that we do, indeed, have the smaller portion of this giant area. Although yesterday it seemed as though we had walked the expanse of the entire earth.

"So here, let's head this way," he continues, gesturing east. "And let's try splitting up today, huh?"

I nod. "I suggested that yesterday, but you were hell-bent on sticking together."

"Well, it didn't work, did it? This is all open terrain, and we can see everything for miles. I guess I gotta let you grow up sometime, huh?" He winks and nudges my shoulder.

"Grow up yourself," I joke. "So what's the plan? Who's going where?"

Jamie chews on his thoughts as he gazes through the lush, watery, tropical vegetation. "The dividing point is the Welcome Center. You take everything north of that. That way you'll be closer to Tamiami Trail, just in case. I'll take everything south. We've got our cell phones, so no need to set a time to meet back up. You got everything?"

I point to my backpack. "Right here."

"Flare gun? Knife? Rope? Water? Pain reflexes?" He winks with a grin.

"I got it all, Indiana Jones. Including this." I pull a small contraption from my pocket and hand it to him.

"A compass?" He turns it over in his hand, then thrusts it back toward me. "You know you have one of these on your phone, right?"

"Yes, but can my phone do this?" I raise one end to my mouth and blow, the antecedent to a high-pitched shriek.

Jamie is quick to swipe my hand away from my mouth. "Nice whistle-slash-compass hybrid. Where did you even get something like that?"

I smirk and slide it back in my pocket. "My job. They give us all sorts of safety gear, since we're on the road a lot and in dangerous construction areas. You're lucky I didn't bring my Kevlar vest and hard hat. I think this was just some leftover promotional item, though."

"Your company gives out glorified rape whistles as swag? Is that to counter other companies' promotional condoms?"

I shove his shoulder. "It's a compass, not a rape whistle. I just found it this morning in my overnight bag, which was also gifted to me from Thompson-Miller. Now, let's do this."

I start trudging into the swamps in my thigh-high rubber boots when he stops me with a hand on my shoulder. I turn around. His face is ashen. "All jokes aside, Noa. Be safe. I don't want to lose you too. Not again."

I wrap my arms around Jamie's neck and hug him tight.

His arms lock so far around my waist that his fingers circle past my sides and onto my stomach. We stand like this for a few moments, just two old friends in the middle of the Everglades, hugging. Then, silently, we release and go our separate ways.

* * *

I'm sloshing through the spongy wetlands, turning around every ten minutes to see Jamie wandering farther and farther away. I doubt I would have been brave enough to separate from him if we were in hardwood hammocks or mangrove forests, but here, it's a prairie of sawgrass for miles and miles. As far as the eye can see. Tamiami Trail is my northbound indicator, unmistakable with the sound of cars whizzing past every now and then, and the Welcome Center and Jamie's truck serve as their own little landmarks. To get lost in this area would be next to impossible—but that doesn't mean things couldn't be hidden in this combination of swamp and sawgrass.

We were fearless as children—running, playing, catching frogs and lizards in our backyards. The Everglades seem innocuous when used for recreation. It's a whole other beast when searching for lost humans. When you're tracking your steps and dividing it into grids, eyes trained on the ground, instead of frolicking aimlessly with eyes toward the sky and boundaries for safety. Without your mother close by telling you to be careful.

Soon, I don't see Jamie at all. With my sense of security no longer visible, my mind wanders. I wonder what I would do if I found a bloated, gray corpse floating face-down. The Everglades are notorious for body dumping and malevolent scandals. Planes have disappeared or crashed here, what with our proximity to the Bermuda Triangle; ancient artifacts from thousand-year-old Natives are said to haunt the swamps; ghost pirates allegedly lurk in these waters. Then there are the legends of gator men and skunk apes.

The supernatural elements don't bother me, but the truth of the matter is the Everglades are a scary, dangerous place full of violent wildlife and sinister murders.

The atmosphere is different today from yesterday; there is no wind to cause the horrific whistling to grate on my ears. Instead, the soundscape is nearly nonexistent—a bit unsettling.

But then a low, ominous thunder rumbles in the distance, breaking my reverie and explaining the unusually quiet scene. I check my watch, it's nine o'clock. We've only been out here an hour.

My eyebrows pucker in confusion when I gaze toward the southerly sky and see its clear blue brilliance—not a storm cloud in sight.

But I jump when the thunder cracks again—loud and threatening now—and I spin toward the north and look up. A swirling black mass overtakes the horizon from everlasting to everlasting, and suddenly the expansive Everglades seem very small.

The pace at which the weather in the Everglades can polarize is one to be revered. I turn and swiftly march south, scrambling for my phone and dialing Jamie's number. When it goes to voice mail, I try again. And again.

I keep calling until my heart is racing and I'm charging through the swamps, my rubber boots no longer effective in keeping me dry.

The storm is chasing me, taunting me with cackling thunder and shouts of lightning. I continue hauling southbound toward the Welcome Center, screaming Jamie's name and blowing my whistle, however fruitless.

Jamie could be anywhere, and I'm just a tiny human in this magnificent, primal landscape with an enormous tropical thunderstorm bearing down on me. Gone is the dormant, whimsical ideal of this place from when we were kids. It's nothing but a creature on its haunches, a sociopathic biosphere.

"Jamie!"

I'm answered with thunder.

"*Jamie!*"

It's like my control has succumbed to the storm, and suddenly I'm falling. I splash face first into some murky water, and my phone goes flying. I burst into tears as my fingers comb through the sloshy sawgrass in search of it.

My thumb finally brushes against something hard, and when I pull it up, I scream. It's a bone. I throw it. *It's not a human bone, Noa. It's just an animal—I hope. Find your goddamn phone.*

Finally, miraculously, I pull my phone with its heavenly waterproof case from the mud, and I run.

All-out sprinting—I don't bother to check if I'm bleeding or hurt, although I'm running funny, which makes me think something is wrong with my leg. The Welcome Center is close now, about three hundred feet. I laboriously reach it, circle it, but Jamie isn't here.

"Jamie!"

And then I hear a scream.

I stop, point-blank. The storm has caught me, its rain pounding me and every inch of the land. A second scream shatters the air, and finally my eyes land on a small, dilapidated shack next to a patch of cypress trees another five hundred feet past the Welcome Center.

I run lopsidedly at the tiny haunt. The screams grow louder the closer I get, and I know for a fact they're Jamie's.

I don't have time to think. I approach the rotting structure and look into the gaping hole that was once a window. Jamie is on the floor, curled up with his arms protecting his head. Another figure looms over him, bludgeoning him with what looks like a bat.

He's killing Jamie.

I drop my bag, and with shaking fingers rip open the zipper in search of my knife. But the rope, it's so big, the knife, so small—I can't find anything, so I grab the rope and burst through the open door.

"This's my property! Imma kill ya!" the looming figure is screaming, and with my brain on autopilot, I throw the rope around his neck and pull.

The figure and I both fall backward, and I pull the ends of the rope in opposite directions while this thing chokes and flails on top of me.

I don't know how long I hold this position. With my eyes shut and my mind in survival mode, the only thing keeping me grounded is my sense of smell. This thing, this monster—he reeks of dirt and earth. He smells of sweat, of human body. I smell his breath—until it stops. Until he morphs from man into corpse.

Eventually, I open my eyes, the weight of the creature heavy on me, his lack of movement heavier. The storm has approached the shack now, raging and relentless. The exposed beams quiver with every crack of thunder. Rain drips through the patchy thatched roofing, and there's a lifeless body on top of me.

I push him off and scramble on hands and knees toward Jamie, who isn't moving. I don't know how long he was being bludgeoned, the extent of the damage, but I push his shoulder. "Jamie! Don't you fucking die, you hear me? Jamie!"

Boom goes the thunder as I shake my friend and scream at him. He finally twitches, rolls over, and I accost him with each hand fisting the shirt at his chest, my legs straddling his torso.

"Get Skye. Save my god . . . daughter," he slurs, his head lolling to the side. Blood drips from his ear.

"Jamie, you fucking asshole!" I slap him as hard as I can across the face. "Get off your lazy ass and save her yourself! Goddammit!" I slap him again.

His eyes flutter and he opens them, staring at me without seeing me. I alter my approach, gently putting a hand on each side of his face, my thumbs resting on his dimples.

"Hey," I coo. "Jamie. It's me. Noa. C'mon, look at me."

His eyes snap into focus, and the moment I realize he's miraculously alive is the moment he winces in pain. "Oh, god . . . Make it stop. Noa, help me!"

I quickly slip off him as he begins writhing. "I did! Jamie. I did. He's dead. You're okay."

Jamie rolls up to a sitting position in a trancelike pivot and drops his eyes to the lifeless lump a few feet away. He collapses onto his back and sobs.

CHAPTER

9

I KILLED A MAN.

It was self-defense, they said—Jamie was in danger.

It's true, Jamie concurred in the hospital once he was able to speak coherently. He'd found that little shack and seen footprints the size of Skye's, he said, and when he was investigating the interior this man burst in and tried to kill him.

Florida has stand your ground laws, Sheriff Muncie told me, so you can legally end someone's life if they are in the process of ending yours or someone else's unlawfully. And after hours of separately questioning both Jamie and me, our answers coinciding and unwavering (and Jamie's injuries confirming our story), I was free to go.

I didn't even find the missing child.

And they're calling me a superhero.

A few nights ago, a missing child found me. I was also called a superhero.

To what extreme must I go in order to just be average?

They ask me if I'm okay. Do I need anything?

No, I'm fine. My knee might be messed up, though. I would like to get that checked out, please, because it *hurts real bad*. And maybe reapply the Dermabond?

Let's get right on that, they say—get me an X-ray, an MRI, then I can get taken back to the station. The tests come back fine. A bit of hyperextension in my knee, according to the MRI. Here, take this ACE bandage. No need for Dermabond reapplication. Do I need anything else?

No. I just want to get home and take off these blasted rubber boots. I want a shower. I'm drenched in swamp mud, and I'm getting whiffs of urine. At some point during this whole fiasco, my bladder must've let loose, because I'd turned off my timer.

Now I wait in the lobby of the Collier County police station. Free to go. I killed someone, and I'm free to go. I laugh to keep from crying. A blanket is wrapped around my shoulders and a complimentary bottle of water placed on the bench next to me—fringe benefits from exercising stand your ground laws.

Blankets instead of handcuffs.

Water instead of Miranda rights.

My head drops in my hands; I can't hold it together for much longer. The bench groans when a body deposits itself next to me, and I look up to see Sheriff Muncie. I wait for him to speak, but he doesn't. It's the first time I'm encountering him without his bombarding me with questions, but that suspicious look is present in his eye nonetheless as he examines me.

Finally, he says, "You sure you're okay?"

I nod.

"You got lucky," he remarks, and before I can ask him what that means, my father enters the building.

He doesn't say a word as I stand, but the moment our eyes meet, I fall into his chest and start bawling.

* * *

The search party command post has moved from City Hall to my parents' house. My mother, despite her scare upon hearing what happened, is in hostess heaven.

For me, it's hell. I'm still absorbing these turns of events. My childhood best friend nearly died. I watched him get almost beaten to death. But he's not dead; he's in the ICU, expected to make a full recovery. Blunt force trauma, kidney damage, broken ribs, bruised arms and legs. They're monitoring for any hemorrhaging.

That man—who was he? And why was he trying to kill Jamie? Simply for trespassing? I remember Jamie's position—fetal with his arms wrapped around his head. He clearly wasn't a threat.

I've been in my room trying to sleep for the past few hours. Voices float from downstairs—the search party filtering in and out, the doorbell ringing from God knows what news station, and the prattling of the media relations officer Shelly Howell so graciously hired on my behalf—and I want to see none of them. I decide to slip out to go see Jamie in the hospital.

The biggest guest room, the Lavender Suite, has a balcony with a spiral staircase down to the gardens. It's remote, with minimal view of the back patio, so I slip down the stairs with my car keys and turn a sharp left toward the front of the house.

I stop in my tracks when I see Zack seated on a low retaining wall, a cigarette dangling from his fingers. He looks horrible, his hair disheveled and greasy from running his hands through it, his jeans and gray T-shirt ripped and filthy. When he looks at me, his eyes are rimmed red and his cheeks are sunken in.

I approach cautiously and sit next to him. "When did you start smoking?"

He takes an extensive hit off the cigarette. "Five days ago. After I was interrogated for hours on the whereabouts of my daughter. The cops in this Podunk town are worthless."

Five days now, Skye's been missing. My eyes drop to the solar-lit pathway in front of us and I bite my lip, stopping when I feel resistance against my bottom teeth.

"In high school, I had to tell you every day to stop biting your lip like that."

I lift my gaze to his face, my lip dropping from my bite.

He smiles, but somehow he looks even sadder than he did a minute ago. "Hardest thing for me to do. Ever."

"Why?"

"Because you looked so beautiful. It always made me want to kiss you. But I didn't want you hurting yourself."

My toe scuffs the dirt. "How incredibly sacrificial of you."

"I'm sorry, Noa."

"Zack, don't—"

"No, I am. You didn't deserve that. I was selfish and an asshole teenager."

I feel his eyes on me, awaiting a response. I'm not sure what he wants to hear. This is just more closure I'm not sure I need. "It was a long time ago," I finally whisper. Then I look at him. "Thank you."

He nods and takes another drag off his cigarette. "What are you doing out here?"

"I was sneaking out to go see Jamie. I didn't know you were here."

Zack puts his cigarette out on the stone of the retaining wall and flicks the butt into the daffodils. "You saved his life today, Noa. You saved my best friend."

I shrug uncomfortably. What was it that Hector said? "I did what I thought was right."

"You're a hero."

I look at him sharply. "I'm a human." Another Hectorial proverb.

"That man you killed is now a person of interest in Skye's kidnapping."

His words slam into me, nearly knocking me off the wall.

Zack sighs and folds his hands. "His name was Morgan Higgins. A hermit, some homeless guy, who lived in this old, rotted shack near Gannet Strand."

"The one where I—where he died?"

Zack shakes his head. "No. You guys were a couple miles west of Gannet Strand. But the beauty of being a vagrant is you basically live by the rule of 'finders, keepers.' He'd claimed Gannet Strand and about three shacks between there and the preserve—that shack being one of them."

Morgan Higgins. I try the name on my lips. Lots of g's. Like in *gurgle* and *gag.* All the things Morgan did as he died.

"Today, after all that happened, they found evidence of a young child being there recently."

My heart thrums violently. "What?"

Zack nods, and his eyes fill with tears. "Um, they found a chicken nugget on the floor with a tiny bite taken out of it, and an empty chocolate milk container. Skye's favorites. Small fingerprints that didn't match up to Morgan's." He whispers the last part, his chin quivering and feet bouncing. "They're testing the chicken nugget for DNA."

My brain feels like it's exploding. I didn't know any of this. I've spent the entire evening in my room, avoiding everyone. When I did speak to the authorities, we simply hashed out the details leading up to Higgins's death. "Zack, you know what that means! Animals would have gotten to that chicken in no time. She's still alive!"

A sob escapes his throat that he tries very hard to swallow. "Yeah. Yeah, if it's her . . ."

"What did Taylor say?"

He wipes at his eyes. "The moment she found out, she drove to the site. After you and Jamie left, while the cops were investigating the place. I haven't seen her since." His head drops into his hands. "I've done everything I could, gone to all the places. But the authorities have searched all the shacks and combed through the whole area, and nothing. So they told me to 'sit tight.' That's my job right now. Sit tight."

I want to hug him, rub his back—something to give even minimal comfort. But there's a history, and he's married. I don't know what's appropriate in a situation like this. I'm sick of weighing high school dynamics with adult logistics. "Come with me to see Jamie. Let's get you out of here."

* * *

The car ride is silent, but Zack's muscles are tense, his breathing heavy. I feel his eyes on me every now and then, but I keep mine pinned to the road illuminated by my headlights.

I'm surprised to see Taylor sitting in Jamie's room when we arrive, and when she sees us, she leaps from her chair and runs toward us. I'm further surprised when she bypasses Zack and wraps her arms around my neck.

"Thank you. Noa, we're going to find her now. You said it, you said we would find her, and we're doing it." She finally releases me and stares at me with a tear-streaked smile. Then she turns to Zack and hugs him. An afterthought. "We're close. We're so close, Zachary."

I cringe at the use of his whole name—everyone knows Zack hates being called Zachary—and slip past them to Jamie's bed, surveying his bruised body. "Hey."

He smiles and reaches for my hand, and I take his. "I told you we shouldn't split up, Noer," he says groggily.

I laugh to distract the tears building in the background. "I bet you wish you had my rape whistle now, huh? Too bad I lost it during that whole fiasco. You all right?"

"Never better," he jokes, then drops the façade. "Noa, seriously. Thank you."

"Stop. Tell me what happened that led up to this." I release his hand and lower into a chair.

"I found that shed. We didn't see it from the Welcome Center where we started, because it blended in with those trees. You had to really be looking for it. Of course, when I finally spotted it, I went inside. And this maniac just came out of nowhere and attacked me. God, if he's got Skye somewhere, I'm going to bring him back to life just to kill him again."

Zack shifts from the foot of the bed. "Did you find the chicken nugget, or was it the cops?"

Jamie opens his mouth, but Taylor pipes up. "No, the chicken nugget wasn't in that shack. There was another shack a couple hundred yards away. Morgan Higgins had been going back and forth between the two."

"Wait, what?" I say.

"Yeah, check this out." Taylor approaches and pulls out her phone, and I watch her punch in her screen lock passcode—0222. Her birthday. Not Zack's, not Skye's . . . hers. She continues. "Morgan had a few shacks he hopped between—"

But Jamie, who has been rifling for the television remote, interrupts. "Look at this!"

We turn our eyes to the news, a female anchor standing on Tamiami Trail in front of the preserve's Welcome Center with yellow caution tape and police lights in the background. I only catch snippets—attempted murder, self-defense, missing child, Noa Romwell—and I nearly collapse when I see Vladimir, the maintenance worker in my Miami condo, appear on screen.

"Noa, she saved little boy last veek. He vas found on zee rrroof. I'm not surrrprrrised she saved someone else."

I stop listening, but Jamie, Zack, and Taylor are glued to the TV. "What did you do, Noa?" one of them asks. But by divine intervention, my phone rings, which reminds me I should go to the bathroom. I excuse myself and step out into the hallway. It's Janna, and I answer.

"Noa, hi. I wanted to confirm you're coming back to work tomorrow?"

"No, I'm still in Everglades City. There's a . . . an emergency."

Janna hesitates. "How long do you think you'll be gone? No disrespect, but—"

"Hey, why don't you turn on the news? That will answer all your questions." I end the call and head to the restroom.

* * *

I kissed Jamie's forehead goodbye and told everyone I was leaving, that I was tired. I strongly insinuated Zack should ride back with his wife.

When I arrive home, I'm relieved to see the house is dark. Assuming my parents are in bed, I stagger inside—my knee locking up briefly—and am surprised to see the outline of my father seated on the sofa, a lowball glass at his lips. He doesn't look up when I shut the door behind me, and I wonder if he's going to acknowledge me at all. But then he says, "You could use some whiskey, huh?"

I sigh. Leave it to my father to ignore me the day of my high school graduation, yet finally be proud of me the day I kill a man. "Yes, I'd love some whiskey."

The very few times I've drunk with him have been some of our best bonding moments. Since my mother doesn't believe in drinking, we had to sneak it—a secret between just the two of us like a treehouse club she wasn't invited to. The first time was the eve of his father's funeral, when I was seventeen. He handed me a glass of wine and clinked it with his own, muttering *Cheers*. Really? I had said, I'm only seventeen. He replied that my mother wasn't here to harp about it because she went to church to mingle with friends instead of supporting her grieving husband. "She thinks she can pray all this away," he'd said.

I'd taken a sip of the sour liquid, feeling it as it slipped down my throat and wondering if that was the burn everyone talked about. But as in all cases, it served as my liquid courage. I asked him, "Why are you and Mom even married?"

He launched into a twenty-minute soliloquy after that, trying his best to explain to his teenage daughter why her parents, who were opposites in every way, had forced themselves into this life together, like polar ends of magnets. "We were young, it was a mistake," he'd said. "But she don't believe in divorce, and I'm not gonna divorce her, 'cause she's good to me, even if she does think I'm going to hell." I'd grinned at that, and he winked. "Besides, there's one thing we have that we both love and will never regret."

I jokingly pointed to my face.

"That gas water heater I installed last year. Saves us a ton on the electric bill." We'd laughed until we heard her car pull into the driveway, so we hurriedly drained our wineglasses and slipped them behind her crystal punchbowl in the credenza, still dirty. I wonder if they're still there, crusted with wine, even more fermented.

Those heart-to-hearts with my father were rare, but they were laden with gold—both literally (because the whiskey) and figuratively. My father buzzed is the only time we can have a normal conversation. He never wanted children; he was already forty when my mother accidentally got pregnant with me. He loves me, but it often feels like he's being forced to.

I move to the recliner as he pours a finger of Balvenie into a second lowball glass. "If your ma saw us right now, she'd flip."

"Yeah, well . . . I killed a man today, so this should be the least of her worries." I accept the glass and take a tiny sip. It tastes awful, but the tingling sensation as it glides down my throat sparkles with a promising future.

We sit in silence, the only sounds being his deep inhales and thorough exhales, the occasional friction of his callused palm rubbing his stiff jeans.

"I killed a man in Nam once."

I know my dad served in Vietnam, but he's never been one to talk about it. I've heard very few stories about the eighteen months he spent there, and his emotion while sharing his tales rivals those of mine when I stub my toe.

"I didn't know that."

"I was driving an M561, a Gama Goat. Drivin' through the jungle when one of those—" He screws his face up as he considers me, ultimately deciding to censor his verbiage in my presence, for which I'm grateful. "An *enemy* was hiding in a tree and jumped in the back of my vehicle. Scared the piss outta me. But I slammed on my brakes and he came rolling forward, like a bale a hay. Crashed into the back of the cab." He chuckles here before his face turns stoic again. "I turned around, and we stared each other down. Just a couple a terrified kids with guns in each other's faces. I didn't want to pull the trigger, but it was him or me."

I'm scared if I ask questions, he won't continue. So I prop my injured knee on the ottoman and wait him out as he drains his glass and pours another. "I didn't sleep for two weeks after that. Just laid on my cot in the barracks and shook like a leaf."

I can tell by his tone that his story has ended. I won't hear about the images of blood and flesh that undoubtedly splattered the bed of his truck, how they haunted him and probably still do to this day. I think about my own victim and am thankful I didn't look at him once I'd ripped his soul from his body. Would his eyes have been bulging? Was his flesh a sickly shade of gray? I'll never know.

I shiver, and my father notices. He leans forward, bracing an elbow on his knee and holding his glass toward me. "Ya did what ya had to do, Noa. Jamie woulda died. People can argue all they want over right and wrong, but I got news for ya—this world will never be a utopia. A utopian society to one person is a dystopian society to another. People like concrete facts, but they don't consider all the subjectives. A rock is a rock, sure, but after years of waves poundin' on it and nature erodin' it, it ain't a rock anymore. It's a pile a sand, and folks call it science. But the fact is, outside events that we don't see—they change what we know to be true. What was once a rock a hundred years ago can't be called a rock no more. And killin' a man ain't murder if your life's at stake. Ask Jamie."

In some strange, slightly inebriated way, I understand what my father is saying. But his theory is just that—a truth established by his own biases. We could ask Jamie all day, but what if we asked dear old Mrs. Higgins what she thought of her son's death?

That leads me down a whole new path of what-ifs—what if she's alive and wondering where her beloved son is? Or what if she was a horrible mother and the reason her son became a homeless murderer? I can't think about this anymore, whether from the whiskey or sheer exhaustion, I don't know. After another round of silence, I tell him I'm heading to bed. Thank him for the drink, the chat.

Finally, I'm lying between my sheets without horror reels running through my head, thanks to my unconventional father and his whiskey. My eyes droop, my body shutting down. Just as I'm about to fall asleep, my phone rings. It's Hector.

"Noa, I've been trying to give you time alone with your family, but I watched the news. Are you okay?" he asks.

I want to burst into tears, but the alcohol. "I killed a man," I reply. "Do you hate me now?"

"Never. You acted in self-defense. It was either that weird vagrant or your friend. You did what you had to do."

My father had said the same thing. As did the cops and everyone else since I strangled Morgan Higgins to death. *I did what I had to do.* On a sigh, I massage an eyebrow. "I still can't wrap my head around all this."

"I understand. But the detectives are right, Noa. You're innocent. Take it with a grain of salt, make an appointment with a therapist, and let them find the girl."

I shut my eyes tight and pull the covers to my chin. "I have congenital insensitivity to pain with anhidrosis."

He hesitates. "I'm sorry?"

"Congenital analgesia. My SCN9A gene never produced the molecular channels that carry signals to the brain that my body is feeling something extreme. Like pain, heat, or cold. And my body doesn't produce sweat. I was born with it, and nobody knew. For the first eighteen months of my life, they thought I was the perfect baby. I never cried, not once. It wasn't until I was a year and a half and my mother found me in my room writing on the walls with a bleeding finger that she knew something was wrong. I had to wear protective goggles to keep from poking myself in the eye, and my baby teeth were removed when I was two because I didn't stop chewing on my tongue and lips. I've had to teach myself all these things, set timers to go to the bathroom and to eat. Zack dumped me because he said he couldn't handle having to be my sensory neurons, and that thing you mentioned the other day that I'm not telling you? It's that."

I count my breaths, waiting for him to respond. One, two—

"Thank you for telling me."

"You're welcome."

"That's a lot to absorb. Looks like I have things to google."

"I also may have told Zack and Jamie that you and I are dating." I wince.

He laughs softly. "Well, in your defense, we are kind of. We've been on dates. That's dating, right?"

"But you don't kiss me," my liquor replies boldly.

"You were hiding something from me, Noa. And I knew it. I wasn't going to get my heart too involved with someone who couldn't be herself around me. But you've told me now. That's huge. I think good things are in store for us. You and me."

For the first time since Morgan Higgins, I smile.

We eventually hang up, and I stare at the ceiling while thinking about Hector—his response to my hefty confession. It was a beautiful response, no doubt, but my smile gradually withers. Will he say that after a month or two once he realizes what a burden it is to deal with this condition? I fall into a dreamless sleep, wondering which I'll come to regret more: taking a life, or telling the truth.

CHAPTER

10

I'M ADVISED TO take Monday off from the search party. I willingly oblige. I'm worried about my knee, because even though it's not locking up anymore, it's still a bit swollen.

New information on Morgan Higgins keeps pouring in (although nothing useful), and while yesterday the leads seemed hopeful, today they bring a new despair. Skye has yet to be found. And if Morgan was feeding her, who's doing it now?

With the alcohol having worn off, so has the comfort of my father's words last night. All the events that led up to Higgins's death—the dynamics and logistics—have blurred into the background, and my thoughts this morning revolve around the focal point of the life I took. The intensity of what I've done is overwhelming, and I know if I don't stay busy today, I'll lose it.

My mother hosted the committee breakfast again this morning, but she looks exhausted. I watch her as she moves about the kitchen, her usual happy whistling replaced with tension in her eyebrows and worry pulling down her mouth.

I sip my coffee and poke at my eggs. "Maybe you should rest today, too," I suggest. While her health is concerning, I shamefully have the ulterior motive of her keeping me distracted, keeping my mind off Morgan Higgins.

She glances up and smiles. "I'm spending the afternoon with Maggie. I'm worried about her. Your father is with the search party down near Chokoloskee."

"What are you going to do with Maggie?"

"Keep her company. Will you be okay here by yourself?"

I nod with eyes dropped toward the floor and dread on my mind. If I tell her I don't want to be alone, she'll stay here instead of going to Maggie, and Maggie needs her more than I do.

In humility, count others more significant than yourselves. The Bible passage I learned in Sunday school pops into my mind, having lain dormant for the better part of twenty years.

"Will you look at my knee before you leave?"

She ends up applying Voltaren as an anti-inflammatory, wrapping it with an ACE bandage, and dropping an Extra Strength Tylenol into my hand with a glass of water to contain the minor swelling. She departs with a kiss to my forehead, and when I'm alone, it's just as I anticipated. All I can do is look at my hands and know they took a life.

I stop staring at them when I notice they're shaking, closing my eyes instead. I try believing what everyone is saying—that I did the right thing—but that's easy for them to say. They've not been put in positions where human lives are at stake, where you choose to either watch your oldest friend die or end the existence of another person.

With a resounding sigh, I commit to doing two things: focusing on Jamie being alive, and staying busy. I move to the desktop computer in the family room and type *Morgan Higgins* into the search engine. I'm unsure if personifying him will make me feel better or worse, but I can at least hope for some closure.

Day-old news articles cascade from the top, some written within the last hour. But none with information I hadn't known already—fifty-eight years old, originally from Key Largo, charged with a third-degree felony for gambling six years ago. I inhale a cleansing breath—my mindset is already switching from one of self-pity to logical, realistic, and I sit straighter and squint at the screen. I'm guessing the gambling is the reason he was homeless, but I wonder why he gambled illegally when the Seminole reservations are loaded with casinos.

The forums and comments are the most disturbing. They are armies of words marching straight for Zack and Taylor with torches and pitchforks—mostly Taylor. *Those parents should be imprisoned. I hope Skye's mother dies. The Flynns deserve to burn in hell for allowing their daughter to walk home from school.* They're the most insensitive comments I've ever heard, and I've heard plenty in my life. I pray Zack and Taylor haven't read these, although I'm sure they haven't. Scouring the internet to see what everyone thinks of them seems the least of their concerns.

The doorbell rings nearly thirty minutes later, and I'm surprised to see Zack at the door.

He looks better than he did yesterday—showered, clean clothes, combed hair. "May I come in?" he asks.

I step aside, and he meanders into the house. Unlike my determined avoidance of scoping out Maggie's house, he takes his time eyeing everything from the guest book and candy jar on the table near the entrance to the books lining the shelves next to the fireplace in the family room. "We spent a lot of time here back in the day. At the height of 'Noer and Zack.'"

"Where's Taylor?"

He leafs through an early edition of *The Grapes of Wrath* and replaces it on the shelf. "Sleeping. She spent all night searching the northern part of the Everglades, up near I-75."

I perch on a stool at the island as Zack continues browsing through my parents' home.

"Remember that time we were watching a movie on your couch and we fell asleep? And your dad woke us up at two in the morning and sent me home?" he asks with a grin.

"I do." I'm not sure why Zack is taking this stroll down memory lane, or why he's forcing me along with him. Like a tour guide, he points out a few more places of interest—the exact spot on the porch where we took homecoming photos, the space on the mantel where those photos later sat, and the corner in the kitchen where we nursed a tiny kitten back to health that we had found tangled in the mangroves off Chokoloskee Bay.

I follow his pointed finger silently, recalling those memories that I thought lived on only in me, having died with Zack the moment he met Taylor. And the *what could have been* hypotheses stir in my chest, the ones I laid to rest years ago and cemented over after their apologies. But those apologies were recent, and I don't know how long it takes cement to dry.

He finally moves to the island and grabs the stool next to me. I find myself leaning away from him, pondering his motive. Wondering why a married man is alone with a former flame in a home where they spent many hours during their years together. "Why aren't you out with the search party?" I ask.

"I just met with Mayor Howell and Sheriff Muncie, and we're calling the search party off. This is the last day. The state is taking over. After what happened yesterday, we're turning it over to the pros."

"Oh."

There's a vase centered on the island with fresh, yellow roses. A petal has fallen onto the countertop, and Zack picks it up and rubs it between his fingers. "Skye reminds me so much of you," he confesses.

I hold my breath, remembering my mother's words about how she could be my child, the canvas in Maggie's home where I confirmed his musings.

"She never cried, Noa. She is literally the happiest, sweetest kid in the world." He drops the petal he's managed to crush and rubs his face. "We even had her tear ducts checked when she was a baby, to make sure everything was working right. They thought she might have Sjögren syndrome, but no. I was scared she had CIPA, even. She didn't, but—"

"Thank God."

"—but otherwise, you two are identical. She loves harder than humans should, feels other people's emotions." He looks at me. "Just like you do."

A realization dawns on me, and I'm ashamed of myself. Zack didn't come here to reminisce about me; he's trying to find solace during the worst time of his life.

He's grasping for anything solid, anything to offer peace, a haven from this relentless torture.

Zack stands and circles the stool. "I have to run down to Smallwood Store. The owner loaned us a few headlamps to use during the graveyard shifts of the search, and I need to return them." He bends down to brace his hands on the stool, rendering us eye level. "Will you please come with me, Noa?"

I gulp. "Sure, Zack."

* * *

Smallwood Store is a little red building on stilts and the oldest store in the Everglades. The interior hasn't changed since the 1920s. Its structure is made entirely of wood and is overwhelmingly covered floor to ceiling in antiques and historical artifacts.

"It's empty," I observe as Zack pulls into the barren parking lot.

"Store's not open yet. She told me just to leave the box in her office. The door should be unlocked, she said." Zack swings into a spot and jerks the shifter into park. I watch as he exits the car and moves to the trunk to retrieve the box of headlamps, wondering if I'm expected to wait in the car or join him.

"Come on," he calls.

We step inside, and I follow his speedy gait past scores of artifacts, our feet clumping across creaky wooden floors. I stop next to a display of boat engines and wagon wheels as Zack slips through a half-open door and deposits the box on a desk. Then he turns and smiles softly. "There."

I smile back. "All done." I make an about face and start toward the exit, but Zack grabs my shoulders from behind and steers me toward a room on the right, causing me to trip over a Seminole canoe. I catch my breath, but when I realize his intent, I playfully resist him. "Keep me away from that wax man! He's scary." But Zack halts at the foot of the disturbingly realistic figure of an old man sitting in a rocking chair.

I study the body made entirely of wax for the first time as an adult, but it's still just as creepy as ever. The hair, his hands, the lines in his face . . . *Crayon-equin*, we'd called it in high school. I'm not sure which of us came up with it, but we thought we were so clever, combining crayons (which are made of wax) with mannequin so nicely.

"You know this place really is haunted, right?" Zack finally allows me to move away from Crayon-equin.

"I know. What was the guy's name? Edgar or something? Who used to murder the people working in his sugarcane fields so he wouldn't have to pay them?"

Zack smiles, and for the first time, it's not laced in sadness. But our footsteps clunking out the door as we leave behind headlamps that never found Skye is the most haunting part of this place.

* * *

We climb into the car, and Zack maneuvers to the exit in haste. "Now where to?" I ask, as he clearly has another destination in mind.

"Do you mind if we head to the observation tower?"

"Um, sure." I cast him inquisitive glances, hoping he'll elaborate on this rather kitschy landmark in Chokoloskee. He doesn't, and I can't bring myself to ask Zack why he wants to go there. Something inside me says I should already know.

We make the three-mile drive to the tower, and after climbing all 108 stairs in silence, Zack heads toward the railing closest to the water and gazes out.

The atmosphere has shifted, taking my mind from a basic confusion to a much darker, nameless place. I linger behind him, giving him a moment to ponder the surroundings.

"I always thought the Everglades were amazing," he muses.

I step forward and place my hands on the railing next to him.

"I mean, look at this," he continues. "It's just . . . majestic. That's what I always thought. But now, the entire place is terrifying. I hate it. It's hiding my daughter from me. Taylor was right. We should've moved a long time ago. None of this would be happening. It's my fault."

I stare out at the vast wilderness, right back in the situation I was in earlier today. Do I comfort him? Have the things we've done today been appropriate for two people with our dynamics? Or do the logistics outweigh the dynamics? "I need to go to the bathroom," I say, thankful I remembered I should go, and make the 108-step descent.

When I exit the restroom, Zack is standing outside, waiting. "I have another idea of where we can go."

I can't read his expression. If he weren't in such a horrid situation, I would think perhaps he was excited. "Where?"

"You'll see. C'mon."

We ride silently in his car until we pull up to his mother's house. Her car is gone, she and my mother waist-deep in their day of catharsis. When we step out of the car, I follow him past the house and down the ramp leading to the boathouse. "We're going out on an airboat," he calls over his shoulder.

As I ponder whether this is intended to be a leisurely joyride or a futile attempt to look for Skye, I stumble down the gravel path and instinctively yelp in synthetic pain. Zack turns around. "You okay?"

"Yeah." I'm getting so caught up in pretending, I'm blurring the lines between what's real and what's not. Is it real that I'm about to skate out into the Everglades, alone with Zack on an airboat? It feels real. Those are the logistics. But what are the dynamics? Well, they're twofold: a married man and his ex-girlfriend are participating in activities they did while they were dating, and a woman is trying to take a father's mind off the fact that his daughter is missing. One of those sounds scandalous, the other valiant.

Subjective and objective. Dynamics and logistics.

There are three airboats of various sizes anchored to the dock, and Zack hops into the ascending captain's chair of the middle one. It's clearly the oldest, as well—I notice the rust dotting the aluminum.

"Why this one?" I ask.

He pats the adjoining seat perched high above the bottom of the boat. "You can sit up here with me." A glance at the other two reveals only a single seat for the driver with additional seating at the bottom. His is the only one that has a second chair next to the driver.

I start to ask if that's appropriate, but Zack has cranked the engine, and the propeller roars to life in its cage behind his head. He tosses me a pair of lime green ear protectors and slips a pair on his own head. Since the entire anatomy of an airboat is above water—and right next to its passengers' heads—I conclude that conversation won't be happening between us on the ride, and therefore, logistics overpower dynamics.

The rudder panels shake with the noise of the engine as I climb up into the chair. Zack grabs the rudder stick and presses the accelerator, navigating us through the glossy marshlands.

The wind whips my hair around my face as we glide across the surface of the swamp. Some areas are so thick with sawgrass that it looks like dry land, but the airboat slices right through, revealing the waters hidden beneath.

Zack speeds through the narrow mangrove paths and makes sharp turns in the more open areas, causing us to skid sideways across the sparkling water. Herons erupt from their nests and shoot skyward, and frogs hop from lily pads into the depths.

He pokes my arm and points to his left at an alligator scurrying through the brush. The blaring engine drowns out my screams.

Soon we swish around into an enclosure mimicking a lagoon. Bald cypresses sprout from the earth with Spanish moss clinging to their low-hanging branches. The roaring engine dies down as Zack releases the accelerator, and the silence is deafening when he shuts it off completely.

I remove my headset and twist toward him. "What are we doing?"

He removes his and breathes in the Everglades. "Sitting."

"Okay." I glance around at our surroundings. For as uninhabited as these swamps are, the population of wildlife is extensive. The birds are loud, cawing over each other, vying to be the alpha. I count three alligators lounging in the water, only their heads visible. Another one is draped across a fallen tree, his skin dry and scaly as he basks in the sun. None are moving—the reason they're not scaring me like the scuttling one did. I study them, and I think it would be strange if they *weren't* here. The native animals are the beating heart of the Everglades and have been for thousands of years. I close my eyes and breathe the biome in through my nose.

Suddenly Zack screams at the top of his lungs. "Skyyyyeeee!"

My heart nearly explodes. I lay a hand on my chest and catch my breath as birds swoop into flight and the rest of nature goes silent.

"*Skyyyyyyyyeee!*"

Now the only sound is the water lapping against the sides of the boat, the remanence of our wake.

"Zack?" I say softly.

He doesn't answer.

"We're going to find her."

His face twists into a sob and he drops his head on my shoulder. My arms go around his torso, and we're embracing. I rock him as he weeps, and after a few minutes he sits up and apologizes.

"What are you sorry for?" I pull a strand of Spanish moss from his hair and toss it into the water.

He takes a moment to control his breathing. "N—nothing, forget it. I was serious when I said Skye reminds me of you. But it's everything, Noa, not just rarely crying. Her looks, her mannerisms, her sense of humor . . . How could I have let this happen?"

His eyes drop to the bottom of the boat, but I grab his chin and turn his head until he's looking in my eyes. "Stop blaming yourself.'"

"I should have married you." I release his chin and sit up. We hold eye contact for a grueling five seconds before he breaks it. "I shouldn't have said that."

I can't respond.

He scrubs his face and runs his hands through his hair. "God. Tell me something, Noa. Tell me something true."

"I still have CIPA."

He looks at me and nods slowly. "I know. I knew you were lying."

My eyes pop. "How?"

"Because I know you better than anyone. You can take the girl out of the 'glades, but you can't—"

"Then how can you say you wish you'd have married me? Isn't that the reason you broke up with me?"

"Noa, I was wrong. I—"

His phone pings a text from his pocket. He fishes it out to look at the screen. "Oh, fuck."

"What?"

"In those ten minutes we were riding, my mom called seven times and Taylor called five. Taylor's sent eleven texts."

"Oh, no." I slip my phone from my pocket to see that both my parents have blown up my phone, too. "Let's go."

By the time we pull back into the dock at Maggie's house, the entire search committee is standing on the lawn, looking at us. My heart flips. Zack navigates the boat to the dock and anchors it to the railing, and by the time we've removed our ear protectors and stepped down from our seats, they've descended the hill like a brigade, Taylor leading the way.

"Where have you been?" she asks. The look on her face is the same nasty one she wore in high school—which I haven't seen since then, and the difference from what I've witnessed the past few days is striking.

Zack steps out of the boat and reaches his hand to help me out, but I decline. "Noa and I went to look for Skye in the Ten Thousand Islands."

Taylor is considering him, and Maggie interjects. "We've been calling you." Then her eyes turn to me. "Both of you."

I feel like we've been caught having an affair. This is exactly what I was trying to avoid. At some point today, I crossed the line from helping a grieving father into entertaining an ex-boyfriend.

Neither Zack nor Taylor will look at me; they're engaged in a telepathic battle of their own. The crowd feels like it's closing in on us, even though there are only six other people, including my parents. I catch their eye; they both look disappointed.

"I'm sorry. It was my fault. I felt guilty about taking the day off from the search party, and Zack was restless, so I suggested we take an airboat and search for her anyway."

Now all eyes are on me, including Zack's. Why do I feel like this lie is more sinister than what it is? I feel like everyone can see right through me, read my thoughts and know that Zack just confessed that he wishes he had married me instead of Taylor.

But strangely, their accusatory stares soften to what looks like acceptance.

"We have news," Maggie states.

Zack and I look at each other. "What is it?" His voice is quivering.

"The DNA test came back from the chicken nugget and milk container. Both are matches to Skye's."

CHAPTER 11

SKYE IS STILL alive. There is a heightened hope and yet a tangible terror skittering throughout the city. We've also received confirmation that the two sets of fingerprints in the shack were indeed Morgan's and Skye's, but we can't interrogate him because I killed him. Everything is slipping away from everyone, and after my airboat ride with Zack, I don't know if I'm still a hero to these people or if I've become an antihero.

It's the following day—day seven of Skye's disappearance. Jamie is being discharged today, and I've just arrived at the hospital to pick him up. In the elevator to his room, I'm sorting through all the information I need to talk to him about. We'll discuss the DNA evidence being Skye's, but should I tell him about the time spent with Zack yesterday? Would he understand? Or would he judge us too?

I step into his room, and the doctor is handing him discharge papers. I catch something about a nephrologist before they both look up. Jamie looks substantially better—the bruises on his face already shrinking, his movements purposeful, and his eyes alert despite the sluggishness of the narcotics. I shiver as I recall the lifelessness in his demeanor just two days ago.

That's not to say he's a hundred percent. His actions are slow, a bit labored. A hand rests over his ribs as he scoots off the bed, his teeth bared as he stands carefully. "Sup, Noer? Here, talk to Dr. Santos. I'm a little high and I'm not going to remember all these things he's telling me." He shuffles toward the exit.

I turn to the older man, his mouth still open from the instructions he was listing off that Jamie so abruptly ended. His glasses are thick, their black frames and his white medical coat complementing his salt-and-pepper hair. Not a whisker is on his jaw, leaving his cleft chin completely bared. I shake his hand. "Hello, I'm . . ." I glance at Jamie, who is still staggering toward the door. "I'm taking Jamie home. I'll just take those." I retrieve the papers once my hand leaves his grip and begin flipping through them. "So what are we looking at?"

Dr. Santos angles himself toward Jamie, who is now lowering into a chair at a snail's pace. "Mr. Camden's injuries are more superficial than we thought, which is good news. Apparently, his assailant didn't have much strength. Not to say he couldn't have killed him; he would have if Jamie hadn't been rescued."

I drop my eyes back to the papers. Blood is rushing to my cheeks, but Jamie hollers, "It was Noer! She killed the sumbitch." He groans in pain and drops his head, and I glance back up at the doctor.

"My name is Noa," I whisper. "Noer's just an old nickname. Sorry about him. Please continue."

His quizzical expression softens to an amused smile, but he doesn't ask questions. "He should take it easy with his ribs. The X-rays of his thoracic anatomy show that his sixth true rib is cracked, but nothing is protruding. Otherwise he would have issues like punctured organs, so that's more good news. My concern is with his kidney—"

"I was pissing blood, Noer. You shoulda seen it. 'Member in school when we'd shake up a Coke bottle and spray it all over that dumbass kid? Daniel something? It looked like that."

I'm mortified. I can't tell what the doctor is thinking of Jamie's crude interruptions or the fact that we allegedly bullied a kid named Daniel. The man is stoic as they come. He continues, ignoring my obvious embarrassment. "It seems to be a contusion on his kidney, but we want to rule out any further renal trauma. Just because we no longer see blood in the urine doesn't mean it's not there. So I'm referring him to a nephrologist in Miami, Dr. Hassan, who is one of the best in the country. She's in Jackson Hospital." He skirts through the pages of discharge papers and points a thick finger to Dr. Hassan's information.

"I live in Miami. I'll be happy to take him to her."

Despite his lack of reactions to, first, my having saved Jamie's life, and second, our incriminating history of Coke wars, his lips spread into a smile at this news. "Well then! That's perfect. Please make the appointment as soon as possible, and schedule a follow-up appointment with his PCP within two weeks. Here are prescriptions for some Vicodin and Extra Strength Advil. Try to administer the Vicodin only if it's necessary." He glances at Jamie; my eyes follow.

Jamie is clutching his ribs, muttering something about a ribectomy. If God can take this rib and make him a wife out of it, like Adam and Eve.

I quickly turn back to the doctor and shut my eyes, but a bubble of laughter bursts through my lips anyway. The doctor chuckles and pats my shoulder, and I feel like a mother whose child just said the f-word in public.

A nurse enters with a wheelchair—our escape route. I shake the doctor's hand again and help Jamie into it, and we make the long, awkward trip to the parking lot.

Once we've situated Jamie in the front seat and I'm navigating toward the exit, I release a massive tension sigh and look at him. He's reclined the seat to about forty-five degrees and has an arm draped over his eyes.

"How ya feeling, bud?" I ask.

He swallows, but it's labored. His head lolls in my direction and his arm drops so he's looking at me. "I'm good. I'm good, Noer. How are you?"

I find myself performing a labored swallow, as well. "Fine. I'm not the one who was nearly killed, though."

He shifts uncomfortably, attempting to sit straighter. "But you . . . I mean, you know what you did. To that dude. I just wanna make sure you're okay." He's still slurring slightly, but I know Jamie—he's genuine under any influence.

I smile at him and squeeze his hand briefly. "Let's not talk about that. You're alive. That's all that matters."

He smiles back, the swelling in his cheek pulling taut and shining a brilliant greenish purple in the sunlight. "Yeah. Getting the hell beat out of me has never killed me before. I guess I can thank my pops for that."

I sputter a laugh. "Whatever, Jamie. Your dad never tried to kill you with a baseball bat."

"Oh, look at you. A girl's capable of feeling pain for six months of her life and she thinks she's an expert."

Now I laugh out loud. "Shut up."

My eyes divert back to the road, but I feel his lingering on me. "Love you, Noer."

"Love you too, Jamie."

The silence is loud and building. Full of anticipation, like overhead lights dimming in an auditorium announcing the start of a play. But I don't know what's coming, don't know what production I've purchased tickets for.

I revel in the quiet—it's ending soon. I feel his eyes on me.

"I was in love with you in high school, you know," he says.

I expel the air from my lungs. "I know." It's the first time I've admitted it even to myself. Jamie is drugged and rambling, but he's speaking the truth. I know because all those years ago, I witnessed that truth. He never said it, never crossed any lines, but I felt it. It was in the way he looked at me, the shadow that would blink across his features whenever Zack and I would hold hands or kiss in front of him.

I told myself that Jamie just wanted what we had, that he wanted a girlfriend. But even when he did date girls, the shadows still haunted his face and his relationships were short-lived. Jamie manifested longing; he made it a tangible entity that only I could see.

I never acknowledged it. Never even entertained the thought of me and Jamie. I was too in love with Zack, and I had known Jamie since third grade. He truly was like a brother, and even once Zack and I broke up, Jamie never made a move. He stayed friends with me, although we didn't hang out nearly as much since his loyalties were with his best friend. His feelings may still have been there, but I was too broken up to notice.

And then we graduated, and I left. Fast forward ten years, and now here we are, in a car together, and he is confessing, breathing life into these words that were never spoken, into the ghosts no one knew existed. It's like another person inhabits the car with us.

I find myself wondering for the first time ever—could Jamie Camden and Noa Romwell ever . . . ?

I slam on my brakes to avoid rear-ending a car at a red light. The lanyard with my Thompson-Miller ID badge hanging from my rearview mirror swings in circles. My head zips toward him, and he's simply looking at me. "How did you know?" he asks, and I've almost forgotten what he's talking about. I'm reminding myself there's a Hector. I have a Hector. Kind of.

"I . . . don't really know," I answer truthfully. "This is the first time I'm really admitting that I knew. I wouldn't think about it back then." I turn my eyes back to the road as the light turns green and we move along, taking shifty glances at him before whispering, "I was with Zack." I don't know why I'm so flustered. It's not like he confessed that he's in love with me now. I could even admit shamelessly that I had a crush on him in sixth grade, but this new person in the car—this ghost he just resurrected—it's spooking me.

Jamie adjusts his position deliberately, wincing through the pain. "I almost kissed you the night of our senior homecoming. Just to teach Zack a lesson."

Suddenly our creepy passenger is gone, and I'm laughing out loud. Jamie and I won homecoming king and queen that year; Zack thought he'd be a shoo-in, but once he'd dumped me so boldly and unabashedly, he lost popularity status. Plus, Taylor wasn't a senior, so the student body collectively decided to stick it to Zack by voting for his ex-girlfriend and his best friend. If there was one sweet moment of my senior year, it was that. "Oh, my god. I can't imagine us kissing. Especially in front of Zack."

Jamie laughs while holding his side. It's easy, carefree. Typical Jamie. He's not flustered like I am; he's simply reminiscing.

I'm suddenly compelled to ask him why he never acted on his feelings once Zack and I broke up, but something inside me tells me to leave it alone. These posthumous emotions are just that, and there is no closure needed.

We didn't talk about it ten years ago. No need to talk about it now.

* * *

It's quiet at my parents' house that afternoon, even though my mother and Maggie are cleaning up the kitchen after lunch. With the search parties in abeyance now that the state has taken over, today was the last meal my mother hosted for them.

I descend the stairs with my overnight bag and keys in hand, stepping into the kitchen to see her and Maggie drying the last of the dishes. I drop my bag and sit at the island while Maggie places the lid over a cake plate, creating a globe around a half-eaten carrot cake. "You're really taking Jamie to Miami tonight?" she asks with a sad smile.

"His appointment is at eight in the morning." I shrug as my mother looks at me with disapproval.

"Where will he be staying?" she asks.

I roll my eyes. "He can sleep in my bed. I'll take the couch. Unless, of course, he wants to have sex despite his broken ribs, bruised up body, and near-death experience, in which case we'll both sleep in the bed."

My mother gasps—"That's not funny, Noa"—and Maggie chuckles.

"Where's Dad?"

"Having a drink with Scott and Marvin down at the tavern." She drapes the damp hand towel over the oven door and surveys her sparkling clean kitchen.

"Be careful, Marley," Maggie warns as she gathers her purse and sweater. "That's what Logan always said he was doing. And you know how that went."

My breath catches, but both women roll their eyes with a patronizing air generally reserved for young mothers who have just shared how their preschool children colored all over the walls. As if Logan's infidelity were a mere inconvenience—nothing that couldn't be resolved with some Lysol and a Magic Eraser.

Maggie hugs my mother before turning to me. "Be safe, and take care of Jamie. Do you know when you'll be bringing him back?"

We retract from the embrace, and I hear her real question encrypted within her words. *Will you be coming back too?*

"As soon as possible." I smile and note the despondence in her reaction, the recognition that I didn't truly answer her question. It's a question I've been avoiding and will continue to as long as possible. The truth is, I don't plan on staying here once I return Jamie. I already killed one person, and the search parties have stopped. I've missed three days of work. There's nothing left for me to do.

As soon as the door closes behind Maggie, I turn to my mother. "Why didn't you tell me that Maggie and Logan divorced?"

She actively avoids eye contact as she arranges the perfectly arranged bouquet of roses on the island. "I didn't think you wanted to know anything about the Flynns."

"They divorced a year ago. I looked like an idiot the other day walking into City Hall and asking where Logan was. You don't think you should've at least given me a heads up?"

She relents and lowers onto a stool next to me. "I'm sorry, I should have told you. Last year when it happened, you were quite disconnected from this place and anything that was going on. I'd recently told you about your old Sunday school teacher marrying a widower from Ireland, remember? And you told me to stop telling you these things."

She shrugs, and I bite my tongue before I can tell her that this is completely different.

She continues. "Anyway, it was a year ago, so when you surprised me by showing up here, it wasn't in the forefront of my mind. Poor Maggie was so mortified when it happened. He's off gallivanting with some young girl, and you know how this town is." She raises an eyebrow and holds up a hand, pantomiming a puppet. "People talk. That made it even worse for her."

"So what happened? How long had it been going on?"

She huffs. "She doesn't know for sure. He blindsided her, you know. It's not like she caught him in the act; he just up and left her. Told her he'd met someone else, a young thing, and that Maggie could keep the house—all through a text, can you believe it? Maggie was willing to work on their marriage, but he had his mind made up. Wouldn't even return her calls. Logan . . . he had a midlife crisis, I suppose."

"Jamie said he moved to Connecticut."

"He did. He rarely keeps in touch with Zack; they talk every now and then. He sends postcards to Skye." She rolls her tongue around in her mouth as if her words tasted like dirty pennies.

I find myself leaning toward her. "Does he know Skye is missing?"

"Yes. Didn't care enough to come down here and comfort his mourning son, but cared enough to share Facebook posts."

I feel the muscles in my face bunching. "That is *not* the Logan I remember."

Her head sways side to side, her eyes locked on the bouquet. "People aren't always as they seem, Noa. You never know what's going on inside a person's head, regardless of their actions."

It's a scary thought. Especially when dealing with the people of Everglades City.

CHAPTER

12

At the south end of Everglades City, just before Copeland Avenue becomes Smallwood Drive and dumps you off in Chokoloskee, there's a small drive leading to the bay and the quirkiest little ranch-style home—one of the very few in this town that is not on stilts.

It is raised, however, as if someone planted it and it grew three feet. A set of five steps leads up to the front door, almost like the house is standing on its tippy-toes to peer over the water. And it's blue, like a Smurf. After dropping him off here this morning, it's the second time today I'm seeing Jamie's house.

And this house screams Jamie Camden—just a happy-go-lucky little thing that doesn't belong here or anywhere, but somehow makes perfect sense.

I'm stepping out of my car when the front door opens, and Jamie lumbers out with a small duffel bag. He grips the railing as he descends the stairs and waves me off when I approach. "Don't go getting any ideas that I need your help. I can still whip your ass in tetherball, and don't you forget it."

I grin as he ambles toward the car. "Oh, that one time in ninth grade? You're never going to let me live that down, huh?"

"I mopped the floor with you *and* Zack." He winces as he tosses his bag in the back and lowers into the passenger seat.

"Congratulations," I snicker as I punch my home address into Waze. "We have an hour and a half to relive it."

He turns to look at me. "Road trip, Noer!"

"Ha! Road trip, indeed."

He reaches into the back seat and retrieves my rooftop emergency hazard light, then rolls down the window as if he were planning to adhere it to the top of my car.

"Put that back, Jamie. I use that when I'm on construction sites at my job." I tug on the cord until he relents and tosses it behind us.

"Thompson-Miller sure does hook you up. If we used that, you could drive a hundred miles an hour. We'd be in Miami in no time."

"That's not really how that works. It's not a toy."

He rolls up the window. "God, *Mom*."

We set off toward Tamiami Trail, making small talk until we are passing the Big Cypress Preserve. Jamie's quiet as he scrutinizes the land, his eyes panning across the area where he nearly died. Where Morgan did die.

I squeeze the steering wheel and press harder on the accelerator, my eyes trained dead ahead.

"They haven't found anything else besides that chicken nugget? And the milk bottle?" Jamie asks.

I shake my head. "No. I killed him before we could get more information out of him."

Jamie pats my thigh and gives it a little rub. "Are you having murderer's remorse?" he teases.

I glance down at his lingering hand, then back at him, laughing nervously. "I . . . I killed someone, Jamie. Sure—he was killing you, and now he's a suspect in Skye's disappearance, but I can only pacify my conscience so much with that."

His hand slides off my leg and joins his other one in his lap. "You want one of my Vicodins? It'll take off the pressure. Make ya feel real good."

I laugh. "Shut up. I wonder if Morgan has any relatives or friends who would know anything."

Suddenly Jamie's hand is back on my leg—squeezing, but not hard enough to have to pretend to wince. "Noa, don't you dare. He was obviously a dangerous man, and if there are others who know what he did, you don't need to be poking around there. Let the authorities handle it."

I start. "I didn't mean me, just someone."

"Can we not talk about this right now, please? It's making me sick." Back toward his lap his hand slides, only this time it goes to his rib.

"Gladly," I sigh as we journey farther and farther away from the preserve. "Have you spoken with Zack? Did he tell you what we did yesterday?"

"No, what happened?"

We went to Smallwood Store, I tell him, where Zack made me confront Crayon-equin. We climbed to the top of the observation tower and took an airboat ride.

Jamie listens to my account with a neutral face, glancing from me to the road every few seconds. When I finish, he says, "So it's high school all over again."

For the first time ever, I can't tell if he's being sarcastic or not. And his expression gives me nothing.

"What does that mean?" I ask softly.

He groans as he rotates his position. "Nothing. Just sayin'. I mean, was it weird? Since you guys have such a . . . *history*?" The last word is grunted as he shifts again.

I find myself pinching the bridge of my nose as I set cruise control and relax my foot. "I mean . . . nothing about this entire situation *isn't* weird, Jamie. Hell, I haven't seen you guys in ten years, and suddenly here I am because his daughter is missing."

"More factors that you 'pacify your conscience' with?"

My head jerks toward him just in time to see his fingers dropping from the air quotes. I definitely detected a sardonic tone that time. "Are you insinuating that something could ever happen between Zack and me again?" I laugh haughtily and shake my head. "Jamie, that's just . . ."

And for the third time, I feel the weight of his hand on my thigh. Not patting, not rubbing, not squeezing—just resting. "You know they're having marital problems. Have been for a while now. It's why they're . . . *were* planning to move. And now with Skye missing, it's even worse."

My jaw clenches, my eyes locked on the never-ending strip of asphalt ahead. "No, I didn't. How and why would I know that?"

Now his hand is doing all those things, patting and rubbing and squeezing—deliberate and arrogant motions of a man who just proved a point, although I don't know what he thinks he's proven—and it retracts back into his lap again. "You wouldn't, and for so many reasons.

Not many people know. I'm just telling you—be careful. That's the situation."

My toes are dancing around in my shoes as anger flickers up my legs and through my arms to my fingertips. "Jamie? I don't give a fuck if Zack and Taylor are having marital problems. You actually just wasted five seconds of my life telling me that, five seconds I'll never get back. I came over here to help find Skye. Not to take advantage of their alleged marital problems and their missing child to seduce my high school boyfriend."

"Not saying you are. Why are you getting so defensive? Sheesh."

I bite down on my lip, probably too hard. He's playing mind games with me. I consciously bring my voice down to a reasonable decibel level. "I'm sorry, it's just that I told you about our day, which was innocent enough, and you're talking to me the same way everyone was looking at us when we got back to the docks."

Jamie laughs loudly and clenches his side. "Ouch! Damn, I'm sick of this rib pain. Noer, you're entirely too defensive for me to take you seriously. Do you mean to tell me that you spent all that time with your ex-boyfriend and didn't once think about him like that? Like, it didn't even cross your mind?"

My mouth drops open as I scramble for something to say, but he continues. "I've seen the way you two look at each other since you've been home. You guys have that same googly-eyed shit going on as you did in high school. Trust me, I saw enough of it back then to recognize it now."

"That's ridiculous."

"It's not. Listen to me, babe. You got this thing going on where you're constantly weighing facts with circumstances. You think I don't know you. Well, I'm just giving you the facts, because you clearly don't have them all. Zack still has feelings for you. Now add that boulder onto your little balance scale."

I'm suddenly claustrophobic. I want to stop the car, jump out, and run, but I'm in the middle of the Everglades on a single-lane road, and all the openness is making me even more claustrophobic. "How do you know that? Did he tell you?" I whisper.

Jamie doesn't answer, but I feel his eyes on me. I don't press; I don't want to know. Zack's confession on the airboat is answer enough.

I can't go back to Everglades City.

* * *

We arrive at my beach condo just before dinnertime. It's good to be home, back to some sort of normalcy, but it's strange having Jamie here. It's like my two worlds are colliding, but I don't hate it.

I texted Hector the moment I parked in the parking garage and invited him over. He responded that he'd be here in thirty minutes. This is the first time he'll be in my apartment too. The awkwardness of that combined with the awkwardness of Jamie's presence cancel each other out, and I decide I'm too drained to foster any sort of discomfort this evening.

Jamie limps around my apartment—*so this is Noer's living room, so this is Noer's kitchen*—and peruses each trinket as if he were in a museum. He finally makes it to the massive wall of windows to behold the infinite Atlantic Ocean and mutters, "Well, shit."

I drop my bags on the counter. "A far cry from Everglades life, isn't it?"

He turns to me and says, "You know, this is the first time I've seen the Atlantic Ocean? I've only ever been to the Gulf of Mexico." He's pulled back to the view, like a magnet.

"That's because we grew up closer to the Gulf. The first time I saw the Atlantic was my freshman year of college. Why did our parents never bring us over here?" I make myself busy, wiping down counters that are already clean.

"Because we grew up poor, Noer. Your folks had the B&B and my dad was a fisherman. A drunk fisherman, but a fisherman."

"I wouldn't say our families were poor. I mean, we certainly weren't rich by any means, but we'd go to Marco Island and Naples. Even Orlando a couple times a year. And Disney ain't cheap."

He clicks his tongue and moves to the sofa. "Maybe our parents just thought Miami would corrupt our innocent small-town minds," he jokes as he braces himself on the arm of the sofa and grabs his side before sitting.

"Ha. Probably."

Three loud raps on the door disrupt our musing. "That your boyfriend?" he asks as I scurry toward the knocking.

I throw open the door, and there stands Hector with a bouquet of flowers and a bottle of wine. He presents them to me like a game show host, and I take advantage of his open arms and throw myself into his chest. He laughs as his arms close around me. "It's good to see you," he says as he kisses the top of my head.

"You, too. Come in. Meet my friend Jamie." I take the flowers and smell them as I lead Hector inside; he closes the door and moves with purpose to the living room. Unlike Jamie, he takes minimal glances at his surroundings, and soon I figure out why—he's eyeing Jamie.

"I'm Hector. It's nice to finally meet you. Noa told me what happened to you. I'm so sorry." He leans to shake Jamie's hand, but I notice the shift in his jaw, because even with a bruised face and a cut eyebrow, Jamie Camden is handsome.

"The pleasure's mine," Jamie replies. "I'd stand up, but . . ."

Hector waves him off and settles in the love seat adjacent to him. He folds his hands and finally surveys the room. He doesn't comment, and I wonder if it's because he hates my décor or because he doesn't want Jamie knowing this is his first time seeing it.

My hands shake as I fill a vase with water and arrange the flowers. There's a tension in the air I wasn't anticipating. "Hector, have you eaten? Jamie and I are starving." It's at that moment I realize—Hector doesn't know that Jamie thinks I've been cured of CIPA. I didn't even think to tell him not to mention it, and I just lied about being hungry.

I frantically think back to how much I'd told Hector, if I mentioned that I don't feel hunger pains. I don't think I did; besides, he's currently listing off restaurants nearby where Jamie can experience authentic Miami cuisine. He's decided on Lario's on the Beach, rambling about how it's owned by Gloria Estefan and has the best Cuban food ever.

"Hector? I was thinking of ordering in. Jamie has a hard time getting around." I move to the love seat and curl up next to Hector as he's verbally kicking himself for forgetting.

"I just got caught up in taking you on a tour of Miami. I'm sorry about that," he says as he pulls his phone from his pocket. "Let me check Uber Eats."

Jamie makes a process of kicking his shoes off and dropping his feet on my coffee table. "Uber Eats? I've heard of that. It hasn't made it to the 'glades, though."

Hector looks up from his phone, like he can't wrap his head around not having the luxury of Uber Eats. But Jamie doesn't notice; he's trying to get comfortable and it doesn't seem to be happening.

"Hey, Jam? You want a Vicodin?" I ask.

"Aw, Noer, that would be amazing."

I stand just as Hector turns his puzzled gaze to me. "Noer?"

"Jamie, tell Hector the story of Noer while I get your pills. Actually, no. Don't tell him."

* * *

An hour later, with bellies full of burgers and shakes from the Big Pink, Jamie suggests we move onto the balcony. He wants to look at the ocean, he says.

The evening has been pleasant, despite the complete opposites that are Hector and Jamie, and the worry of my CIPA coming up in conversation. I've been successful thus far in steering the conversation away—especially when Hector asked Jamie to tell him embarrassing stories of me as a child and Jamie rubbed his hands together and said, "Oh, brother, lend an ear"—but something else isn't sitting right with me. There's a tension in the air I can't put my finger on.

The three of us are seated in the Adirondack chairs surrounding a small propane firepit I don't use often because it's against the association rules, and the ocean view is perfect, with the waning crescent moon and the twinkly lights I've strung along the railing.

"I've been following the story of Skye," Hector says as he twirls the wine in his glass. "What else is going on that the news isn't telling us?"

Jamie and I look at each other despairingly. "Nothing," I say. "What you're hearing is all that's going on. They found her DNA in a shack near where Morgan attacked Jamie, but it's like she disappeared."

Hector's demeanor turns full-on attorney—he props his ankle on the opposite knee and rests the base of his stem glass on his shoe. "Have they ruled out the family? A high percentage of—"

I nearly drop my own wine. "Hector!"

"Are you kidding me?" Jamie says between clenched teeth.

Hector drags his hand down his face and plants both feet on the tile. "Look, I'm sorry. Just hear me out, okay? I'm an attorney, I work with the law, and I know from experience that it's easy to be biased when family and friends are involved in a situation like this, but—"

"Zack and Taylor are my best friends. They are working night and day to find their daughter. They don't eat or sleep, they don't even shower," Jamie says calmly, although I know he's holding back his fury. Whether it's for my sake or for his rib's sake, I don't know, but that underlying tension I've felt all night is beginning to manifest.

Hector sighs and leans back. "You're right, I'm sorry. I shouldn't have brought my job into this." He stares into the empty firepit and snorts a laugh. "Noa's told me about you and Zack. I've heard many stories of all the fun times you guys had together as kids. I'm glad she has you."

Although I'm puzzled because I've never told Hector any stories about us as kids, this seems to relax Jamie. His dimples are puckered against his smug grin, and he winks at me. "Yeah, she's real lucky to have me around to keep her in line. This girl is trouble."

Hector gives a courtesy chuckle and pats my knee, but then Jamie eases out of his chair. "I hope you don't mind, but I think I'm gonna go to bed. Noer, we gotta get up early tomorrow for that doctor's appointment. And I'm not gonna lie—the Vicodin is kicking my ass right now."

Jamie and Hector engage in a cordial handshake with empty promises of doing this again sometime. I tell Jamie good night, then he slips inside and it's just Hector and me.

I listen to the breeze and the waves lapping against the shore as I think of something to say.

"He likes you."

My head swivels toward Hector. "What?"

He smiles, and it's the same smile as when we're about to depart from a date and we both want to kiss each other. "Jamie. He's carrying a torch for you."

I drop my head into my hands. I'm going to go crazy. I feel it in my stomach; it's bubbling higher and higher, up my throat, onto my tongue, and suddenly I'm laughing—and I can't stop. It's one of those silent laughs where tears stream from your eyes and take over your whole body. It's both cathartic and torturous.

Jamie told me earlier that Zack has feelings for me, and now this. It's all so ridiculous, and now I understand that tension I felt all night—a primitive pissing contest between these two. This whole thing is absurd.

I wipe my tears and catch my breath. "Hector, Jamie is like—"

"—a brother to you, yes. I know. How is it that you could sense—and prevent—the murder of your oldest friend, but you can't see the love-struck puppy look in his eyes?" Hector chuckles and pushes a strand of hair behind my ear that got caught up in the breeze.

"Hector, you've known Jamie for a couple of hours. I've known him my whole life. If he had feelings for me, I'd know. Trust me. Jamie and I have had crushes on each other at different times during our childhood, but nothing romantic has ever happened between us, and it never will."

Hector's been refilling our wineglasses and hands me mine. "Touché." He clinks them together, and his eyes sparkle brilliantly with a grin I can hardly resist. But then he drops his eyes to his glass and his smile slowly drips away. "Can I be honest with you?"

All traces of flirtation evaporate, and I sit up. Perhaps I went too far. I shouldn't have admitted that to him, it was too soon. Jamie just confessed to me yesterday about his bygone crush, and I haven't even fully processed it yet.

Hector glances toward the patio door and turns back to me. "I stopped talking earlier because I knew I was offending him. But, Noa, have they checked into Skye's family?"

"Hector—"

He holds up a hand. "I'm not saying it's for sure, but I've been following this story and I know how these things work. They need to rule everyone out. There is no motive for anyone in that town to take her. There hasn't been a child abduction near that area for over forty years. A body hasn't been found, which means whoever took her either is hiding his tracks very well or is keeping her alive for a reason."

"But what motive would Zack and Taylor have for kidnapping their own daughter? I've seen the tears they cry, Hector. You can't summon grief that explicit."

"You haven't seen them in years, you have no idea what kind of people they are anymore. And from what you told me of them, they already sounded cruel and heartless."

"We were stupid teenagers when they did that," I whisper. "And they've both apologized."

"Well, I'm glad, that's good. And I hope it's true. What about any other family members? Grandparents or aunts or uncles?"

I shift my weight until I'm leaning into Hector's shoulder and gaze out over the water. "His mom, Maggie? I don't see her kidnapping her granddaughter. Zack's dad, Logan, lives in Connecticut and doesn't give a shit about any of this. I don't know Taylor's parents, but I know they moved away once her father's construction company finished their project in Naples. And if I remember correctly, Zack has a couple of aunts and uncles, but none that were around the area often. I think I met Maggie's brother and sister once during the holidays. Logan didn't have siblings. Besides, why are we discounting Morgan Higgins? Her fingerprints were found in the shack he was squatting in. And he tried to kill Jamie in cold blood."

Hector wraps his arm around my shoulder and sets his empty glass on the table. "I'm not discounting him. He obviously was involved in the kidnapping, but there may be others. There have to be others, otherwise they would have found her by now in one of his campouts. My fear is that she's in some sort of trafficking ring. She could be anywhere."

"Oh, god. Stop." I snuggle deeper into his side, and he pulls me in to kiss my temple.

"So Jamie has his appointment tomorrow, then what? Are you going back to Everglades City? Or staying home?"

I smile. I like his use of *home*, and he feels like home. "I think I'll drop Jamie off and say goodbye to everyone, head back here. This whole situation is out of our hands now. I have a job. And a Hector." I twist my head up to him, and it's at that moment he leans down and plants his lips onto mine.

CHAPTER 13

I'M SITTING IN the waiting room of Dr. Hassan's office. Jamie was called in twenty minutes ago, and I can't stop thinking about Hector.

We didn't have sex last night. For many reasons: Jamie was in the bedroom, the couch would have been awkward, and it was the first time we'd done anything physical since the night we met.

We did do a lot of kissing on the balcony, though, among other things, and it seemed like the first time because neither of us was drunk.

I open Safari on my phone, because in addition to Hector's lips being on my body, I can't stop thinking about what he said last night—that family members are usually involved in child abductions. Initially, his accusation made me angry. But I reminded myself to step back and look at it from his point of view. He's only known Taylor as a teenage homewrecker, Zack as a heartless bastard who dumped a girl because of her serious health condition, and Logan as a cheating husband who has minimal contact with his family. It's with a sinking feeling in my stomach that I realize—he might be onto something.

I google Logan Flynn. The only items to come up are a football player and a child gamer. So I swipe out and head to Facebook. There are too many Logan Flynns to scroll through, so I navigate to Maggie's profile and go to her Friends page. I don't expect them to be friends, but I'm sure they have some mutual ones. After ten minutes of sleuthing, I finally find a Logan Flynn from New Haven, Connecticut, with a sailboat as his profile picture.

Of course, the settings on his page limit what I can see since we aren't friends. I'm unable to see any of his photos, and only minimal posts. The latest was two days ago, when he shared Taylor's post about Skye's disappearance.

My thumb hovers over the *add friend* icon, but the door opens and Jamie emerges. I notice he's walking better than he has been, and before I think better of it, I send Logan a friend request. I lock my phone and stand. "Well?"

"Let's get breakfast. I'm hungry."

"What did the doctor say?" I ask as I chase him out the door, his ADHD in full swing.

"They'll call within a couple days to give me the results."

* * *

Three hours later, we're driving through Ochopee past the smallest post office in the United States. It's smaller than my father's shed in the backyard. We've been quiet on this drive, Jamie and I. But he turns toward me now. "Thank you for driving me there. And for letting me crash at your place. I really appreciate you, Noer."

I glance at him and smile. "You're welcome. That's what friends are for."

He turns back toward the road. "So what are you going to do now? You're probably not going to stay in Everglades City much longer, huh?"

I sigh deeply and slide my hands to ten and two. "No, I'll probably go home this evening. Spend one last day with my folks and you guys." I'm hesitant to admit that I'm coming around to Hector's theory of familial involvement. After his reaction to Hector's accusation last night, I decide not to.

Twenty minutes later, I'm pulling up to his blue house. As he steps out of the car, I lean toward him. "Hey, I want to come inside and see your place. I showed you mine, now you show me yours."

He laughs as he grabs his bag from the back seat. "Do I look like I'm in any condition to be a tour guide? I can barely haul my ass from the couch to the john. Besides, it's a total mess right now. Can you swing by before you go home tonight? Give me a chance to clean it up? Then we can have a proper goodbye."

I roll my eyes. "Fine. I'll text you later." I wait until he's in his house before backing out and heading to my parents'.

Neither is home when I arrive, and phone calls to both of them go to voice mail. If I know them, my mother is at church and my father is at a bar. It's eleven in the morning, but that's never hindered either of them.

I pour a glass of sun tea and head out onto the back patio, deciding to call Janna to tell her I'll be back at work tomorrow, but when I reach for my phone again, I see a Facebook notification: *Zack Flynn has sent you a friend request.*

I'm not exactly sure how strange this is, I think. But I swipe it open and accept it. This is the first time I've ever seen Zack's Facebook page; I only saw privacy restrictions the few times I stumbled upon it through the years—including today while searching for Logan.

I sit at the table on the deck and study his profile, the photos of him with Skye posted sparsely throughout her life and those of him with Taylor. There are a few of him with Jamie from a few years ago, but his most recent posts are obviously of Skye's disappearance.

I click on his Friends list and begin scrolling, recognizing names of the ghosts of people past—friends from high school, neighbors, even a set of twin boys who moved away shortly after Zack came to our school. Then I see an interesting one: Logan Flynn.

I click on him again and am puzzled when the blue icon glows brightly: *add friend*. I added him this morning, so it should say either *request pending* or indicate that he accepted it and that we are, in fact, friends.

He declined it. I can't help feeling a bit hurt, especially after the kind things he said to me after Zack broke my heart. Maybe he declined it by accident. Or maybe while Jamie was barreling out of the doctor's office at lightning speed, I just thought I hit the friend button but missed.

With desperation overpowering my pride, I friend request him again.

Just then the patio door opens, and I look up to see my father sauntering onto the deck, wearing worn jeans and a blue flannel shirt. "Hi," he groans as he lowers himself across from me. "How was Jamie's appointment this morning?"

I lock my phone and set it on the table. "Fine. I think I'm going to head home tonight."

He strums his fingers on the tabletop, the ticking sound buffered by his callused fingertips. "I don't blame ya. This place just gets more and more depressing."

I nod. "Yeah."

"Your ma's out planning a vigil with Maggie and Taylor for tonight. You really should at least stick around for that, ya know."

"Oh, she is? I didn't know there would be a vigil. Of course I'll come. That will give me a chance to pay respects and say bye to everyone. Where is it?"

"In that big open space in front of City Hall. She's down there now, putting those paper discs around candles, if you want to go help her."

"Yeah, that's a good idea."

* * *

Four minutes later, I'm driving through the giant roundabout and parking in front of City Hall, where my mother, Maggie, and Taylor sit among a sea of candles and flowers like a human assembly line. Three sad smiles greet me as I approach. I shove my hands in my back pockets. "Need any help?"

Taylor scoots a box of candles toward me, and I kneel next to her in the grass and begin spearing tiny candles through small cardboard circles that say *Bring Skye Home*. I slip glances at her, monitoring her to see if she's upset with me for taking the airboat out with Zack, but then chide myself for the narcissism of thinking she is upset with me rather than the fact that her daughter is missing. We work silently for a few minutes until Taylor scoffs.

"What's wrong?" Maggie asks.

Taylor is rifling through the box of finished candles and says, "Some of the prongs on these drip protectors are facing up. It looks tacky." She begins plucking candlesticks from the discs and inserting them into the other end—prong down—before tossing them forcefully back into the box.

I start, my eyes turning to Maggie, who says, "Oh, that might've been me. I didn't think it mattered."

My mother cocks her head. "I don't think it matters, Taylor," she says softly as if she were approaching a tiger. "Both sides say Bring Skye Home. They're just meant to keep the wax from dripping onto people's hands."

"Tacky," Taylor repeats as she determinedly rectifies the wayward candles.

The rest of us exchange glances—our eyebrows raised and jaws tightened.

The moment passes, and we continue working until there's one box left, at which point my mother and Maggie decide to go arrange the flowers around the centerpiece of the vigil—a giant portrait of Skye.

As they step away, Taylor leans into the box to grab the remaining candles, and that's when her shirt rides up her back and reveals a huge black bruise. Without thinking, I blurt out, "Oh, my god, Taylor. What happened to your back?"

Those are the first words we've exchanged since our visit to Jamie's hospital room.

I lift the hem of her shirt and run my finger along the discolored skin, and she cranes her neck to observe it. "It happened during the search party. It was really dark, and I tripped over a huge stump and landed on an even bigger one."

She doesn't look at me as she tells me this lie, but it wouldn't matter even if she stared me dead in the eye as she said it, because everyone knows when you trip, you fall forward. Not backward.

I want to call her out on it, but the sound of crunching dry grass causes us to look up and see Zack approaching. He's in distressed jeans with a navy sweater, the shirttails and collar of a gray dress shirt rimming the edges.

"Hey, Noa." He squats down next to Taylor, and after Jamie's revelation of their marriage problems and Hector's legal advice to suspect the parents, I don't know if I'm imagining the heightened tension between them or reading things more accurately than ever.

"Hi," I whisper and continue impaling the last of the *Bring Skye Home* circles.

"Taylor, can we talk?" he asks softly.

Without answering, Taylor stands and struts away at a brisk enough pace to insinuate that she doesn't want to be followed.

Zack plops from squatting to sitting as we watch her retreat, and I don't know what to say. When she disappears inside City Hall, we look at each other. Zack raises his eyebrows and sighs apologetically.

I turn back to the last candle. "These are tough times," I say, because asking him if everything is okay would be insulting.

"I guess she's mad at me. Again."

I glance up to see his elbows propped on his raised knees, his hands running through his hair. I can't speak for a grieving mother, but Taylor seems to be angry at everyone lately. It's getting harder to deny that this grieving mother bears a striking resemblance to the snotty teen she once was. "I'm sorry, Zack. It's not because we went on the airboat, is it?"

He waves me off. "Nah."

I wait for him to continue while folding the empty boxes.

He doesn't; instead he stands to help me carry the finished candles toward our mothers, who are adjusting the easel with Skye's portrait next to a table littered with photos, flowers, and more candles.

"Zack, why does Taylor have a huge bruise on her back?" I ask as we walk side by side.

"What? She doesn't," he replies.

Maggie approaches and takes my box from me. "Let's get these inside so they don't melt out here." And Zack and I curve our steps to follow her into City Hall. I want to press the issue, tell him there's no mistaking what I saw, that she acknowledged it with a pitiful lie, but the way he answered makes me think he either doesn't know about it or doesn't want to talk about it.

How could he not know his wife's back is severely bruised?

Upon entering, Maggie beelines to a folding table and sets the box on it, and Zack follows suit. I look around for Taylor, but I don't see her. Maggie, preoccupied with the vigil, mentions something about going across the street to the church to borrow their hymnals.

"I'm going to head out, too," Zack says and follows Maggie out the door.

I ponder his behavior as I stand alone in City Hall. His departure seemed rude, abrupt. He may have been avoiding any further interrogating over Taylor's bruise. Or perhaps he's simply upset about Skye. I rub my eyes and decide to head to the bathroom, since I haven't gone in a while and I've nothing else to do here.

The stalls in the bathroom are thick with floor-to-ceiling dividers. I push the heavy door open on the first stall, and it slams behind me. I've just gotten my jeans unzipped when I hear the bathroom door opening and a person crying, and I freeze.

"So now what? She saw the bruise," Taylor's voice cries, muffled through the thickened walls. I plant both hands over my mouth and strain with everything I am to hear her. She's mumbling something, I hear a series of *no, no, no* before it's quiet. And then: "I just want my daughter back."

But the way she says it causes the hairs on the back of my neck to rise. It wasn't a wistful plea; it was more of a demand.

I'm so quiet I can hear the echo of her locking her phone. She hung up on whoever she was talking to, and suddenly the silence is split by a guttural scream. It scares me so badly I feel the wetness begin to saturate my jeans, and the slamming door marks her exit just as I shimmy them down and finish relieving myself in the toilet.

I never sit on public toilets, but I can't hold myself up. I am on the porcelain with my elbows on my bare knees, my shocked face cradled in my hands. What did I just hear? So many thoughts are going through my head at once. That bruise is sinister. Something happened that she doesn't want anyone to know about, and whoever she was talking to knows about it too—might be responsible for it.

I can't fathom Zack being physically abusive. He never raised a finger to me while we were dating.

Noa, you have CIPA and hitting you wouldn't faze you.

Oh, my god. Would Zack have hit me if it would have had the effect he wanted?

No, I know Zack, and that's just not who he is.

Ten years changes people . . .

I pull my jeans back up and button them, then flush the toilet as another thought crashes into my brain. Did I imagine the way she demanded her daughter back? I observe the stall door's thickness as I open it. Her words made it through the barrier, but did her tone somehow get lost in translation?

I barely register washing my hands and hustling to my car. It's not until I'm back at my parents' house and showering off the urine and public toilet seat that I realize I cannot leave Everglades City tonight. Not yet.

CHAPTER

14

Zack's been on Facebook, because he liked my latest post. If that's not weird enough, he had to have gone to my profile to see it, because I posted it two weeks ago. It's a simple photo of me Hector took at a restaurant, a martini glass in hand. I can't even remember what restaurant it was, until I zoom in on the photo and see the menu still on the table—Yardbird.

A knock on my bedroom door startles me from my cross-legged position on the bed. "Yeah?" I call.

My mother pops her head in and smiles. "Your dad and I are heading over to the vigil now. Do you want to ride with us?"

I check the time and see that it doesn't start for another hour. "I'm not ready yet. I didn't know you were leaving early."

"No worries, we'll see you over there." The door clicks shut.

I turn back to my phone and stare at the notification: *Zack Flynn liked your photo.*

Just below is a list of people I may know. I'm reminded of that second friend request I sent to Logan, but I'm not seeing that he accepted it. I try navigating to his page, but now I can't even find him.

I jump when the screen goes black and suddenly the whole device vibrates and jingles. Hector is calling.

"Hi," I answer.

"Hi, beautiful. Are you still planning on coming home tonight?"

I hesitate. "I don't think so. Some weird stuff is going on. Can you do me a quick favor?"

"Um, sure."

"Go to Facebook and see if there is a Logan Flynn from New Haven, Connecticut. He's got a sailboat as his profile picture."

"Hang on."

I wait, staring at the graduation photo of Jamie and me on the dresser. After thirty seconds, I hear the *ping!* of an incoming text.

"Check your phone," Hector says. "I just sent you what I found."

I pull the phone from my ear and sure enough—Logan blocked me. My shoulders slump forward—I can't believe he'd do this. He was always so nice to me, so gentle. Perhaps time does change people.

"What's going on?" Hector's voice says through the phone as I stare at the screenshot of the damn sailboat.

I return the phone to my ear. "Nothing. This guy blocked me, apparently. But listen—you don't know the can of worms you opened when you suggested not ruling out the family. Weird things are happening, Hector."

"Like what?"

I tell him about Taylor's bruise, her and Zack's reactions to it, and the phone call I heard from the bathroom.

"Uh, Noa? I think it's time you back away from this and come home."

"But you said—"

"I know what I said. I didn't mean for you, personally, to look into the family. You're not a detective, Noa. What you're doing is playing with fire. Remember, you have a history with this family, a bias. I told you those things because there is also a legal, objective, *unbiased* side to this situation that I was fearful you were rejecting *because* of your ties to them."

We're both silent as I register his words and he lets me.

"Listen, Noa. What you saw on Taylor's back and what you heard in the bathroom is her own business. I'm sorry if that sounds misogynistic and old fashioned, but it's not your place to intervene. Not from a practical standpoint nor a theoretical standpoint. Altruism is a virtue, yes, but it can also be detrimental to your well-being."

I mull his words over, acknowledge the truth behind them. I've put too much into this situation—my time, my heart, my soul—but the truth is Zack and Taylor chose each other over me ten years ago, and this is their life now. Mine is back in Miami.

For a woman who is constantly weighing dynamics versus logistics, I've failed miserably.

"I'll be home after the vigil tonight, okay?"

He chuckles smoothly. "And I'll be waiting with open arms."

* * *

Despite the two hundred people standing outside City Hall, the evening is stone cold silent. I'm one of the last to arrive, apparently, and I slip to the back of the crowd gathered around Skye's portrait. Pink balloons float around like guardian angels, and flowers are sprinkled like fairy dust around the photos and candles lighting up the area. I believe the photo of her is from the same photo shoot as the picture in Maggie's house, as she's wearing the same green linen dress and wreath of flowers in her dark, flowing hair. It's a headshot of her, though, with a solid black background that makes her eyes pop.

Mayor Shelly Howell takes the makeshift stage up front, but I'm too far away to hear her. I look at the people surrounding me, and I don't recognize any of them. I'm sure my parents are with Maggie and the family—Jamie too—and I wonder if I should be up there with them instead of here in the back among the fourth and fifth degrees of separation. But then I remember I've gotten too involved already.

The mayor continues speaking—words I still can't hear—and suddenly everyone holds up the little candles we put together this afternoon. Empty-handed, I glance around and spot a large basket I must have missed, with a sign: *Take One*.

I move away from the crowd and extract one of the few remaining candles. But when I turn back I nearly bump into Taylor. She's been running. I reach to steady her and notice her eyes are swollen and red. "Hey," I say softly.

She swallows and shakes her head, her eyes filling with tears again. "I—I just need to step away from all this for . . . for just a second. It's too much for me." Her lips tremble as she tries fruitlessly to hold back her tears.

I pull her into a hug. "Of course. Take your time. We'll all be here when you're ready."

"Thank you." She sniffs and releases me. "Will you hold my purse, please? I'll be right back." She shoves a small black bag at me and heads straight for City Hall.

I watch as she scurries toward the building, bumping into at least three people without so much as an apologetic glance.

I have a flashback to the lunch line at school, how she'd plow past people as if they weren't there, and I wonder—how much has she changed? But this isn't the same. She's mourning now, I have to remember this. Those tears seemed very real. Still, her phone call in the bathroom was real, too, the one that sounded like she was bargaining for her child. Backing out of a negotiation. Does Taylor know who was helping Morgan Higgins?

I consider following her, but no. I'm staying true to my word, staying out of this mess and going home after the vigil. I return to the crowd, Taylor's purse feeling foreign in my hand.

A tap on my shoulder reminds me that we are lighting candles, and I hold mine out for an elderly lady to light with her illuminated one. I look up and notice the sea of tiny orange dollops lighting a broad pathway up to the angelic face of Skye.

My breath catches, and suddenly, the orange flames begin swaying while a multitude of powerful voices begin singing "Amazing Grace."

It's soul-stirring. I feel the emotions in the air, the heartache as palpable as a living entity. Sobs break out like surround sound among the lyrics—*I once was lost, but now am found*—and I'm losing control of my facial muscles as I try in vain to swallow my tears.

Was blind but now I see . . .

I grip my candle with both hands, Taylor's purse a burden on me now. I glance at the building, hoping she'll return to claim it soon. When I don't see her, my eyes turn down to the handbag—a black leather thing with silver rhinestones.

Why would she give this to me simply to go to the bathroom, I wonder. There's no reason she couldn't have taken it with her, although nothing should surprise me after witnessing her behavior these last few days. And why give it to me, of all people?

Suddenly her purse buzzes—one long, muffled vibration. It's like a call for help, and I'm struck with the realization that I'm the current keeper of Taylor's phone. Wax drips onto my hand as I inadvertently tip the candle to illuminate the contents of her bag, but I don't feel it. It's probably burning me, but at this point I don't care. Her phone is the first thing I see, the very device that delivered her obscure demand: *I just want my daughter back.* The device that holds all her secrets.

I pluck it from her purse and glance toward City Hall. Her phone is in my hand, the screen lit up as brightly as my dripping candle.

Bright shining as the sun . . .

I don't see her. I look back at it. I could go into her call log and see who she was talking to earlier; I know her password—her own birthday.

I slip past the elderly woman and immerse myself farther into the crowd, blending in, inconspicuous.

Through many dangers, toils and snares, I have already come . . .

About twenty people in, I'm near the center of the mass. Taylor won't find me anytime soon, and I scramble to push the magic digits.

0222

And just like that, her home screen shines brilliantly in my face.

'Twas grace that brought me safe thus far . . .

I touch the green call icon down at the bottom, and with shaking hands, touch *Recents.*

There must be five hundred verses to "Amazing Grace," because the crowd drones on as my hands shake and I try to calculate with my frenzied mind what time it was when I heard that cryptic phone conversation.

It was around noon, I remember, and I drag my eyes down the time stamps and land on one at 12:06 and one at 12:10.

One is Zack.

The other is Logan Flynn.

'Twas grace that taught my heart to fear . . .

My candle drops to the earth and immediately snuffs out, and I turn to push my way out of the crowd. "Excuse me, sorry," I mumble to the mourning carolers, and they step aside with grace for the woman they assume can no longer handle the heavy sorrow hovering over us all. But when I reach the outskirts of the crowd, I head to the small building in the middle of the clearing, the one with the sign that says *Stone Crab Capital of the World.*

I duck behind it, fully hidden from the hundreds, and click on his name. He's kept his Florida number, according to the area code, and I copy it into my own phone and hit *Call.*

My heart is pounding. The first ominous ring drags out forever, the tone a clashing harmony with the singers. Four more times the ring tone mocks my ear drums, and then an automated voice tells me this mailbox is full.

I call it again.

Again and again until even the automated voice sounds annoyed, and with a loud growl, I swipe out of Taylor's phone app and lock it, slipping it into her purse and sneaking back out into the multitude.

My eyes scan the crowd for Jamie, for my mother—anyone I can recognize. But I'm among strangers, drowning in them, and the sadness is overpowering, and the singing is monotonous, and I'm too overwhelmed to stay here a minute longer.

My legs carry me away from the mob, away from the heaviness of the roundabout. The night gets darker as I move farther and farther away from the oceans of fire, those miniature torches that mock me with their melancholy tunes—*when we've been there ten thousand years*—and I run until my feet are no longer pounding pavement but instead are clomping on the wooden planks of the docks at the canal, where I finally feel like I can breathe.

I could run right off the dock and into the swampy waters, swim to Bear Island. Anything to get away from this torturous town. I need to leave, go back to Miami. I miss my bed, my Hector, but I can't get to my car without passing through that purgatory again.

A nearby bench catches my eye, and I drag myself to it. I sit and look at my feet, consider the raw mess they must be after sprinting nearly a quarter of a mile in strappy sandals.

The content of Taylor's phone is too unsettling, and I stare at the creepy black waters and the skeletal mangrove forests across the way as I catch my breath. I gaze out into them, trying to glean from their wisdom, empathize with their caliber of darkness.

I can't just abandon Skye. Oh, I'll go home, but I'm calling the cops when I get there. Sticking to Hector like glue. This is far from over.

Footsteps are approaching, rapid ones. Angry ones. I turn around, but I only see the black form of a silhouette before it swings an object and bashes it against my head.

CHAPTER

15

AMAZING GRACE! HOW sweet the sound, that saved a wretch like me . . .

These dream-like lyrics swirl rhythmically throughout my brain, twirling and braiding themselves among my wormlike gray matter.

"I once was lost, but now am found. Was blind but now I see."

I'm singing it now, trying to wake myself up. I've heard of incubus, that scary stage between sleep and awake, but this is the first time I'm experiencing it. I'm in a sitting position—unbelievably rigid—but I can't move, can't open my eyes. I'm stuck like this. Forever, it seems.

I force myself to blink, but either I'm still asleep or it's pitch dark. I can't move my arms or legs, but I'm moving my fingers, my toes. I rub my fingers together, acknowledge the pressure of my thumb against the pads. I grate my toes over one another, feeling the tendons and ligaments pulling and slinking through my feet and into my shins.

I'm awake, I know it. I also know that I'm blindfolded and bound.

I scream as loud as I can.

"Help! Help meeeeeee!"

I scream until my voice is gone, thrash my shoulders, my head, because they're all I can move.

"Lemmeooouuuuut!"

There comes a point where rationality succumbs to irrationality, and now the irrationality is your new norm. You must accept this irrationality as rationality, lest you die. It's a survival tactic, the mind's way of continuing to function by shutting down awareness.

I did that when I first moved to Miami—the traffic. Twice a day I nearly lost my mind to the sluggish cars, the crazy drivers, the long bouts of idling, the terrifying sideswipes I narrowly missed for two hours. Then after a while, I forced myself to accept it, to become numb to it. Not because I liked it any better, but because I needed to preserve the majority of my sanity, even if that meant sacrificing a percentage of it. So I traded a part of my sound mind to the devil, in exchange for a small token of madness to efficiently get through my day.

This metamorphosis has begun in my mind now, as I realize I'm comparing this horrible, terrifying situation to traffic in Miami.

I'm screaming like a crazy person—which I realize I am—and as the chrysalis of former rationality unravels away to this new, warped form, I begin hearing birds chirping, can see specks of sunlight through the fibers of whatever is hindering my sight.

I don't know how long it takes before I'm fully granted a quasi-sound mind, but eventually I find myself scrutinizing the details of what got me here. The vigil, Taylor's phone. I was onto something, I knew it. But I still don't know what it was. Just that Taylor has a bruise, and at one point she called either her husband or her father-in-law and said she wants her daughter back.

And why wouldn't a mother who is missing her child say that?

I've learned nothing. I'm no closer to finding Skye than I was when I first came to Everglades City. I've only allowed my mind to play games with the circumstances and went from suspecting nobody to suspecting everybody.

Hector was right. I'm not a detective, and I should have left. I should have left.

Fear of the unknown creeps in as I become more aware of my surroundings. I hear no people, no cars, just the sounds of wildlife and hints of light whispering through the blindfold. This means it's daytime, and I've been held here an entire night, at least. Is this where I die? Why haven't I died yet?

I try again to move against the restraints, but it's useless. I realize it's quiet—the birds have stopped and the specks of light are dulling. Is it getting dark already? But soon I hear patters of rain, and at least I'm in some sort of shelter. I taste the humidity, so wherever I am isn't air conditioned.

Thunder cracks, and within minutes a drop of water splatters on my forehead. Another on my foot. The roof is leaking, and there's no air conditioning . . .

I'm in a shack in the middle of the Everglades. Tied to a chair.

Despair, that's my new norm. People must be wondering where I am by now. Is my mother crying? Is my father? And what about Hector? Does he think I just didn't come home last night like I said I would? He probably thinks I'm ghosting him.

How long until they have a vigil for me?

A long, drawn-out sob pushes through my strained lips. Tears soak the blindfold.

The rain, it's coming for me. It pounds on the roof, letting me know it's trying to get in here, trying to rescue me. I wish for the rain to come, to break down the doors of this place. Remove these shackles, rescue me.

What feels like hours go by, but it does none of those things. No one comes for me. My body is bound but my mind runs wild. Rationality is losing, and I drift in and out of consciousness.

I once was lost, but now am found. Was blind, but now I see . . .

Yeah, right.

* * *

I awaken to sounds that are not of nature. No birds, no rain, no whistling of wind through sawgrass in major and minor keys. Instead, I hear a creaking of door hinges. Footsteps. Someone is here. The door slams so sharply that this thing I'm strapped to vibrates. I strain to see through the blindfold, even a fragment of light, but this darkness is otherworldly, an infinite black hole. I wonder what time of night it is.

"Wh—who's there?" I ask, my voice strangled.

There's no reply.

"I hear you, goddammit! Tell me who you are!"

Footsteps—only one set—scuff almost hesitantly. Closer.

"Why are you doing this? What are you going to do to me?"

My voice is desperate, unlike the slow, calculated movements of whatever is happening around me.

"Wh—what are you doing?" I breathe.

The footsteps come to a stop with an awkward scuff sound. They slowly start back up again, making a scraping noise, and I feel a presence hovering over me. Something touches my arm. I jump.

Then, in my ear, a whisper: "Shhh. He'll hear you."

The words roll around my head, the high-pitched pixie voice of a child, until they're completely unraveled to reveal an epiphany.

"S—Skye?" I utter.

They're on my hands now, those fingers, my hands that are bound behind me. I hear her little grunts as she works at the restraints, whatever they are, but at this point, I don't care about them. I want this blindfold removed so that I can behold her with my own eyes.

I try again—"Are you Skye Flynn?"

No response. But I hear her breaths—tiny and sweet.

"Honey, please answer me. Please."

But all I hear is the warfare of hemp and fibers gnawing against each other, rubbing at my skin. The smell of synthetic earth and oil permeates my nose.

Then slowly, gaps. They form between my arms and this death chair, the centimeters of space growing by infinities. I twist my wrists, dancing with the loosening ties, her tiny fingertips brushing against mine with dexterity.

And then her touch is gone, replaced by her footsteps scampering back toward the door or wherever they had initiated.

"Skye, no! Come back!" I hiss.

The scurrying ceases—she obeyed. Just like everyone said she does.

Freedom never felt so sweet as my right hand escapes first, and I can't remove this blindfold fast enough. And there she is—I'm staring at the image of a dark-haired little girl, swaying on the other side of this small cabin. It's too dark to see the details of her features, but I know it's Skye.

She's here. Alive. We're being held hostage out here in the middle of the Everglades—by someone who could walk in at any moment.

But before I can speak, she throws open the door and is gone.

I jump up to chase her, but my feet refuse to leave the chair and I fall forward, taking the chair with me. Stars explode when I land hard on my forehead, and the earth spins a quick, violent rotation.

I fumble around in the darkness until my fingers find the rope knotted around my ankles. It's so dark, and I don't know up from down right now. A thick substance drips down my forehead into my eyes, distracting me from navigating my way around the knot. The longer this takes, the farther away she's getting.

I manage to slip off the sandals I wore to the vigil, which enables me to make sense of the ropes in relation to my feet. I abandon the knot and focus on the intricate loops around my ankles, wiggling and manipulating them, warping my feet into dangerous positions, until my heel breaks free and one foot is loose. My other foot slips out, and I'm running to the door, barely registering the barren log walls and thatched roof, the filthy window with blacked-out glass—a tiny rectangle. I sprint for the door and nearly fall. "Skye!" I whisper-yell.

I throw it open and am met with three poorly structured steps leading to the soft marshland, illuminated by moonlight. My ankles pop and crack as I step to each one. Blood drips from my head and soaks my dress, but I've no time to assess the severity of damage I've done to my body. I turn and look at the shack that's been holding me hostage. It's dilapidated, with a low roof, spray painted brown and green. The midnight hour gives it an even more eerie feel, the moon a lamp casting haunting shadows. Fear grips me as I swivel around and see that I'm surrounded by these chilling structures—five of them in total—hidden among a thick forest like a coven.

I'm choking with fear, and even if I could call out Skye's name I wouldn't dare. I don't know what sort of demons are lurking around. But I've seen her; she rescued me, and now I have to rescue her.

I hobble toward the next haunted cabin. My ankles feel thick—so does my brain. I have to work to maintain balance. But I ascend the stairs and open the door hanging haphazardly from its hinges. I wince at the loud creak.

"Skye?" I whisper into the darkness. One step inside reveals a barren shell of a cabin with a stone floor covered in rusted cans and broken bottles. Red graffiti covers the walls. No sign of Skye. I shiver deeply before retreating.

A bird shrieks as I quickly tiptoe to the next shack, and I push the door open and whisper her name again. This one is completely empty—simple wooden walls and a dirt floor. The next two are nearly the same, and the last one is half burned to the ground. I check it anyway, chirping out Skye's name sporadically as I poke my head in the door. Ferns and vines grow through the cracked and charred flooring, and I back out when the first step inside results in crumbling floorboards.

When I've searched all five cabins, I stand in the middle of them, head spinning. What's happening? This child is living among this evil neighborhood of ghosts, a monster is on the loose, and she's disappeared. I circle the collection of shacks, squinting in the darkness and whispering her name until I hear the rumbling of a car engine.

A car engine.

My subconscious picks a direction, and I run. My hands are slick with blood and swamp mud, I lose count of the times I trip and fall, but still I run. My brain tells me to stay and find Skye, but all rationality has surrendered to this maniacal will to survive.

I'm unaware of where I'm going, of where I am. Seven thousand eight hundred square miles, these Everglades. And with my sense of direction lopsided, I could be running in circles for all I know. Two things are certain: Skye is out here, and there is another predator besides Morgan Higgins prowling around.

My entire body is soaking wet. The bacteria in these stagnant waters are surely festering in these wounds on my head, the cuts on my ankles, the withering Dermabond, and the healing gash beneath.

It's shutting down, my body. The head trauma, the lack of food and water. And although I feel none of the repercussions, I know I can't hold out much longer. Tears spread across my face, dripping into the swamp, my bare feet scraping and tearing over God knows what, my eyes rendered useless from the thick canopies of the hardwood hammock.

Something slithers into a small solution hole nearby, maybe a snake. Alligator. I can't keep my eyes open, whether from exhaustion or trauma I don't know. But I can't stop. I'll either die of tetanus or be eaten by an alligator. And the longer it takes me to get to the police, the longer Skye is stuck out here.

And then, just as the black sky morphs into a dense, hazy gray, a break in the trees ahead has me running harder. I nearly leap for joy when I stumble into a concrete wall and flip over it onto the asphalt of a main road. My bloated, bare feet continue thrusting me forward, leaving a trail of crimson footprints, until they stop right on the broken line down the middle. I turn toward a set of headlights blasting in my eyes, waving my bloody, mud-covered hands frantically.

The driver flashes the high beams at me and honks a series of angry blares. But I'd rather be run over than left like this in this primitive swamp. The vehicle is close enough now to see that it's a huge bucket truck—*Florida Power and Light* displayed in blue on the side—and by the grace of God, it slows and pulls off to the shoulder.

I limp toward it as a middle-aged man with thinning black hair throws open the driver's side door and jumps down. "What the hell?" he says as he marches toward me, arms outstretched.

I fall into him and sob, blood and swamp smearing all over his rugged blue jeans and khaki button-up with the FPL logo. He smells of coffee and cigarettes. "Help me" is all I can manage.

"What's your name?" he asks as he carries me to his truck.

"Noa Romwell. I was kidnapped. I escaped and need to go to the hospital. I saw the little girl, Skye—"

"Damn right you need to go to the hospital. Jesus Christ, you looked like a zombie walking across the street. Scared the shit out of me." He helps me up into the passenger seat of the truck, and I shiver as he sprints in front of the headlights and jumps in the driver's side. He pulls out his phone and dials three simple numbers, and he stares in awe as I continue crying, my head dripping blood all over the cab.

"Yeah, I just found a woman who says she's been kidnapped. She's . . . she's real bloody. We need an ambulance," he says into the phone.

My eyes are locked on a foam cup of coffee, a random gas station emblem stamped into its skin. Behind it, his knee parades around in edgy bounces while his rough hand rips apart a matching napkin.

"Tell 'em about Skye," I mumble.

His face twists as he gazes up through his windshield. "Yeah, she's conscious, but talking real crazy. Wants me to tell you about the sky, doesn't even care about all the blood coming from her head. She ain't even in pain. How long 'til the ambulance gets here? I think she's going into shock. Yeah, we're on I-75, Alligator Alley." He punches buttons on his navigation system in the dashboard. "I just hopped on about twenty minutes ago from Fort Lauderdale heading toward Naples. Hang on! There's a mile marker ahead."

He jumps out of the cab and sprints toward a small rectangular green sign as I process his words. Alligator Alley, just outside Fort Lauderdale . . .

It's so far north, so far east of Everglades City. Easily sixty miles away, maybe more. My breaths hitch as I realize that the area we were scouring like a bunch of fools is nowhere near where Skye actually is. Despair rises from the floorboards, a poisoning mist, smothering my air and polluting the cab.

He jumps back in with no phone to his ear. "They're coming, sweetie. Just hang in there."

"Did you tell them about Skye?" I grit through chattering teeth.

He nods patronizingly as he reaches beneath his seat and extracts a jacket with a matching FPL logo. "I did. Told 'em the sky is blue, and they believed me."

I acquiesce by allowing him to wrap his jacket around my shoulders, because there's no use challenging the beliefs of anyone who argues that the sky is blue.

CHAPTER 16

IT WAS THE Lost City, most everyone is sure of it. A place of legend and folklore. A place where Al Capone allegedly ran a bootlegging operation, peddling moonshine during Prohibition. Others argue that a few dozen Confederate soldiers, rebels, had stolen a wealth of gold and were hiding out there, only to be ambushed and slaughtered by Seminoles for setting up camp on sacred ground.

No one knows for sure, but there's one thing I know—I wouldn't use the word *sacred* to describe my experience in that little domain where I was held captive.

They comb the area while I'm here at Memorial Regional Hospital near Fort Lauderdale. Once again, they've found no sign of Skye.

My mother stays with me, and Hector makes the forty-five-minute drive after work. They exchange pleasantries, and afterward Hector says my mother seems nice, and my mother doesn't say anything at all.

Zack calls my mother repeatedly—is there anything he can do? Pay us a visit, bring Jamie, anything?—and I shake my head ardently at my mother. No visitors, please. Jamie was recently bludgeoned, and it's an hour and a half drive. Stay there and look for Skye.

X-rays. CT scans. IVs. MRIs. Do you have preexisting conditions? I try to say no, but my mother says yes. Congenital insensitivity to pain, she says. Whoa, the doctors say. That's a real thing?

Cops! Detectives! And until Hector-attorney-at-law kicks them out, lawyers! Their initial questions revolve around Skye: Are you sure it was her? Did she say anything? Tell us again what she said. Is that all? Are you sure that's all? What was she wearing?

Later on, they ask about my mental health history. If I or anyone in my family ever suffered from schizophrenia or the like. They ask for permission to see my CT scan, ask the doctor how severe the concussion is.

Did I see the person who abducted me? No. Go find Skye, please.

I'm surprised when the questioning circles back to the death of Morgan Higgins. A spritely woman enters my room with jet-black hair slicked back into a severe ponytail. She introduces herself as Officer Nash, and though she apologizes for "having to ask these questions," she doesn't sound very apologetic. Her tone is accusatory as she asks for a detailed account from the day I saved Jamie's life.

"Stop there," she says when I'm relaying the part about seeing Morgan beating Jamie through the window. "How clearly could you see the assault happening through that little dirty window?"

Puzzled, I glance at my mother, who is shriveled up in the corner of the room, and then Hector, who seems to be more agitated by the minute. "I mean, I could see that someone was hitting someone else with a stick or a bat. The window was clear enough to see that something was wrong, and that was confirmed when I actually entered the shack and watched it happening."

She cocks her head. "So once you entered the shack, were you able to determine whether the implement the assailant was utilizing was a stick or a bat?"

I pause because I don't know where she's going with this. "Honestly, no, I didn't stop to label the weapon that was killing Jamie Camden. It wasn't until later that we established that it was actually a bat. Check the police records."

She doesn't look at me as she absorbs this answer; instead, she scans page after page of her notes while shaking her head. "It's peculiar," she says more to herself than to us, but it makes the three of us straighten our spines and widen our eyes.

"Wh—what do you mean?"

"There's a pattern, Ms. Romwell, of you not seeing things clearly. You *couldn't tell* what Skye looked like, you *couldn't tell* what the weapon was—"

"Nope. Nope." Hector catapults from his seat and approaches Officer Nash. "The minor details of the implement the assailant used to attack Jamie Camden are irrelevant, considering his wounds speak for themselves. To claim that she must be confused about seeing Skye because she was confused about the weapon is ludicrous and totally illogical." He throws a hand in my direction. "My client—erm, Noa is clearly recovering from severe mental and physical trauma at the moment. Unless you have hard evidence otherwise, kindly leave."

She does.

* * *

After nearly two whole days, I'm released. Stitches in my forehead and temple, concussion, rope burn on my wrists, cuts and bruises on the bottoms of my feet and my two sprained ankles, and one tortured mind.

My mother and I are quiet as she weaves through the labyrinth of the hospital parking lot. My gaze catches a sign near the entrance: this way to Miami, that way to Naples.

She turns that way.

"I want to go home," I whisper.

"Are you serious?" She drifts to the shoulder and jerks the gear into park. "Noa, you are severely injured, and you have CIPA. You need help right now. And aren't you scared to be alone? You were just kidnapped."

She speaks slowly and deliberately, as if she can't believe my audacity. As if my mental state were just as damaged as my physical one for even considering going back to Miami. But with injuries of this degree, it's true. I can't be alone. I'll have to go back to the place where kidnappers and sadists dwell—for now.

I swallow hard. "I'll stay with you tonight, but I'm going home as soon as possible."

Her lips pucker, but she doesn't reply. She simply puts the car into drive and continues our westerly trip, back to Everglades City.

* * *

I'm lying on the couch in my parents' living room, my feet propped on the ottoman. Neighbors stop in to visit, but Jamie is the only one who stays. I feel my forehead pulsing, wonder if I have a headache. I touch the bandage and look at Jamie, who is perched in the wheelchair I'm to use until my ankles have healed. His foot pushes against the floor to create a makeshift rocking chair.

"What are you doing?" I ask as he scrolls through his phone.

"Looking for a two-bedroom apartment on the beach. I told you, I can't leave you alone for a second."

"Ha. Funny. You are *not* moving in with me."

He locks his phone and slips it in his pocket. "There you go, talking crazy again. I think they should recheck that concussion of yours."

I huff. "There's no way I got a concussion from that tiny spill when I fell out of that chair. It bled because that's a sensitive area."

He looks at me funny. "Yeah, not from that . . . from when whoever captured you whacked you upside the head with a plank? The one that knocked you out and left you unconscious long enough to haul you like sixty miles away and strap you to a chair before you came to? You definitely have a concussion, Noer."

I blink. "It was a plank?"

He shrugs. "That's what they said."

My mother enters with a bowl of broth and hands it to me. "How are you feeling?"

I accept it and nod. "I'm fine."

Jamie clears his throat. "Mrs. Romwell, I'm concerned. Noa doesn't remember getting whacked in the head."

We both look at him, the spoon halting between the bowl and my mouth.

"It's not that I didn't remember. It's just that I forgot."

I realize how silly that sounds when they both stare at me nervously.

My mother places a hand on my forehead. "Honey? It's the same thing."

I roll my eyes. "I'm saying I forgot that I had been hit in the head before being kidnapped. I've been so focused on the aftermath. Stop worrying so much."

Tears fill my mother's eyes, and she says softly, "You have no idea what worrying is until you can't find your daughter and her car's been abandoned in a parking lot and her purse is found on a dock next to the bay."

Emotions cloud my vision, and I reach for her arm. "I'm sorry. I'm going to be fine, I promise. I'm here, and I'm alive. But Skye . . . She's out there somewhere. I saw her. I *saw* her."

Jamie and my mother exchange tentative glances, and I perk up. "What?"

He takes a deep breath and leans forward, shuffling his feet to bring the wheelchair closer to me. "They can't find any sign of Skye within a two-mile radius from where you were picked up. Nothing. That whack you took to the head . . ."

It takes me a moment to see the correlation between these two separate events, but when I do, I nearly flip the soup bowl. So that explains the detectives' behavior, the constant rehashing of what I did and didn't see or hear, the inquisitions of my mental health. Jamie saying that I'm talking crazy *again*. "Are you saying I imagined her? Jamie! We don't know exactly where I was being held hostage. I don't know which way I ran, where I was to begin with, and it was the middle of the night. I just happened to come across Alligator Alley, and they were only able to search near the area where I was found. It may not have been the Lost City at all, but I know what I saw." I swing my gaze to my mother. "Is that what they're saying? That I hallucinated her from a concussion?"

She lifts a shoulder. "Your story is solid, Noa. You retold the same story verbatim each time you were questioned. No one thinks you're lying about being abducted. I mean, look at you."

"That's not what I'm asking," I growl.

Another exchange between the two.

"They didn't find her in the shacks near the preserve, either! But no one questioned whether or not she was there," I continue.

"But they found DNA evidence in those shacks. They've found nothing up north where they picked you up." Jamie is bouncing his fingers together, his elbows on his knees. "But the good news is they have a lead on who may have kidnapped you."

I freeze. "Who?"

Jamie rubs his chin. "Some dude named Howard something."

"Who is he?" I toss blinks between him and my mother.

Jamie shrugs.

I look at him cockeyed. "So why hasn't he been arrested already, or even interrogated? Why hasn't she been rescued? I was tied to a chair for an entire day with no food or water, and who knows what would have happened to me if I didn't escape. If a monster of that caliber is the same person who's been holding Skye, then I don't understand why militaries and SWAT teams and the freakin' president of the United States aren't out there inspecting every blade of grass and every speck of dirt looking for her."

Jamie sits back. My mother lowers onto the edge of the sofa. "They are, Noa. They are. These things take time," she says.

The front door slams in a fashion typical of my father. The three of us look toward the door as the floorboards squeak in the same manner, and he appears in the entry. He smiles sadly at me. "How ya doin'?"

"I was fine until these two told me no one believes me about seeing Skye."

A shadow falls over his face as he leans against the wall. He drags a disappointed gaze between Jamie and my mother. "Don't know why you'd tell her that right now. Marley, come here for a second. There's a reporter outside."

"At eight o'clock at night? Send them away," she says.

"I tried."

She stands and marches toward the front door mumbling, "No you didn't," and he follows her.

Jamie and I stare each other down once we're alone. "Are you mad at me?" he asks.

"I'm not mad. I'm hurt."

He wheels the chair closer and grips my fingers in his. "I believe you. Okay? I'm sorry. It's just . . ."

"What?"

"It's kind of like . . . that Millie chick all over again."

I glance up. "How do you know about Millie?"

He makes a face. "I've known you since forever. I definitely remember Millie."

"Oh." I drop my eyes in embarrassment. I must've forgotten I'd shared my imaginary big sister with Jamie. "Well, this is nothing like Millie. She was fake, and I knew she was fake. This was a real person, and it was Skye Flynn."

He nods then pokes my ribs. "How's the pain? I bet you wish you were never cured from CIPA at this point, huh?"

My mouth opens, and I stare. I completely forgot about this lie. I don't feel like playing along, but I also don't want to tell him the truth because I'm still a little upset with him. "Jamie? I know what I saw."

"I one thousand percent believe you." He sits back again and props an ankle up on his knee, folding his hands behind his head. "How did she look? Did she seem . . . okay?"

"I don't know. I only saw her for a second."

He sighs and pinches the bridge of his nose, like he's trying to keep his thoughts from spilling out of his mouth.

"It's not just that I saw her for a second. I heard her and felt her, too. I'd been in that chair for . . . hours. I don't even know how long. In and out of consciousness. But I was awake when I saw her, I know it because the sound of the door opening woke me up. My hearing was very alert—it's all I had since I couldn't see anything. I *heard* birds chirping, I *heard* frogs croaking, and I *heard* her voice."

He nods again. "And you said she untied your hands, right? Not your feet?"

"Right. That's what I mean—I know what I felt. I felt her little fingers on my arm and my hands when she was untying me. And her tiny body and brown hair—I recognized it from all the pictures."

"So it was it daytime?"

"No, it was night."

He pauses. "Were there any lights on?"

I shake my head. "There's no electricity out there."

Jamie scratches his chin. "Did you actually see her face?"

I answer by shutting my eyes. "I know what I saw."

He absently studies the rug, then runs a hand down his face. "God, this whole thing. I'm sorry this happened. I know how scared you were out there. I felt like that, too. When Morgan . . ." He looks up with sympathy. "I thought I was going to die. It was . . . awful."

My lungs deflate as I recall the battle of sanities, the warfare and unfathomable fear wrapped around my brain. For a moment, I close my eyes and wish that I could trade this insensitivity to pain for insensitivity to emotions. Anything to escape this mental torture. "I was scared for my life. My mind, it was going crazy. I was fighting for sanity but wanting to give in to the insanity at the same time. I can't explain it."

"Yeah, okay—you're shaking. Let's change the subject." He pulls a knitted throw off the back of the sofa and drapes it across my lap. "You cold?"

I just nod. *Sure, I'm cold.*

"What were you doing down at the docks during the vigil?" He places a hand back on my fingers.

I pause. I need to figure out where I stand in all this before I tell Jamie anything. I don't know if I should tell him my suspicions about Taylor or Logan because nothing I heard or saw holds any validity beyond my gut. So Taylor lied to me about a bruise. She doesn't owe me any explanation of its origin. Maybe she got it during sex or something—which would make sense if it was Zack on the phone during the restroom call at City Hall. *How embarrassing, Noa saw the bruise you accidentally gave me during our intimacies!*

And big deal—so she spoke with her husband or father-in-law on the phone and said she wanted her daughter back. That doesn't mean whoever she was talking to knew where Skye was. And so what if Logan blocked me on Facebook? We had no mutual friends, besides Zack now, and maybe he's blocked everyone from his past life with Maggie. Maybe he's trying to avoid their judgment on his affair and life choices. Regardless, after being kidnapped and held hostage, after witnessing Skye with my own eyes, I'm even more confused about what these things could mean—if they mean anything at all. Jamie made it clear he thinks I'm losing it, and I'm reluctant to raise any more red flags.

"I just needed to step away from all the people. I was getting claustrophobic."

He squeezes my fingers. "But the docks? That's not stepping away. Stepping away would be going to City Hall or the street. The docks were a quarter mile from the vigil."

My mother enters the room again. "Noa? It's a detective, not a reporter. He has something he wants to tell you. Are you up for it?"

I glance at Jamie, who frantically shakes his head.

"Send him in," I answer, and my mother retreats.

Jamie slaps my hand. "Why would you do that? Don't talk to anyone yet. Wait for Hector or some other lawyer." He frowns at me.

"I have nothing to hide," I bite out.

He rolls the wheelchair away with a defiant foot shove. "Can you at least not talk crazy? I told you I believe you, but when someone gets rocked upside the head and can't even describe what this 'girl' looked like that they allegedly saw, it doesn't—"

A portly fellow appears, a red mustache, and introduces himself as Detective Lawson. He shakes my hand, and I notice a plastic bag clutched in his other.

My folks follow him in, and all three take a seat around the living room. Before anyone can speak, there's a knock at the door. My mother rockets from the chair muttering various euphemisms, disappears to answer the door, and returns with a chagrined Sherriff Muncie.

"Sorry," he mutters while hovering in the entryway. He leans against the wall and falls silent, then my mother returns to her seat and we turn our attention to Detective Lawson.

"There's something I want you to see, Ms. Romwell." His voice is loud, deep, and he opens the bag to reveal the sandals I'd left in the cabin. "Do you recognize these?"

I sit up straight. "Yes! Those are mine! Does that mean you found that creepy set of cabins? Did you find evidence of Skye?"

Hope rises, straightening all our spines and widening our eyes and mouths. But Muncie's eyes are aimed at the floor, and Detective Lawson's puffy chest deflates. "Ms. Romwell, these shoes were found twenty miles south of where you were picked up. In the back of an old warehouse near a stormwater treatment area, along with a chair and rope that both tested positive with your DNA."

My brain twists and marvels at this information. "It . . . it wasn't a warehouse I was in. It was a cabin. Small, five hundred square feet, tops."

He shrugs and breaks eye contact with me. "Well, Skye's DNA was not found on the rope. Unfortunately." He turns his eyes back on me, contemplating. Studying.

My mouth opens and closes. I shift my gaze from him to Jamie to my parents. Then to Muncie, who's quiet. Every eyeball in this room is on me, each jaw masticating this turn of events, each brain questioning my testimony. I want to cry. "Maybe that was just the rope around my feet. She didn't touch that one. You should have two ropes."

Detective Lawson tips his head apologetically. "Just the one."

"What about other DNA?" Jamie asks. "Perhaps the abductor left fingerprints or something behind."

The man strokes his mustache like he's petting a cat, then shakes his head. "None that we know of yet. Just Noa's."

My hands drag down my face. "This is impossible."

Sheriff Muncie finally speaks. "You're sure it was a cabin and not a warehouse?"

I grip my soup bowl and glare at him. "I explained in great detail the cabins I saw." I turn back to Detective Lawson. "There were five of them—four and a half, to be exact, because one was partially burned down. Has anyone found them?"

A head shake.

Another from the doorway.

I drop my head back against the sofa before it pops back up. "Twenty miles, do you hear yourself? Did you see the condition I was in? There was no way I could walk or run twenty miles looking like that."

Muncie clears his throat and pushes off the wall. "Don't you have a history of not feeling anything? Or something? So you could move a lot more efficiently than someone who can feel stuff."

My mother steps in. "It's called CIPA."

"And she doesn't have it anymore," Jamie adds.

"And that has nothing to do with moving at an inhuman speed," I bite out. "It's impossible for anyone with any condition to—"

My father holds up a hand before I'm able to fully lose my cool. "What is this about a lead?"

The detective stands and adjusts the belt squeezing his round middle. "He is under investigation, believe you me. Look, we're still investigating. We're not ruling anything out, Noa. Maybe someone moved them there, who knows. How has your head been? Is the concussion getting better? The headaches? Have you been hallucinating or hearing things that aren't there?"

My sigh is clipped. "No."

"Not that we know of," Jamie says, and I glare at him.

The detective asks if he can keep the shoes for further testing, and I tell him yes, please do.

"Great. I'll return them to you within the next week."

I clear my throat. "Well, I'm going back to Miami soon."

He gives a pause, exchanges a look with Sheriff Muncie before eyeing me. "Ms. Romwell, can I give you some advice?"

Sheriff Muncie steps into the room. "You may want to stick around for a while."

I glance at Jamie, his creased brows mirroring mine. My mother steps forward. "Why?" I ask.

Detective Lawson sighs. "Look, your alibi is solid. You were absolutely in Miami when Skye was abducted."

"What? My alibi?"

He holds up his hands. "Don't worry, you're not in trouble. I'm just suggesting you stick around to avoid any suspicion."

Muncie interrupts. "You killed a man—I know it was self-defense—but then you got kidnapped soon after, and the facts are hazy. Your name is now on a bunch of different cases in connection with Skye."

The detective moves toward the entryway, blocking Muncie from my line of vision. "Just trust us. Stick around."

My parents walk them outside.

I rub my face with both hands. "I can't believe this is happening."

"Welcome back to small-town drama," Jamie remarks. "I'm not surprised they just handed you an alibi—practically gift-wrapped. This is like your initiation." He smiles. "Don't even worry about them. You'll be back home in no time."

"Yeah, right. They all think I'm crazy." I throw a pillow at him. "Why did you say that? 'Not that we know of,'" I repeat in a mocking tone.

He stands. "You were being too adamant! No one trusts a girl they think is in denial. And it didn't help that all these things were found nowhere near the area you told them you were, and with no evidence of Skye." He throws his hands up and circles the room.

I watch him until he stops and turns to me. We simply stare at each other for an eternity, both of us struggling with what we know and what we want. Their bias versus my bias. The subjective versus the objective. Finally he strolls over, kisses the top of my head, and mutters that he has to go.

That night I have strange, reoccurring dreams—the same ones I had back in Miami, the first night I learned Skye was missing. I see her and try running to her, only to see dracaena plants whipping in the wind.

But like most dreams, I don't recognize the setting. It could be anywhere. That cabin. A lean-to. Maybe a barn.

Perhaps a warehouse.

CHAPTER

17

A FLOWER ARRANGEMENT ARRIVES from Janna and the girls from work the next morning, and I call to thank her while I'm still in bed.

"I'm so sorry to hear about everything that's happened," she says.

"Thank you. I should be fine. I'm gonna need a few more days off work. Still recovering . . . both physically and emotionally." I squeeze my eyes shut tight enough to feel the stitches pull in my forehead.

"Don't worry, I put you on sick leave already. Aren't you glad now that you weren't hired for the PIO position?"

She's joking, but still I scowl. *Too soon, Janna. Too soon.*

"Keep us posted on your recovery, and let me know if there's anything I can do."

"Will do. Thanks again. Bye." My phone clunks to my nightstand, and I yawn.

I haven't used the bathroom since yesterday, and I'm surprised I haven't had an accident. Especially with all the fluids I received from the IV in the hospital.

I gingerly move off the bed and stand. Staring at my bedroom door, I wait for the vertigo to twist me in circles, but the door just sits there, like a normal door should. Relieved, I grab some fresh clothes and a clean towel and head toward the bathroom.

My mother exits her room as I'm in the doorway, wearing a burgundy dress and black pumps. She gasps. "Noa, sit down! You are not to be standing for another week!"

"I need to use the bathroom. Shower."

"Use your wheelchair."

"It's downstairs. Where are you going dressed so fancy?"

"It's Sunday morning. I'm going to church."

I stop, consider that. I've been here over a week already—nine days. Skye's been missing for twelve. "I want to go with you."

"You do?"

"I need to get out."

"Praise Jesus!" She skips down the hall and claps. "The Lord always knows what it takes to bring us back to him."

I doubt that God would work through a diabolical kidnapper to bring someone to church, but there's no use arguing with her. I'm not going to point out that she basically just blamed me for being kidnapped because of how I spend my Sundays. *This is all your fault, Noa.*

I continue my trek to the bathroom.

* * *

It's true that I should let my ankles heal. So I allow my mother to wheel me up the ramp of Everglades Community Church. I also conclude that using the wheelchair in public will remind everyone that I've been "healed" from CIPA and discourage them from asking about it.

Because I took my time showering and dressing, the service has started before we enter, and the congregation is singing "O for a Thousand Tongues." She parks me near the back in a wheelchair accessible area, and I gaze around the sanctuary I haven't been in since I was a child.

Not much has changed, except the attendees. The parents from back then are either gone or gray-haired, and the children we once were are now adults with careers and families burdening our shoulders. There are many people I don't even recognize.

My eyes stop on a couple at the end of the pews near the front—Taylor and Zack. I'm surprised they're here, but I don't know why. Tragedies tend to send people flocking through church doors. Or maybe they've always attended. I study their posture—rigid, uncomfortable. More is happening between these two than a missing child. They're not even sharing a hymnal. I can't tell if they're singing since I'm looking at the backs of their heads, but the tension is palpable.

I tear my eyes from them and look at the floor. I'm done getting involved. Done trying to read people for cryptic clues as to Skye's whereabouts. I hate that no one believes me. I hate that I'm questioning my own memory. I hate that I'm in Everglades City. That someone here is after me and I don't know who.

The song ends and the congregation sits, and I continue pondering the true versus the abstract in a game I seem to be losing time and again.

* * *

There's a potluck after the service on the lawn, where I'm approached often and by many.

Thank you for your prayers.
Yes, it was a very scary time.
Thank you.
The pain is pretty bad, mainly in my ankles/head.
All the time . . . and God is good.

They ask about my head injury and my Skye sighting in the same sentence, and in a patronizing manner. I've barely touched my burger, not only because I'm constantly talking to people, but because I'm choking back tears. It's clear they're all convinced I hallucinated it, and I'm realizing that coming here was a bad idea. Nothing here has changed; even though they've left me alone about the CIPA they think I'm healed from, they're now convinced I'm mentally unstable. And nothing I say will change their minds.

When the gathering finally dwindles down to around a dozen people—mostly the self-proclaimed cleaning crew that includes my mother—I'm left alone with my wheelchair parked at the end of a picnic table, staring at my raw, red wrists outlined in rope. I swallow my Diet Coke, wishing my dad were here to spike it with some rum. But he told me many times as a child that he would spontaneously combust if he ever darkened a church doorway.

Taylor approaches and sits next to me, evidently having exempted herself from the cleanup. "Hey," she says.

"Hi."

She eyes my state of being—all the trappings of the recently abducted—and my nearly full paper plate of various side dishes.

She places folded hands on the table, tightly bound. "I'm sorry, Noa."

"For?"

"Everything. God, everything. I felt guilty enough that you came to help, and now this horrible thing happened to you." She plants elbows on the table and rests her forehead in her palms.

My fork pokes around at the multicolored dollops of food—green bean casserole, corn succotash, baked beans, coleslaw—and my heart feels weary. Too worn out to engage. "Did you get your purse back?"

She nods. "It was lying near yours at the docks."

"Good, good."

I wait for her to ask why I ran off with her purse, study her for any sign that she thinks I was trying to steal it, or if she has any idea I went through her phone. There's something in her expression, but I can't pinpoint what it is. "I, um, wasn't trying to . . . steal. Steal your purse."

Now her expression is clear: surprise. "I didn't think you were." A small smile. "It's not your fault whoever took you threw it down by the docks."

"Oh, no—that's where I was when I was abducted."

She tilts her head. "Really? I knew you'd stepped away from the vigil but I didn't realize you went there on purpose. Why?"

I pause when a woman's voice carries across the yard—*Taylor, can you help me?*—and she waves the woman off—*No, thanks for asking though*—and turns back to me.

"Umm . . . ," I stutter. "I was just . . . Whew. I was overwhelmed at the vigil. I just followed the shoreline and ended up there. I needed to get away." *And wrap my head around the fact that Logan Flynn was in your call log.*

She nods sympathetically.

"Do you and Zack ever keep in touch with Logan?" I blurt.

She's casually poking at a staple in the picnic table with a tiny strip of red plastic trapped beneath, but I clock her shoulders tensing. "Sometimes. Not often," she says softly.

"He blocked me on Facebook."

She looks up. "He did? When? Have you spoken with him?"

"No. He blocked me after I sent him a friend request a few days ago."

She moves to get up. "I should go help clean up."

"Stay." I lay a hand on her wrist and consider censoring my next question, but I don't have the emotional capacity to care. "Why isn't Logan a suspect in Skye's kidnapping?"

She slowly sits back down. I don't need to analyze her actions to know she doesn't want to talk about Logan Flynn. "For the same reason the Olsen twins aren't."

I assume that means because he lives in another state, has a life of his own now, is completely disconnected from this family. Including Skye.

"Have the police contacted him?"

"Yes, they said they were working on it. But then I never heard anything about it again, so I'm assuming they got in touch with him and he's off the hook." She sighs.

Something about this doesn't sit right with me.

"Hey, Noa?"

Taylor's directness breaks my troubled thoughts. I look at her.

"When you saw Skye in that cabin—or warehouse, whatever, were you—"

"Taylor."

We both turn to see Zack approaching, a frown on his mouth and a furrow in his brow. He looks at me and manually removes the creases, forming an artificial smile. "Hi, Noa. Will you excuse us?"

His pleasantries toward me clash with his grip on Taylor's arm. I force a smile of my own and refuse to allow my eyes to witness their interaction.

Taylor stands quickly—whether of her own accord or with Zack's help—and she grins at me as if everything is right in the world. "We'll talk later?"

"Of course." I stare at their backs as they head toward the parking lot, puzzled when Zack's hand moves from her arm to her lower back and he caresses it.

Taylor quickly skirts his gesture. "Ow, be careful."

"Oh, right. Sorry." Zack grabs her hand instead.

So it seems Zack has discovered the bruise. But whether he knew of it before or after I pointed it out is still a mystery. But I digress. I don't know when I began analyzing every little detail—if it was when I decided to take Hector's advice and suspect the parents, or when I was kidnapped and strapped to a chair. Perhaps both are contributors, but my mind is torturing me by constantly analyzing everything and everyone.

I hear my name called from somewhere on the lawn and look up. My mother is carrying multiple casserole dishes and somehow still manages to wave at me. "I'm putting these in the trunk," she calls. "Then we can go home."

* * *

The house is quiet when we enter. A quiet house is the only note my father would ever leave to let us know he was gone. I haul myself up the stairs and collapse on my bed. I can't be here anymore. I don't know who to trust out here; I can't even trust myself when I'm here. Regardless of whether or not I'm ready to be alone, regardless of what Detective Lawson and Sheriff Muncie think, I need to step away from the chaos and allow my mind to heal along with my body.

The display of flowers catches my eye, and I find myself fixating on the focal point of them all—Hector's giant spectacle of blue delphinium, white roses, and pink lilies. I drag my phone from my pocket and call him.

"I need to come home," I say the moment he answers.

He laughs, but it's unclear whether it's nervous or amused. "Uh, is it because you miss me?"

My voice becomes a whisper. "I do. I miss you. But I can't stay here anymore, Hector. I'm losing my mind."

He pauses. "You've been through a lot these last couple of weeks. You could've died, Noa. Your body is recovering from serious trauma. You're going to have days like this."

I shake my head. "No, it's more than that. I don't know if it's the hit I took to the head or just the distress from being kidnapped, but I can't"—I break down sobbing, and am barely able to get out—"do this anymore."

Hector waits as I succumb to the mental and emotional storm. After a while, he says, "Look, Noa. Here's the truth. You are a loving, selfless, giving person. That's a fabulous quality."

Convinced this is his preface before ending things with me, I try frantically to backtrack, but he stops me.

"But it's becoming your own detriment."

"What do you mean?"

"Think about it and tell me what comes to mind. How have your generous efforts toward finding Skye affected you?"

The list is endless. Besides having taken a life, gotten abducted and tied up, and being lost in the Everglades with multiple injuries, I've also left my home and my job, submerged myself back into the high school drama I left, somehow come to need a "solid alibi," and now I'm nearly having a mental breakdown.

"Has it been worth it?" he asks after I rattle these outcomes off, and then some.

I hesitate, and he takes that as my answer. "You're going to sacrifice yourself to death. Nothing should be as important as your well-being."

It hits like an arrow to a bullseye, this awakening. It's that simple. I'm not helping anyone if I'm not helping myself. I jumped into a lion's den when I decided to come back here, not realizing I would end up sacrificing every single piece of me.

I can't do it. I'm really not a superhero. I gave it my best shot and failed. I drove myself crazy, weighing the facts with the ideas, the dynamics to the logistics, when all it comes down to is one simple fact OR it all comes down to one simple fact—Zack and Taylor's child has been abducted, and one simple idea—it hurt my soul and I wanted to help.

"You're right. I came out here on a mission, and that mission hasn't been fulfilled. But I've got to set limitations. I'm not going to die over this. I'm going to come home, recuperate, and do whatever I can for Skye from there."

"That's my girl," he says through a smile I can hear. "When?"

"Tonight. I mean, you'll take care of me, right? You can learn how to be my nociceptors until I'm well."

He laughs. "Sounds good. I've always wanted to be a . . . a . . ."

"Nociceptor."

"Right, a nociceptor."

* * *

A while later, I clomp down the stairs with resolution and inform my parents I'll be going home. They're both shocked at first, but when I tell them I'm much safer over there than I am here, they eventually acquiesce. My father asks about the detective's advice to stay put, to which I reply, I owe that man nothing. A tight-lipped nod is his reply.

He then runs through the inventory of my arsenal—do I still have the Smith and Wesson? How about the hunting knives? The rifles? And the folding knife? I have all of it, the whole collection, under my bed. No, I'm not afraid to use it.

They both help me pack, and once everything is downstairs, my father slips a bottle of tequila in my luggage while my mother is busy packing snacks. I catch his eye, and he winks at me. "Think of me as you enjoy that at home," he whispers.

I wrap my arms around his neck. "I will."

My mother comes around the corner with a Publix bag. She hands it to me. "Should you be driving with sprained ankles?"

I shrug. "Don't know. It won't hurt me, either way." Avoiding her look of disapproval, I gaze into the bag—an egg salad sandwich, two pears, a water bottle, and homemade snickerdoodles. "It's only an hour and a half drive. I don't need this replica of a fourth-grade school lunch."

Her laughter tinkles around me like a wind chime as she pulls me into a hug. I squeeze her and realize I don't want to let go. "I love you, Mom."

She pulls away with tears in her eyes. "I love you, Noa. Be safe. I'll come over there in a heartbeat if you need me."

"And I'll send your ma in my place if you need me," my father jokes.

I grin and head to the door, and they follow me down the porch steps. My mother puts my bag in the back seat as my father loads the wheelchair into the trunk—you never know when a good wheelchair might come in handy, he says.

My mother closes the back seat door. "If you were still a minor, I'd forbid this."

"Hush up, Marley. You forbid everything," my father barks.

She rolls her eyes and I laugh as I shut the door. My father knocks on the window, and I lower it.

He leans down until his head is almost in the car. "Hey. I'm proud of you."

I smile, kiss his cheek, and give a small wave to them both before backing out of the driveway.

They are two of the quirkiest people I've ever met, and I'm not sure I'll ever understand them. But their relationship and worldviews are none of my business. The simple truth—they both love me the best way they know how.

CHAPTER

18

HECTOR IS STANDING in my designated space in the parking garage when I arrive. He makes haste removing the wheelchair from the trunk and my bags from the back, but not before kissing me deeply. "Welcome back," he whispers.

"It's good to be back."

"Get in the wheelchair. I'll wheel you upstairs."

"No."

"Yes."

We compromise—I push the empty wheelchair, leaning on the handles to take most of the weight off my ankles. We're quiet as we step into the elevator and then down the hall, and I hand him my keys as we approach my door. It's not until I'm inside that I realize how much I've missed this place. He moves my bags to my bedroom as I drift into the kitchen, past the island, and toward the majestic view of the ocean.

I feel his hands on my shoulders as I stare mesmerized at the vast, endless waters. "You want to sit outside?" he asks.

"No. I want to sit with you on the couch."

He happily obliges by grabbing my hand and leading me to the sofa. And I realize this is the first time it actually feels like we are boyfriend and girlfriend, and not two people who are casually dating. There's no awkwardness, no formalities. Like we've been doing this for years.

I take the opportunity to study him, Hector—how Hector relaxes (with socked feet on the ottoman, a tumbler in one hand and me in the other), what Hector likes to drink (single malt whiskey neat), and what Hector enjoys watching on TV (basketball and Adrien Brody movies).

This is where I belong, and when he excuses himself to use the bathroom, I unlock my phone and turn my *restroom break* alarm back on. It feels good to shed the façade.

When he returns, it's with a blue T-shirt in his hands. "Looks like your buddy left this here when he was visiting."

"Oh, well. I'll give it to him—oh, shoot! I didn't even tell him I was leaving. I didn't tell anyone I was leaving, except for my parents. They all think I'm still there."

He places himself back on the sofa and pulls me into his shoulder. "But you're not. You're here." Then kisses my forehead.

The matter-of-fact way he said that makes my guilt ebb away as another realization dawns upon me. I don't need to tell them what I'm doing. I don't owe them any explanations, the Everglades City folk. How easily I slipped back into the toxic, small-town mentality. I thought I had overcome that, but I see now that I only ever ran from it. Ten years running is not equivalent to healing.

* * *

Hector sleeps over, ultimately, saying he doesn't think I should be alone. I agree. Under any other circumstances, I would assume he had ulterior motives. But since it's clear I'm a bit on edge, sex is not in the cards for either of us. He does climb into my bed with me, though, and when his arm is wrapped around my shoulders, I wonder what I was ever scared of.

I wake early the next morning, well before he does, and check my phone; it's six AM. I take the opportunity to study Hector sleeping (on his stomach with his arms stretched up and wrapped around his pillow).

I wonder if I'll hear from anyone in Everglades City today. Granted, Jamie will probably be mad at me for leaving without saying goodbye, and Zack and Taylor should be focusing on their marital problems, both legitimate ones and those conjured by my overthinking.

I roll onto my back. As peaceful and cathartic as it's been to be home the last twelve hours, I'm still disturbed as to the haunted subdivision of cabins I remember versus the warehouse twenty miles away that everything was found in. My father suggested that perhaps I managed to escape the ropes myself, having dreamed Skye had entered. But I tell myself I can't think about this now; I need to give myself time. I have other priorities that need tending to, like work.

I called Janna last night to let her know I'll be taking that co-PIO position and working from home. She was delighted and said she'd email me in the morning.

At seven o'clock, my alarm alerts me to go to the bathroom, and consequently wakes up Hector (a morning person). He kisses me, then goes to make coffee and breakfast. I take the opportunity to shower and dress, and by the time I've made it to the kitchen, two mugs of coffee are on the table along with two plates of bacon and eggs.

"It's like we're playing house." I sit across from him.

He chuckles through bites of bacon. "Hey, do you have follow-up appointments?"

"Not yet. I have to make those today, now that the weekend is over."

"They should be soon, though, right? You don't feel pain, so you don't know if your wounds are infected or not."

I sip my coffee and nod my confirmation. "I'm planning to call my PCP today. She'll know which specialists to send me to after a routine physical. I generally get one once a month anyways."

We continue eating in silence, and I watch Hector eat (left-handed and scrolling through his phone). It's not until I'm taking my last bite that he speaks. "Hey, this is kind of weird."

"What?" I lean across the table as he turns his phone to me.

"Look at this."

He's got Facebook open and is on Logan Flynn's page. I squint and move closer, peering down at another shared post about Skye's disappearance. It's the same one he posted last week: her most recent school picture, her description, and a call to action with phone numbers. He posted this last night. "It's her missing person flyer. Why is it weird?"

"Not that. This." He points near the top, next to Logan's name. "His location is New Haven, Connecticut."

"Yeah . . . that's where he lives . . ."

"But isn't it weird that he felt he had to 'check in' while sharing a missing person in Florida? I don't know, it just seems like you wouldn't take the time to specify your location unless it was integral to the post."

I feel my face contorting as I process that. "I don't know. Sometimes boomers are awkward on social media. They don't know Facebook etiquette."

Hector grins as he moves our plates to the sink and rinses them. "Definitely a possibility. I've just been keeping an eye on this guy. Something doesn't feel right about him."

That I thought the same thing yesterday spooks me. I'd attributed it to the fact that my mind was glitching, paranoid and over-scrutinizing. But if a sound-minded lawyer is coming to the same conclusions as an unstable layperson, I may not be as unstable as I'd thought.

Hector asks at least five times if I need him to stay with me today, and I assure him I'm fine. Go to work, I say, you've got personal injuries there to deal with. He states that he handles general liability and his partner does personal injuries. Would I like his partner to come stay with me instead?

That results in a playful punch to his arm, which escalates to a fabulous goodbye kiss and a promise to see me this evening.

I'm finally in my recliner—drinks and snacks on the end table, phone in hand, and laptop on lap. I won't need to get up for another four hours until my restroom alarm goes off. I kick back in the recliner and realize I've actually missed having that alarm.

It's nine thirty, and I still haven't heard from Janna. After calling my PCP and making an appointment for tomorrow morning, I decide to look Logan up while I wait. I navigate to Facebook, log out, and create a new profile with my work email. Within minutes, I'm on his page and looking for anything I hadn't seen before.

It's true that he has some privacy settings, because I'm still unable to see his profile pictures or his Friends list. The only public posts are his now three missing persons flyers for Skye, a picture from last Christmas of a snow-covered colonial I'm assuming is his house in Connecticut, and another from two summers ago. It's a selfie of him and Skye. They're in an airboat—one of his, no doubt—and his left hand rests on her shoulder as they both smile into the camera. He must have still been with Maggie, not only because he's pictured with his granddaughter, but because a thick, tungsten band adorns the ring finger next to Skye's cheek. I remember that wedding ring. I'd never seen one like it before, but since my father never wore one, that wasn't saying much. A thin channel of tiny blue sapphires ran through the middle of it, and I remember wanting to get Zack one like it.

I've come to the bottom of his profile, wondering what else is on this page I could be missing.

A sinister idea crawls into my head like a tarantula. Logging out of my fake profile, I type Zack's email address in the username field. And for the password I try *monkeybread10.*

My brain nearly explodes when his page loads and I'm staring at his news feed—not only because he hasn't changed his password in over ten years, but because monkey bread was an inside joke between the two of us when we were dating. It involved a child's birthday party with an excessive chimpanzee theme and monkey bread instead of birthday cake.

This feels too intimate, like I've trespassed too far already. But because Logan and Zack are friends—thus, Logan's restrictions are lifted from Zack's profile—I hurriedly navigate to Logan's page and scroll down to see a surplus of posts that had been hidden from public view. Not many, but definitely more than five.

They're boring. All links he's shared dealing with politics. A photo of a little dog. Then one of a blonde woman with the caption, *Love.*

Avenging anger captivates my insides. I glare at the woman—early forties, bleached hair, bosoms overflowing from a too-tight red tank top, martini glass in hand. She's sitting in a bar. She seems everything that Maggie is not, and Maggie is wonderful. How could he do this to her?

Hardly any of his posts have any likes, but then again, he only has forty-six friends. Zack hasn't liked any of them.

Another idea—I click on the message icon to see if Logan and Zack have corresponded through Facebook Messenger.

They have.

My email inbox pings a new message, a notification that Janna has finally emailed, with the subject: NEW POSITION. I exit out of her notification window and scroll up past the cascading blue and gray bubbles of their conversations.

I finally reach the top and see that they began eleven months ago, shortly after Logan left. The first three are from him and went unanswered.

Zack, did you change your phone number? My calls and texts aren't going through.

Zack, answer me please.

Please answer. I'm so sorry I did this to you. Let me explain.

On day four, Zack finally answered. *Leave me alone. You're dead to me.*

"Damn."

I scan through the rest, which basically consist of Logan begging for forgiveness and Zack grudgingly agreeing after much persuasion. He tells Logan he'll unblock him from his phone with strict stipulations, mainly—*Don't pretend like everything is fine between us. I'm doing this for Skye.*

He must have unblocked him at this point, because there are no more messages. I log out of Zack's account, having just made myself incredibly uncomfortable. I shouldn't have done this.

Janna's message is long, with eleven attachments. They're all copies of the contracts she's signed with the Department of Transportation and the other subcontractors who won the bid for this project. There are links to paperwork I need to e-sign—privacy notices, disclosures, affidavits, and a fifty-six-page outline of the entire four-year project.

I can't wrap my head around this right now. I'm so far behind at work, but I don't even know where to begin. Another ping, and a second email notification pops up. It's from Shelby Seville. *Welcome back, Noa! Glad you're feeling better! Can you write up a press release for the local businesses in the Westchester area with the attached dates and information? I've copied Angela on this email, so you can just reply all and she'll be able to make the graphics and put the press kit together . . .*

I'm fuming. Shelby is supposed to be my co-PIO. She doesn't get to tell me what to do. My laptop slams shut, and I pick up my phone instead. I go to recent calls and tap Logan's phone number from when I stole it from Taylor's phone and send him a text message.

Hi Logan, it's Noa Romwell. I wanted to reach out and make sure everything's okay.

I shouldn't have sent it. But it's too late now. Skye has been missing for thirteen days. I fear that the state will start getting distracted with other things once it hits the two-week mark. I reopen Janna's email and start reading again.

* * *

Each time my phone chimes throughout the day, I rush to see if Logan's responded. But it's never him. Hector texts, my mom, even my dad sends me a winky emoji. Then at six o'clock, just as I'm about to shut my laptop down for the day, I get a text from Jamie. *You left.* ☹

My shoulders slump. *I did. I had to go home. Sorry I didn't say bye.*

He doesn't respond. Worried he's angry, I text him again: *Don't worry, Jamie. We will see each other often. We won't let ten years go by again. And I'm still going to help with Skye, just from here in Miami. I'm able to think a lot more clearly from here, and I think I might be onto something. Will tell you about it later.*

I lock my phone and remind myself that if he's upset with me, that's not my problem. I have a life to live. And so does he, thanks to me. And no thanks to Morgan Higgins.

Morgan Higgins.

I reopen my laptop and type his name into Google, including the word *Everglades* to avoid being subjected to every Facebook and LinkedIn profile connected to anyone with that name. But I fooled myself, because various news stories pop up with his death. It was low key, our story in the media, because we somehow missed the algorithm wave that made us nationwide news. I've read these articles, and if you've read one, you've read them all: *Woman Saves Best Friend, Kills Assailant.* I scroll past them all until I'm knee-deep in the fourth Google page.

Okeechobee Obituaries catches my eye, with the tag: . . . *survived by siblings, Haggart and Morgan Higgins.* I click the link. The tribute is for one Esmerelda Higgins-Joel, who passed nearly three years ago. I marvel at those names—Esmerelda and Haggart. But the silver lining is that the names are odd enough to google and not be overcome with thousands of title doppelgängers.

A quick search of Haggart Higgins shows that he passed nearly a year after his sister. A deeper search of *Haggart Higgins family tree* shows that Morgan was part Seminole, part Irish. But any further names related to the trio result in dead ends—it seems I ended the Higgins lineage with Morgan.

You had to do it, Noa. He was killing your friend. It was him or Jamie.

Plowing on, I'm able to glean that Morgan's middle name was Edward and that he was a member of a Seminole chapter during his heyday of working at the casinos in the late nineties. Connecting the dots, I assume he became the vagrant he was when his remaining family passed away and he was arrested for illegally gambling casino money on dog races shortly after Haggart died.

Another quick search in the Monroe County Clerk of Courts confirms his arrest, term served, and release—which was six months ago. With no family and no descendants, it's clear how Morgan was able to hop from abandoned estate to abandoned estate—or shack to shack, in his case—having been the sole heir to each of them.

With this information, I search *Morgan Edward Higgins Seminole.* But the results are the same information I've already read.

My ringtone dissipates this world of Morgan I've exhumed, and my wall of windows tells me it's dark outside. A glance at my ringing phone reveals that Hector is calling. He tells me he's leaving the office now, that he's bringing dinner to my house. He hopes I'm hungry. Do I need anything else? I don't, thank you so much. And hurry! He will—he promises he will.

Turning back to my computer, I scan the articles again. They're all highlighted purple—all information I've read. So I click images.

Surprisingly, quite a few photos of Morgan Higgins cascade down my browser, mostly from his younger, prevagrant days. The height of his pitiful life.

Then my eye catches something strange. Familiar, yet incongruent. It's a photo of six men, and I'm reminded of the *Sesame Street* song I heard so often as a child, the one about one thing not being like the others . . .

Four of the men I don't recognize, but next to Morgan stands a man I know. Logan Flynn flashes his million-dollar smile, his arm draped across the shoulders of Morgan, who stands a half a foot shorter than he.

"What the . . ."

I click the article and am taken to a newsletter from *The Greater Everglades Chronicles.* It's commemorating the twelve-year anniversary of a networking club called the Panthers—a group of businesses that form charities to conserve the depleting population of animals in the Everglades. It's dated six years ago.

I stare at the picture for so long, the other four men disappear, and it's simply a portrait of Morgan and Logan.

I jump when my phone screams that I've received a text message. I look down.

Logan Flynn.

CHAPTER

19

IT'S BEEN A *long time.*

I stare at them, the five words. Count them—one, two, three, four, five. Count each letter. Sixteen. Each character. Twenty-two. I squeeze my eyes shut, look again. Ensure I'm not hallucinating this.

I'm not.

I look back at the picture on my screen. Logan and Morgan. *It's been a long time.*

My thumb lingers over the notification, swipes. I stare at the five words again, all circled in a light gray bubble, hovering below my innocent blue one—*Hi Logan, it's Noa Romwell. I wanted to reach out and make sure everything's okay.*

So naïve, I was. Back a hundred years ago when I sent that. But I'm older now, wiser. I chew on my lip—stop, Noa. It'll bleed eventually—and start typing.

How have you been?

His response comes immediately: *What do you want?*

I blink, read it again. He clearly doesn't fancy me, but he's responding, so that's something. I tread carefully. *I'm sorry if I've offended you. I thought we parted on good terms all those years ago when Zack broke up with me. I heard about your granddaughter. I'm so sorry.*

Another text comes in, Hector. *I just made it to your complex. I have sushi! Are you able to open the door?*

My fingers fly across the screen: *The key is under the mat.* And I move back into Logan's texts to see if he's responding. He's not.

Hector: *Okay, wow. Well we'll talk about that when I get up there.*

Yes, we will, won't we? Back to Logan's texts. A bubble pops up and disappears.

"No!" I shout at my phone. It lies dormant for the next few minutes until the door opens and I hear Hector's voice.

"You know, my mother taught me never to disrespect women. So let me start by applauding you for so boldly leaving a key under your mat shortly after you've escaped a sadistic kidnapper." His beautiful form appears, and he sets a brown paper bag on my dining room table. He meanders toward me—a couch potato in my recliner—loosening his tie with a smug grin. "Allow me to continue with how mesmerized I am by your bravery, and a respectful inquiry regarding what you were thinking."

He leans down to kiss me, and I melt. I could get very used to this.

"Your mom sounds like a wonderful woman," I reply.

He winks and starts to work on his cufflinks. "Now where were we . . . Ah, yes. What were you thinking?"

"I'm sorry, I forgot it was there. I locked myself out once, not my brightest moment. So I put it there just in case," I confess as he moves to the kitchen to retrieve plates and pour two glasses of merlot. "Besides, this building has top-of-the-line security. Between Vladimir and the chain-smoking guy, I'm in a vault of protection."

His laugh puts a smile on my face, and soon he's serving me a plate of rolls and sashimi, chopsticks, and a glass of wine.

"Thank you."

He tinks his glass against mine. "Cheers. To geriatric security guards."

We discuss our respective jobs as we dine on sushi and sip our wine, he regarding a case about an employee falling at her employer's home during a holiday party, I regarding all the paperwork and the details of this new position. I tell him how Shelby messaged me at least three times today, asking about basic protocol that any self-respecting PIO should know before delving into a project of this caliber.

"You know, Hector, any other day, I would have sucked it up and walked her through it. Even if that meant putting my own workload on hold. Not anymore. Janna gave this job to her, not me. So I sent her to Janna."

Hector wipes his mouth and nods, pantomiming a slow clap. "Good for you. Tell that party planner to stay in her lane."

I laugh as I finish the last of my sushi. Since I never feel hungry, I also never feel satisfied. But at this point, my stomach is bulging, stretching, and that's my sign that I've overeaten.

Hector takes our empty plates to the kitchen. "I have a surprise," he calls.

I wait in anticipation until he comes back with a long, flat, rectangular box with *Mojo Donuts* inscribed in colorful lettering. "Shut up! You did not!"

"Oh, but I did. Pick your poison." He opens the box and presents me with a dozen types of huge gourmet donuts, each one the size of a small cake.

I eventually choose guava and cream cheese, and Hector decides on cinnamon sugar with dulce de leche.

"I'm so stuffed," I mumble when I'm halfway finished. I surrender my remains to the box and collapse back in my recliner. Although not painful, my stomach protrudes, and I feel the lining stretching to near capacity.

Hector finishes his and brushes crumbs off his hands. Without warning, he picks me up from the recliner and sets me next to him on the couch. I'm lying against his chest as he speaks into the TV controller's voice command—ESPN!—and I feel like a woman who's been married for twenty years.

I'm nearly falling asleep while he consumes NBA highlights, but his phone dinging an email jostles me. He opens it, and after a few seconds he says, "Wow. Are you ready for this?"

I turn my face up to his. "For what?"

I see his typical lawyer façade breaking through—the pouty lips, puckered brows. "For information on Logan Flynn."

If I weren't so comfortable against his body, I would jump off the sofa. "What did you do?"

His tongue rolls around in his mouth as he stares at the television. "I did some more investigating today, looked him up. Contacted some friends outside of Google, if you know what I mean. You ready?"

I have to manually control my breathing; my heart rate spikes. "Tell me."

"It seems Logan Flynn has no address in Connecticut. There is no trace of him ever being there. His last known address is in Everglades City."

The universe tilts sideways. I stare at my quiet phone, the phone that's been conversing with this liar, this Logan Flynn.

Hector continues. "So that hunch I had about him constantly 'checking in' to New Haven, Connecticut? I was right. It was a ploy. I think he's still here in South Florida."

My whole body begins shaking, shrinking into Hector like a puppy. I can't speak, can't admit that I've been conversing with this lunatic. I'm too scared. I know with everything that I am that Logan Flynn kidnapped Skye, that he kidnapped me. He knew Morgan Higgins; they were in on her kidnapping together. For what reason, I don't know. Morgan is dead, but Logan is very much alive.

"Noa?" Hector places a finger under my chin and coerces my head up until my eyes meet his. "No more keys under the mat. And please keep your door locked."

I nod. And with a quivering chin, I say, "Stay with me again tonight."

* * *

I dream I'm back in the cabin. I can't move. I'm tied to the chair. I'm not blindfolded, though; I see everything—the barren log walls and rotted wood floors. The gaping black window. The heaps of straw hanging limply from the thatched roof in disarray.

This time, there's not just one chair confining a victim. There are two. A matching chair is erected next to mine, only half the size. A small girl is perched on it, each fragile limb bitten into by heavy ropes. Her head rotates until she's staring into my eyes. "Shhh. He'll hear you."

I shoot straight up in bed. Hector sits up a split second after I do (a light sleeper). "What's wrong?"

My eyes are locked on the patio door to the balcony where my dracaena plants dwell. A girl is standing there. I know her. I saw her in the cabin, after she loosened my restraints.

"Noa? What is it?"

"Look," I whisper, pointing at the girl.

A pause. "Look at what?"

I finally rip my gaze from her, and it lands on Hector. Handsome Hector. "The patio." I watch him as he pivots his dark eyes toward the moonlit balcony, his long lashes squinting, full brows dipping. He's got that flustered attorney look again.

"What about the patio?"

My eyes rotate back to the balcony—empty. Just my plants, that's all. No girls, no Skye. I'm beginning to despise all things dracaena. "I—I was dreaming."

"Shh, it's okay. I'm here. You're safe." He guides me back onto my pillow and curls his arm around me. Within minutes, he's sleeping again, but my eyes remain locked on the ceiling.

I just hallucinated Skye. She's not on the balcony, that's ridiculous. I'm aware that I was in a state of partial sleep, the same as I was the first night I heard of her disappearance and imagined her out there on that balcony.

There are many things I don't know. What pain feels like, hunger, cold. I can't comprehend the universal fear of those things.

But one thing I do know—Logan Flynn kidnapped the both of us. And I am afraid of him.

* * *

The next morning I wake up focused. After committing to what I know to be true, it's empowering not to have outside influences making me question my sanity. It's overcast, the sky. Rain spatters in spurts against the windows. Hector shifts next to me, a deep inhale, and I feel his arm wrap around my stomach. I could lie here all day.

I reach for my phone on my nightstand, unplug it from the charger. My intent to check the time dissipates when I see I have another text from Logan, sent at four in the morning. My hand shakes as I look at the name of my kidnapper. The sick bastard who knocked me out and tied me up and left me to die in the middle of nowhere. The one who has Skye at this moment.

I slink out from under Hector's arm and take my phone to the bathroom to read it.

Thank you. Wish I could be there. Zack tells me you've been helping them out a lot. That's very big of you.

I read the message again. Surely I'm missing something. Yesterday he was rude and short, and suddenly at four AM he's pleasant and inquisitive. I ponder a response and finally decide on: *Why can't you come down from Connecticut?*

If the man was awake at four in the morning, I assume he's not now. So I don't anticipate a reply; instead, I head back to bed just as my alarm goes off to use the restroom. I'm quick this time to avoid waking Hector. I retrace my steps, and once I'm settled, I google *Skye Flynn* to look for updates.

Disgruntled Ex-Employee of C-44 Reservoir Suspected in Kidnapping of Everglades City Child is the first article, posted yesterday.

Authorities are now investigating Howard Zilnich, 44, of Palm Beach in connection with recent Everglades City abductions, including that of Skye Flynn, a young girl beloved by her small community.

Zack and Taylor Flynn, natives of Everglades City, Fla., have been on a desperate hunt for their six-year-old daughter for nearly two weeks. Friends and family have gathered from all over the state to help in the search, during which a fatal confrontation leading to the death of former convict Morgan Higgins named him the main suspect in her disappearance. But the story took a strange turn when an unidentified friend of the family was abducted shortly after and was discovered wandering near I-75 Alligator Alley just over twenty-four hours later, having sustained multiple injuries and head trauma. The victim claimed to have sighted the child during her time in captivity, but rescuers could not pinpoint the location she described. Soon after her rescue, articles of clothing that proved to belong to the victim, as well as the implements used to imprison her, were discovered in a building near Stormwater Treatment Area C-44. "Authorities aren't sure of the victim's mental stability during her time as a hostage," says Pete Farrington, engineer of the South Florida Water Management District. "All we can do is stay positive and hope for the best."

At this, I roll my eyes. I fight the urge to close out of the article, because I already know their suspicions regarding this Howard Zilnich, but I'm curious to know what's come of their investigating.

Further forensic testing has revealed trace amounts of DNA on the implements that do not belong to the victim, but to Howard Zilnich, an employee of Palm Beach County until his termination last month due to aggression and creating a hostile work environment.

"Howard had a temper," Farrington continues, "and just because a motive isn't clear yet doesn't mean there isn't one. If he's capable of kidnapping a woman, he could very well be capable of kidnapping a child, too. We're searching everywhere for this little girl, and we're confident she'll be returned home safely." The good news is that a body has not been recovered, leading investigators to believe that Skye Flynn is still alive and well.

I lock my phone and wash my hands. The article irritates me, not only because my sanity is still under fire, but the heart of my heart knows there is no Howard Zilnich involved. This is old news that I've already discredited. I was held hostage in a cabin, not this Stormwater C place twenty miles away. It's quite possible that my abductor simply abandoned my shoes and one of the ropes in there, having planted Howard's DNA to throw off investigators. They've only uncovered one of the two ropes—Detective Lawson told me this. Skye's DNA wasn't on it, but mine was, and they were going to investigate for further DNA. If my DNA was on this rope and Skye's wasn't, then it was the one around my feet.

They're wasting so much time, investigating these rabbit trails, when Logan Flynn is not even registered as living in New Haven, Connecticut. When Logan Flynn had a tie to Morgan Higgins. When Logan Flynn had a motive to kidnap Skye after being cut out of her life.

For reassurance, I quickly google Howard Zilnich. When I find nothing that could overtly tie him to Skye's disappearance, I navigate back to the photo I saw of Logan and Morgan together to see if any of those other men might've been Howard—they're not. I combine their names, different variations and locations, but everything is pointing to poor Howard having used a rope that would eventually be used to tie my ankles together.

Quite calculating, this perpetrator. Planting evidence clean of his own fingerprints while hiding the rope used to tie my hands—the one with Skye's DNA. It was a great plan, to build a cacophony among the authorities and the media to throw doubt on my eyewitness accounts.

Hector is stretching from the bed; I hear his drawn-out moans. I exit the bathroom and climb back under the covers with him, nestling into his chest and smelling his scent (testosterone and a piney aftershave). "I don't want to go to work," he mumbles.

"Don't," I whisper.

"Okay."

The rain picks up, the pattering against the windows upgrading to pounding, then a crack of thunder.

It's a trigger, dropping me right back in the Big Cypress Preserve when I couldn't find Jamie, when that tropical storm bore down on me. When I heard Jamie's terrified scream and I killed someone.

I killed someone.

"You okay?" Hector asks. "Your heart is pounding."

His palm lies flat on my chest as my heart rocks against it. I close my eyes and focus on the weight of his hand, his comforting vibes seeping into my skin. And I smile. "Yeah, I'm good. You hungry?"

* * *

I'm ladling batter into a waffle iron when he emerges from my bedroom, having showered and donned black dress pants, a white button-up shirt, and a gray tie. A thick strand of wet, black hair flops onto his forehead as he pours a cup of coffee. "Waffles?"

"And eggs. And bacon." I load two plates and set them on the table.

He tucks a napkin into his collar and grins. "I made bacon and eggs yesterday. You gotta one-up me with waffles?"

I wink and sit across from him. "What? I like waffles."

It's becoming a habit, our comfortable, quiet breakfasts. A habit I rather enjoy. But then he speaks, and I realize this is also part of the newly established habit—Hector surprising me as we finish.

"Shoot. It looks like I might have to go out of town for a couple of days."

I look up at him, a syrupy, fork-speared waffle hovering in front of my mouth. "What?"

"There's a workers comp conference in Vegas. I was sending a paralegal, but he fell ill this morning, apparently. My assistant is asking if she should rebook everything under my name." His head tilts, his lower lip tucked between his teeth as he monitors my reaction. "I would leave tonight, and I'll be back Friday evening. I'm sorry. Do you want me to cancel?"

I set my fork down. "Wow, I—yeah. I mean, no. You should go. I'll be fine."

He's chewing the inside of his cheek, his fingers rubbing together. "Are you sure?"

I wave a hand. "Don't be silly. You've done more than enough for me. I really appreciate everything you've done." I smile—genuinely, despite the turn of events and the sinking realization I'll be spending my first evening alone since the kidnapping. “And I can’t wait to see you Friday.”

His sigh is a relieved one, his smile full of gratitude. A deep, beautiful kiss, and he leaves for work. But not before scouring the entry in search of any more rogue keys.

CHAPTER

20

THE VISIT WITH my doctor went as I expected—routine with a splash of drama, thanks to the events that brought me there. I leave with a stack of referrals for various specialists that I'll call later today.

The workday flies by as I continue familiarizing myself with the new project, contacting contractors I'll be in close communication with for the next four years. The tone between Shelby and me has shifted considerably in the last twenty-four hours, her high horse having bucked her off and left her in the dust.

"Shelby, Angela is waiting for the information for the press kit, and we can't coordinate anything until you give us a location for the meeting."

"Did you get a permit to hold it there? Of course you have to have a permit."

"Yes, that is *your problem. It happened on DOT right of way, so it has nothing to do with the property owners."*

"No, send it to me before you email the engineer. I'll need to proofread it."

My frustration is nearly at capacity when Dave, the project coordinator, calls me. "You need to have a chat with your new information officer," he spits.

My fingers freeze over my keyboard. "What happened?"

"She came out to the site today with her hard hat on backwards. Just traipsing around like she owns the place—and everyone is there, mind you. Architects, engineers, construction workers, county officials, commissioners—with a backwards hat. Of course I say something, trying to do it quietly, you know? And you know what she said? 'How do I put this thing on?' She said it real loud and then laughed like a donkey. The gotdamn USDOT rep was right there, almost fired her on the spot."

My palm slaps against my forehead, and I'm so distraught I don't know if I should laugh or cry. "Dave, I'm so sorry. I'll take care of it right now."

"Well, I'm letting Janna know she did the wrong thing putting that imbecile out here instead of you."

"I appreciate that, Dave. Thank you. Thompson-Miller cannot lose this contract. Trust me, I'm calling Shelby right now, and I'll set up some training for her."

We end the call and my thumb smashes into Shelby's contact.

"Thompson-Miller PIO," she answers haughtily, even though she knows it's me.

"Guess who just called me?" I snap.

She hesitates. "Who?"

"Dave Moffitt from LJD Group. Did you seriously go out onto the site with your hard hat on backwards? You made a fool out of yourself and the entire company, and we could lose the contract over this. You really don't know how to wear a hat?"

She's quiet, and I think she's hung up until I hear her sniffling. "I can't do this, Noa," she whispers.

My shoulders slump and my heart thaws just a bit. "Shelby," I say more softly. "You wanted this job. You swore you were qualified for it."

"I thought I was! But there's just so much more to it than I expected."

An email pings in my inbox from Janna. Subject: *Shelby did what?!?!*

"Shelby, stand by." I mute her and open the email.

Just spoke with Dave. Shelby to be removed from this position. You're the lead PIO on this project as of tomorrow.

I squint at the screen. No apologies, no admitting she was wrong. Suddenly I'm the person for this job because Shelby doesn't know how to wear a hard hat? Part of me is elated, while another part is wondering what the *stockholders* have to say about this—the *stockholders* who denied my application to begin with. Perhaps my *condition* is no longer a concern to them, now that their precious *contract* is threatened. I read the email again, the audible Janna just called.

I'm a team player. I'll jump into action during an emergency. But I'm not sure this constitutes an emergency so much as a poor judgment call—one I saw from a mile away. One I warned them about. And their lack of planning doesn't translate into an emergency on my part.

I unmute the call. "Listen, you wanted this job and you got it. If you're really wanting out of it, call Janna and quit. But if you're just overwhelmed and feeling emotional, try harder. Learn. Ask questions. Fake it 'til you make it. You're giving up a big opportunity here. One you'll probably never get again if you quit."

We hang up and I reply to Janna's email: *Please send over the new contract. I'll have to look over the conditions, not sure I'll be finished by tomorrow. In the meantime, let's set up some training for Shelby.*

What Janna doesn't realize is that I'll only accept this under certain terms. For one, I want that hundred percent pay increase I was promised, no sharing it with Shelby or anyone else. In addition, I'll need better insurance and gas reimbursements—no, a company car. My self-worth was slaughtered the day I was passed over for this job, and had this happened before I'd gone to Everglades City, I would have kissed Janna's shoes at an email like this, even if it did mean a shared salary with Shelby. But not now. I'm a different person now that I've saved Jamie's life, killed a man, been kidnapped and bound and concussed—and dismissed.

I deserve better than this, and as a person who fights for her value, I'm about to demand it.

I swear out loud when my phone rattles from the end table, then I realize it's my alarm—restroom break. It's seven PM. Wondering where my day has gone, I gaze out past the balcony to the never-ending ocean. We get the sunrises over here, no sunsets, so I imagine the glistening glow the Gulf of Mexico is experiencing right now—that Everglades City is experiencing.

I think of Zack and Taylor, day fourteen ending without their daughter. Maggie, going to bed in her big, drafty house, alone. I use the restroom and fix myself dinner as I wonder what another night would have looked like if I'd stayed. But the thought depresses me, so I take my spaghetti for one onto the balcony and text Hector. *How's it going?*

He replies: *At a meet and greet. Call you later?*

I reply of course he can and move back inside to finish eating. There are too many bugs out here and not enough Hector.

It's quiet tonight, and I'm moving about the kitchen, cleaning the dishes and wiping the counters when a loud boom startles me. I drop the rag and place a hand on my chest, my eyes scurrying to locate the key Hector brought in. It's sitting on the table. *It's just the neighbors, Noa. They do this sometimes.*

An octogenarian voice reverberates through the wall—Nancy yelling at Mose, no doubt—and I try to laugh off my nerves. But the darkness continues descending, the quietness getting louder and louder, until I find myself in bed at eight o'clock.

I look at my phone, wonder when Hector will call.

I remind myself that no one is going to break in. I'm safe here. There's Vladimir, and the gentleman with the electrolarynx.

This does nothing to calm my nerves, but then a grin spreads my lips apart as I grab my phone and call Jamie.

"Yo, Noer. What's up? How's My-hammy?"

My body relaxes into my sheets, the tension vaporizing up through the ceiling. "Hey. It's good. I'm doing well. How's everything there?"

There's a steep inhale, like he's smoking or vaping. "Same. Sad, depressing. I can't imagine why you left."

I smirk. "How are your ribs?"

He yawns. "Good. I'm back to work now. I'm either getting used to the pain or it's healing up. How's your head?"

I touch the stitches until I remember I'm not supposed to. "It's okay."

"You still getting headaches?"

"Yes," I lie.

"Sucks. I guess I can't blame you for giving up."

He's joking, but still I bristle. "I'm not giving up, Jamie. I'm still working on it, just not from that pit of vipers over there. One murder and one abduction are plenty for me, thank you very much. I've been doing some research here. I don't know, I think I might be on to something."

"Yeah, I saw that in your text. What is it?"

"I don't want to jinx it. Let me do a little more digging first."

He laughs. "God, you're such a Nancy Drew."

"Well, I don't see you puffing on a Sherlock Holmes pipe."

"That's because I'm playing marriage counselor over here. Imagine, Noer. Me, a marriage counselor. That's where we are, over here in the 'glades."

There's movement in my peripheral vision, and I glance up to see my dracaena plant waving from the balcony. I tell myself to order some blinds and turn my body in the opposite direction. "With who? Zack and Taylor?"

"Yeah . . ."

"Is it really getting that bad?"

"Yup. Taylor's crazy and Zack's in love with you and their kid's missing—"

"Why would you say that?"

"Because their kid is missing."

"Not that, idiot. You know what I mean. You've got to stop saying Zack loves me."

"Fine, I'll stop. Doesn't make it any less true, though."

"But why do you think it's true? What has he told you?"

Jamie laughs menacingly. "Oh, you want to know, huh? Does Jamie get to be the mediator between Noer and Zack again? 'Zack, Noa wants to know if she can keep your football hoodie?' 'Noa, Zack says to stop giving Taylor dirty looks during assembly.' 'Zack, Noa says she's not looking at Taylor at all and to stop causing drama.'"

I roll my eyes throughout his performance. "Are you finished? I'm not asking you to relay any information between us. I want to know what he's done that makes you think he has feelings for me."

"Fine. He told me. He said he should've married you instead of Taylor."

I groan and throw my arm over my eyes. This isn't news to me, unfortunately. I contemplate whether to tell Jamie, but in the end I decide that was something Zack told me in confidence. Even if he confessed it to Jamie, as well. Besides, Jamie's reaction the last time I told him Zack and I had spent time together isn't something I want to relive. Instead, I say, "That doesn't mean he loves me."

"Well, you can interpret it however you want, kid. Speaking of being in love, how is Henry?"

"It's Hector, and he's fine. He's in Vegas for a couple of nights for some lawyer conference."

"So that's why you're calling me, I see how it is."

I laugh. "Shut up."

"You need me to come protect you? Say it, babe . . . Oh, shit."

There was something ominous in his words, and I sit up. "What's wrong?"

"Someone's here."

"Where? At your house?"

"Yeah . . . hey, Noa. Hold up. Hang on a sec."

I push the phone harder into my head, listening as Jamie moves around his home. My pounding heart relents slightly when I hear him greeting someone with familiarity. And then his voice is loud in my ear—"Yo, Noer. It's Zack. He wants to say hi."

"Noa?" Zack's voice says before I've registered this trade-off.

"Hi—hey. Hey, Zack."

"Man, I feel like such a dick."

"What? Why?"

But then my phone jingles the high-pitched, tinkling FaceTime tune, and I look to see that Zack has taken this conversation a step further. I frown. My finger hovers over the accept icon before tapping it. A short, sharp chord, and I'm staring at Zack's downtrodden face. But the moment he sees me, it brightens.

I smile, tilting my phone to avoid any double-chin illusions. "Hi. So why do you feel like a dick?"

A cameo of Jamie fades into the house as Zack moves off his front steps, and now just the big blue house is in the background. Zack runs a hand through his hair. "Because I never thanked you for everything you did."

I shrug. "Well, I did just kinda take off. I didn't say anything to anyone."

Zack sits on the bottom step of Jamie's house, and I have to tell him to angle the phone a different way to keep the porch light from whiting him out. He does, and now it looks like he has a halo.

"I meant before that, though. That day we spent some time together? That was good for me. I needed that."

My lips purse together in discomfort, and I force them into a smile. Taylor didn't seem to appreciate that day so much, and Jamie's words are still echoing around my semi-lit bedroom. "Zack's in love with you" is currently ricocheting off the corner and getting caught up in the whirling blades of the ceiling fan.

"I enjoyed it, too," I confess unabashedly. That is my truth, and I don't have to apologize for it.

Zack bats a mosquito out of his face. "God, I wish we could've talked more."

"About what?"

"Everything. High school, after high school . . . You've always given great advice, and I could've really used some."

I think carefully before answering. "Well, talking about high school would've probably just conjured up bad memories for the both of us. Me, specifically. And after high school would have been worse. And honestly, there's not much advice I can give to a guy in your situation."

He plants a fist over his mouth. "I tell myself night and day that you really did see Skye in that warehouse."

I grimace. "Cabin."

His fist opens, fingers flicking. "Cabin, warehouse, wherever you were. Jesus."

"You're blaming yourself again," I say without working that one through. But it's true—I can read him just as easily now as I did back then. And the more I think about it, the more I realize I shouldn't have to apologize for that, either. My entire teenage years were invested with him, and no matter what happens in the next hundred years, we will always be the owners of each other's virginity. I continue boldly. "You've always been that person, the one who blames yourself for everything. All the effort you're putting into crucifying yourself, put it into finding your daughter. There is truth, and there are ideas. Stop focusing on the ideas and start working with the truth. The truth is your daughter is missing."

He stares at the phone—or through the phone, it feels like, right into my soul. "I've missed you so much."

My breath halts. Not only because he shouldn't have said that, but because I'm battling with my own truths. I've missed him, too. But the dynamics—his rocky marital status, our exhumed history—are transforming before my eyes into solid, palpable truths. And dynamics that become logistics . . . they don't play well with others.

He ducks his head, his fingers doing the scratch of shame on his scalp. "So, uh . . . Hey! Great job pulling off that little charade while you were here. The whole, 'I've been cured of CIPA' bit." He grins now, boyish and roguish.

I laugh loudly, grateful for the change of subject. "Well, you country folk believe whatever you want to believe. I'm sure everyone would've figured it out eventually. Especially after I got whacked in the head with a plank and then fell headfirst into the floor of the *cabin*—not warehouse—and complained only of the vertigo and not the headaches."

He nods amusedly. "A plank, huh? I must've missed that part. You're the world's most interesting woman."

I cock my head and contemplate that. "It's better than being called a superhero."

"Oh, you're a superhero." His thumb presses into his bottom lip, and I'm forced to look away. But his next words bring my eyes right back: "You see? You've made me feel a million times better tonight already. And you're on the other side of the state."

His charming, sparkling demeanor shifts like a slippery mask, and his grieving soul manifests through his face. "I don't have anyone here that I can talk to like this, Noa."

"What about Jamie?"

A crooked grin hooks up the side of his face. "Ha, yeah. Jamie helps, but only so much. Especially when he's off the Ritalin. My friendship with Jamie doesn't hold a candle to what you and I . . . I mean, he helps with the guy stuff. It's not like it's a superficial level, but it's not what we—it's not like this."

"What about your mom?"

He smirks. "She's my mom. Like, what exactly am I supposed to talk to her about? And my dad is fucking dead to me."

I know. I read it in your Facebook messages. I wonder what he would think of my theory that Logan is still in South Florida and has kidnapped Skye. But like I told Jamie—I'm not bringing this up until I have solid proof. Especially considering this is his son.

His head dips to the right; he's digging something out of his pocket. He tells me to hang on, and I'm forced to stare at the black night sky for a few seconds before his face pops back on the screen, a cigarette dangling from his mouth.

He concentrates on that first big inhale as I prompt, "And Taylor?"

He shuts his eyes, smoke wafting from all his facial orifices. "Can I be honest with you, Noa?" He takes another hit.

I nod numbly.

He shakes his head on the exhale. "I think Taylor—"

The door behind Zack opens, and two bare feet and yellow interior light flood my screen. "What is this? How is it that ten years after you guys break up, I'm still the third wheel?" Jamie whines, and Zack twists his head back to look at him. I stare at his elongated neck, the muscles and tendons stretching and bulging, and force away the memories of my lips running across them.

Jamie's face fills the screen, and I'm staring at a grinning two-headed monster. "You guys go and do whatever it is you guys do. Weirdos."

Jamie laughs and tells me he loves me. Zack winks and says, "I'll see you soon."

I don't know how to respond to that, so I end the call.

I lie in bed, wondering what my life will be like now that my Everglades City people are back in it. Things won't be like they were then, obviously, but I have to admit I'm not nearly as jumpy and nervous as I was before the call.

I look at the time—nine thirty. My eyes stare inattentively at my TV—a home makeover show—as I snuggle down in my sheets. Why hasn't Hector called? Surely his meet and greet is over by now. But then I remember the time difference, that it's only six thirty in Vegas. So instead, I pursue my goal of searching for Skye from a distance and google Howard Zilnich again.

As expected, I still find nothing that leads to him ever being in the same area code as Skye. There are no new updates, which means either they're taking their time questioning him or he's been ruled out so quickly that the media is too embarrassed to admit their mistake. So much for journalistic integrity.

At nine forty, a text pops up—not from Hector, but from Logan. Pillows and blankets fall to the floor as I leap out of bed. His text message doesn't make sense at first, until I look up and remember my last text to him: *Why can't you come down from Connecticut?*

And now, his five simple words make too much sense. A sense only I would understand, and he knows that. Like he created an encrypted portal from his mind's eye to mine. And for the first time ever, I actually feel cold.

I think you know why.

CHAPTER

21

I'M WATCHING ALL my strength and courage evaporate from my body and dance toward the ceiling until it's like they never existed. I want to throw my phone in the ocean, hide under the bed, plug my ears, close my eyes, and la-la-la like a child.

My chin quivers as I stare down at his menacing words, and I picture the man on the other side of this portal, his and mine, the man who is harboring a small child who hasn't seen her parents in two weeks. A righteous anger sparks, ignites my heart and explodes through my veins. With a bloodthirsty roar, I return his text: *Could it be because you never went to Connecticut at all? You never even left Florida?*

His following text is a location. A red teardrop shape on a blue and green rectangular map surrounded by quite familiar words: Big Cypress National Preserve, Carnestown, Everglades City, Chokoloskee.

The red teardrop pulses. A living, breathing heartbeat.

He.

Never.

Left.

My head sways back and forth. No, I'm missing something. Surely he wouldn't freely give me his location that easily . . .

I drop my phone and take a lap around my bedroom. I need to breathe.

I need to call the cops. I run back to my phone and cannot find the call icon fast enough because another text from him pops up.

Pay attention because I'm about to tell you the truth.

My hands shake so badly I can't read it. I'm forced to place it back on my bed and simply stare at it until I'm capable of calling the police. The text bubble dances, mocking me. Teasing me. Then it explodes into a cloud of words:

> *Connecticut was a lie. The whole thing was a lie. I left Maggie a year ago and have been lying ever since. I've been hiding out in the Everglades. And I have a secret for you.*

Somehow, I don't know how I do it, but I reply: *Do you have Skye?*

Why don't you come see for yourself?

I scream. Urine saturates my leggings. My knees buckle and I fall, sprawled on my side, my cheek on the carpet, my eyes glued to my glowing iPhone lying inches away. This. This is how I felt as I zigzagged through the Everglades after escaping this monster. Dizzy, terrified, not knowing what to do, where to go. My sanity dangles from a string.

With energy I don't have, I sit up and type back: *Calling cops*. But he's texted something, a photo.

Skye.

A horrified numbness washes over me as I stare at her little face. Her eyes are open, she stares into the camera. I know with everything I am that this photo was taken just now, because the ghosts in her eyes were not there in all her flyers. She's aged a thousand years. Her silent mouth speaks horror stories only I can decipher. The photo is from her chest up, the background dark and undecipherable.

Another text—*Call the cops and she dies.*

I'm frozen in this hell.

He sends another. *I tried telling you my secret once and you escaped.*

My quivering fingers move clumsily across the letters. *Why me?*

You'll find out when you come here. Here's how this will work. You have two hours to arrive at the location I sent you. If you're not here in 120 minutes, exactly at midnight, the kid is shark food. If someone comes with you, or the cops show up, you're all shark food. If you breathe a word of this to anyone, you'll never even find Skye's body.

It's happened again, that phenomenon where irrationality overthrows rationality and holds a tyrannical reign over your universe. And I adapt because it'll annihilate me otherwise.

He's giving me two hours to drive to a location at least an hour and a half away. He doesn't want me thinking about it, doesn't want me to have a moment to plot against him.

My fingers, with minds of their own, type out: *Too late. I'm at the police station now. They've read all your texts and found your location. They'll be there any minute.* And then I delete it because Skye's life is on the line and I shouldn't bluff her to death.

I lie on my bedroom floor in a puddle of urine, staring at these threats on my phone while my time ticks away. There are no logistics or dynamics to weigh here. Only life and death.

He's forcing me to go. If I don't, she dies. He thinks he has all the power with his threats—*Come alone! Come now! Tell no one! Or else!*—because this waste of flesh, this man who left his wife and son, who knocked me out and tied me up, who plotted with Morgan Higgins to steal his grandbaby from her family—is threatened by me and wants to take me on. Fifty-year-old man versus twenty-eight-year-old girl.

Real tough, Logan.

I'll do it. I'll go along with his little game, because Logan isn't the only one with cards up his sleeve. I don't need cops. He has a secret? Well, so do I. He can't hurt me, but I can hurt him.

I look back at my phone to see that he's texted again: *You have 118 minutes.*

I smirk and reply: *I'll see you in 117.*

This is happening. The first thing I do is shower. It's a quick one, but a necessity. I don't miss the irony that the girl who is going to kill yet another man to save Skye just peed her pants.

I dress in black jeans and a Kevlar vest I received from one of my first construction projects in Liberty City. It's a dangerous area, Janna had said, and you'll need this in case of, God forbid, any drive-bys or stray bullets.

How thoughtful of her, I think as I put a black sweatshirt over it, to be so concerned for my safety and not at all for her underwriters. I pull my hair back into a low ponytail, thinking of Shelby wearing the vest incorrectly, too—either backwards or as a diaper.

I send up a prayer of thanks for my country-girl upbringing as I slide a long box from beneath my bed and open it to reveal several hunting knives, a Benelli Nova, two Remington rifles, and a Smith and Wesson M&P 9mm. I grab the Bowie knife first and slide it in a holster. Once it's secured snugly in the back of my pants, I move toward the pistol but spot the folding karambit knife my father gave me—almost circular with its claw-shaped blade and rounded handle. It's tiny and compact, and it won't weigh me down any more than everything else does. The more the merrier, I think, and shove it in my jeans.

I have two magazines for the Smith and Wesson, both loaded and lying next to the little contraption. I pop one in and rack it, slip it into a second hidden holster in the front, and grab the extra magazine and another box of ammo for good measure.

Last, I strap a tracking device around my ankle—also a fringe benefit from the generous Thompson-Miller Corporation—that's connected to my company network. I sit down at my laptop and schedule an email to be sent to Janna in twenty-four hours: *If you receive this email, check my tracking device and call the cops.*

If all goes well, I'll cancel the email. If not, Janna can be the new superhero.

Keys in hand and phone in pocket, I head for the door.

* * *

It's ten fifteen. My preparation has eaten at least fifteen of my 117-minute promise, leaving me a little over an hour and forty-five minutes. I buckle my seat belt and tap the location Logan sent.

One hour and thirty-six minutes.

"Plenty of time."

I smile and wave to Vladimir as I pull out of the parking garage onto Ocean Drive. Always on duty, Vladimir. No days off. It's quiet tonight, relatively, and I flip the radio to an easy listening station as I plan how I'm going to gut Logan and scatter his intestines all over the Everglades.

I wondered if my GPS would take me through Alligator Alley, but no. It has me exiting the Florida Turnpike onto SW 8th Street heading west. Good ol' Tamiami Trail. It feels like I'm going home.

Twenty more minutes gone, and I'm passing Krome Avenue and the Miccosukee Casino, the lights and life of Miami behind me. Nothing but darkness and death ahead.

My arrival time keeps dropping the closer I get—one minute, now two—and I realize in horror the reason when my rearview mirror suddenly erupts in red and blue flashes. I press the brake and move my eyes to the speedometer, which is quickly plummeting from eighty-five miles an hour.

I maneuver to the shoulder, and the cop follows. I shut my eyes—the flashing lights are blinding—and place a hand over my heart, which could outpace my previous speed. I am a Christmas tree of concealed deadly weapons.

A tap on the window makes me jump, and I turn to see a uniform peering in with a flashlight. My jittery hands manage to roll down the window. It's a young kid, not a whisker in sight. Which could mean one of two things: either he's still trying to prove himself, or he's easily swayed. I pray to the millions of stars above that he's the latter. "Where are you headed?" he asks, and the tone of his voice makes my heart sink. He clearly has to compensate for that squeaky, prepubescent voice. I can hear his mantra already—*despite my high voice, I am not one to be trifled with.* A Barney Fife complex.

I clear my throat. "To visit my parents. In Everglades City."

He straightens, and I can no longer see his face. "May I have your license and registration please?"

And I left my purse at home with my license. My heart rate leaps through the roof. He's going to arrest me, and Skye is going to die.

I take my time searching the center console for my registration, trying to conjure up a legitimate story as to why I don't have my license. I could tell him right now about my mission. Show him the texts. We could plan a way to capture Logan and save Skye. *Who are you kidding, Noa? This kid is shorter than you. Probably weighs less too. He couldn't save Princess Toadstool from Bowser's castle.*

And then the most brilliant idea comes to mind.

"Here's my registration"—I hand it to him—"but my purse was stolen last week. Not sure if you heard about it. The kidnapping that happened? On those docks southwest of here? That was me."

He drops into a squat, his eyes as wide as the flashlight lens. "The one they found wandering up near Alligator Alley?"

I nod and continue to milk his sympathy by pointing at the stitches in my head, by rolling up my sleeves and revealing the rough, red marks on my wrists.

But his sympathetic face quickly turns suspicious. "And you mean to tell me you're back out here, driving alone and at night? With no identification? I'm going to need you to step out of the car, please."

My heart is a rocket, soaring through time and space. He steps away from the car, but I can only hover my finger over the unlock button.

"Miss? Please step out of the car."

As if on autopilot, I unlock the door and open it. My limbs shake as I plant one foot on the ground, then another, and stand. "P—please don't . . . touch me."

He freezes. His expression softens and he holds up a hand. "Don't worry. I'm not. Are you carrying any weapons?"

My eyes lock on his, and I reply boldly, "After being kidnapped? You bet your ass I am." And I pull up my shirt to reveal the gun. "I have a concealed weapons permit, and it's right here." I pull the small piece of plastic from my driver's side door and pray that this is my ticket to redemption.

He studies it then looks up at me, then back at the photo. "Noa Romwell. Yup, I remember that name. And this is you. Well, that makes sense, you driving these deserted streets, because you're armed. Good for you." He hands me my permit as I collapse back into the driver's seat. "I know your purse was stolen, so you wouldn't have a driver's license yet."

I bob my head. "Yeah, it should be arriving in the mail any day, Officer."

"Well, then I think you've been through enough. I'll let you go this time, but please drive safely. I know you're trying to get home to your parents and escape these Everglades, but there's a speed limit and you need to abide by it." He's retreating to his car, his already small frame getting smaller and smaller.

I want to hug him. I want to cry, to laugh, to jump around for joy. "I will, I promise. Thank you."

"You have a good night, now." And he's gone.

There isn't enough air in all the Everglades to fill my lungs right now, as I relax onto the headrest and shut my eyes. "Thank you, thank you," I whisper to everyone and everything. Then reality hits me and I jerk my eyes open to look at the time. Eleven thirty. Thirty minutes left.

And according to the GPS, my ETA? Thirty minutes.

CHAPTER 22

I'M TURNING OFF Tamiami Trail now, facing the real deal—back roads. The speed limit drops from sixty to forty, so I do thirty-nine. Logan will just have to deal with it, because I can't risk getting pulled over again. My hands are still shaking when my GPS tells me to make a left in five hundred feet.

I squint at the road ahead while slowing, but even with my high beams on, I can't see where I should be turning.

Two hundred feet.

One hundred feet.

Turn left here.

But it's the same soupy sawgrass I've been seeing for miles. My car is at a complete stop in the middle of a gravel road. "Something's not right." I push the gearshift into park and hit overview on the GPS. Supposedly, once I turn left here, I need to go straight for another half mile before turning right, then in four hundred feet should be my destination.

I'm second-guessing all this. I assumed I'd be meeting him at an actual address, but I don't know why I ever thought that; he doesn't have an actual address. I decide to dial him.

Of course, he doesn't answer. I text instead.

I'm a half mile away. It's telling me to turn left but there's no road.

No response.

I have ten minutes left, and I didn't come all this way for her to die. I take a deep breath and notice a broad scenic pull-off just ahead. I maneuver my car into it and kill the engine. I'm almost sure it will be towed before I return, so I give it a little pat as I hit the lock on my key fob. It chirps and winks at me—goodbye, Noa—and I follow my phone's navigating finger into the mushy sawgrass.

The flashbacks are haunting and repetitive—the last time I wandered through these swamps in the dark. This place doesn't offer trigger warnings, and the mocking caws of vultures and melancholy whistles are vying to drop me right back into the night I escaped the cabin. I force them out of my mind. I survived it once, I'll survive it again.

For a person who can't feel pain, and therefore doesn't fear it, these swamps could be my best friend or my worst enemy. Pick your poison. But for the sake of Skye, I must become allies with these lands—I can't have them working against me like they did before. I remind myself that the Everglades aren't the Everglades without the wildlife. Tonight, I am the wildlife, becoming one with this vicious atmosphere. I won't be the prey like last time, but the predator.

I check my GPS. I'm to turn right in a hundred feet. And in a hundred feet, I do.

In four hundred feet is your destination.

I look up but see nothing more than I've seen since I started this hike. Gumbo limbo trees loom like skeletons, their branches weaving together like millions of broken fingers. I take my first spongy step toward them.

In two hundred feet is your destination.

I'm fully immersed in the canopy made by this thick hammock, using the flashlight on my phone. "Logan?" I call. A stick cracks beneath my feet, and I jump.

In one hundred feet is your destination.

I'm power walking now, because I can't take much more of this. I reach for my gun and yank it from the holster. Safety off. The ground is sloping downward, and my flashlight catches something up ahead—something made of wood. I run.

You've arrived at your destination.

My eyes behold the wooden thing, my destination—a boat. I stare at it. This can't be right. It sits on the bank of some stagnant body of water and is completely empty. Was this some sort of joke? To get me out here in the middle of nowhere for nothing? I scream and kick the boat, sending it rocking.

The water ripples and slaps against its sides, but I hear another sound—something from out in the water that makes my neck prickle. A scream. I gaze out into the black liquid. The new moon does nothing for visibility, but there's definitely a small island nearly two hundred feet away—my fairly educated estimate after having walked two hundred feet this way and that way for the last ten minutes.

Another shriek pierces through the night like a flare gun from the little island.

"Okay, Logan." I return my gun to its holster. "You want a scavenger hunt? Let's go." I wade into the ankle-deep banks and drag the small boat back inland. One thick hiking boot swings over the side, balances, and then the other. A long oar rests in a burrow at the bottom. My fingers wrap around its rough shaft as I use the end to push off the bank.

The waters are shallow, some areas hidden among scores of sawgrass, most likely barely visible even in the daylight. I perk my ears, listening for more screams, for any sign of Skye or Logan. But all I hear is the paddle cutting through the calm water, the groan of its mass fighting against the wooden blade and losing.

The island is desolate, I can tell from here. And the closer I get, the lonelier I feel. Perhaps those were the screams of ghouls I heard, spirits marooned here for centuries. All too soon, the stern of the tiny boat faceplants into the island, but my heart has sunk somewhere in the murky waters. There's no one here. The foliage is so thick I can't imagine any man has ever stepped foot on it.

Another scream peals throughout the night, intensely louder than before—it's coming from this island. I'm frozen in my boat, one foot hovering over the edge. My eyes dart around the expanse, and I jump when a nearby tree rustles. An owl soars through the air and shrieks another haunting tune, and I shut my eyes on an exhale. It was only an owl.

My phone chimes a text, slicing through the silence, and my startle jostles the entire boat.

Welcome. And with 30 seconds to spare.

"Son of a bitch," I breathe and step out of my little vessel, retrieving my gun with trembling hands. I pan across the island. It's a small thing, its length spanning not much more than the width of the Florida Turnpike. I click flashlight mode again on my phone, shining its bright scope across the mangroves.

A little ways to the left, there's a break in the mangroves. A path. I slosh my booted feet through the muck until they're standing on solid earth and recheck the safety. It's definitely off.

It's short, this little road, and speared at the end is a hut half hidden behind a banyan tree. My heart pounds as I shine my flashlight across it. It's built of rotted wood and packed with mud in the crevices, two windows that look like eye sockets and a gaping doorway with splintered planks nailed to the side. It looks like it was once boarded up until someone took an axe to it.

The light from my flashlight skitters across the spooky façade, and I realize I'm shaking. If I'm thinking correctly, I'm in the Ten Thousand Islands and this is an old Calusa mound. I can't do this. With one hand gripping the gun, I use the other to call Logan. No more games. He either shows himself or I leave.

The ring tone drones in my ear once. Twice. And then something strange happens. A cell phone rings in the distance. It's coming from the hut. I quickly end the call, and the ringing stops.

"Logan?" I take a tentative step closer, my gun aimed right at the skull-like structure, and I call his phone again.

The ringing starts back up. He's in the hut. "Logan!" And I sprint toward it now with hell's fury, my trigger finger raging.

I'm at the entrance when I stop. Because right there—seated at the foot of the banyan tree and grinning at me—is Logan. His phone is in his lap, tinkling and dancing merrily, the glow glinting against the ring on his finger, that wedding band I loved so much—tungsten with sapphires. It's the only part of him I recognize, and my feet are moving backwards, phone and gun dropping into the mushy earth, and a scream erupts from my bowels, because Logan's body has been decaying for at least a year.

This island is evil, and I'm running on it. I have only tunnel vision, and it's aimed right at my little boat. My screams, they're unmanageable, these noises coming from my throat something from another species.

Boat, boat, boat, my wild brain chants.

My eyes remain locked on it, my only lifeline away from this realm of demons and back into a world that will forever be tainted.

It's so close now, I take a flying leap into it, but my leap is halted. A hand is wrapped around my heel. I'm suspended in midair until my body comes crashing down and my face collides with the stern of my precious, precious boat.

A split second of stars, then nothing.

No tunnel vision, no boat. No pain.

I'm officially in hell.

CHAPTER

23

Sometimes I really miss Millie. She was the best imaginary big sister. My childhood was a lonely one, and I didn't realize it then, but I harbored a lot of depression. Millie talked me through a lot of it.

There was this one time I remember when I was around eight or nine. My grandmother had passed, my maternal one. My mother was a wreck, as would be expected. It was the first funeral I'd ever attended, and while I didn't know my grandmother that well, it was strange seeing her body lying in that casket. Her face looked like it was molded from clay, and I waited and waited for the rise and fall of her chest that never came.

My mother's siblings—my aunt and uncle—joined her at the casket, the three of them weeping quietly. Their father had died before I was born, and my uncle threaded his fingers through both of his sisters' and said, "It's just us now."

I watched them from the first row of pews, the three of them holding hands, and I pondered their collective bond—their shared childhood, Christmases and birthdays, the fights and the laughs, and now this.

"At least they have each other." An older woman said that, a distant cousin, and it made me think—what will I do at my parents' caskets? I'll have no siblings to hold my hand, tell me it's just us now.

I closed my eyes, but the tears came anyway. When I opened them, Millie was sitting next to me. We wore matching dresses, although hers was a size bigger since she was a year older, and she smiled at me. "It's okay," she said. Then she held my hand and whispered proverbs that would rival King Solomon's, and I felt so much better.

I still don't know why I ever invented her. Perhaps it was a consensual trade-off of the rational for the irrational. Regardless, I could use her companionship and her sound advice right now. Because nothing about my mind is sound. And I've never been more alone.

It's the first kidnapping all over again. I'm completely blindfolded. Only this time, I'm lying flat on my back on something, a bench or a table maybe. Each limb is clamped down—no flimsy ropes this time, and no sharing restraints between my hands or my feet, no. Four limbs, four restraints. Each arm is splayed out to either side, just like my mother's were when she would tell me as a small child, *Jesus loves you THIS much!*

My legs, though not spread apart, are imprisoned in their own respective shackles, and the way my back sticks to the table and the air contacts my skin makes me wonder how exposed I am. These are the only things I'm sure of, my only truths left. That, and the fact that Logan Flynn is dead.

Upon initially regaining consciousness, the metamorphosis of the rationalities was a slow, torturous one.

I screamed until I thought I would die, then screamed myself back to life again. And now here I am—hours? Days? Years? later—just waiting for death.

Logan. Dead. For a long time. My body clenches when I think of his corpse—his empty eye sockets, the skin rotting and melting off his skull.

I have a secret for you, his text had said. And boy, did he.

Who in God's name is doing all this?

I squirm a little, as if it would make me less of a hostage. I can't imagine who is behind this, or why, but this person clearly has an agenda because they have Skye, too.

I wonder why I'm still alive, why this monster hasn't killed me. Why it insists on tying me up and blindfolding me. Then I stop wondering things and go mad, and the cycle continues.

I've given up trying to listen for signs of life. The birds, the inhabitants of the Everglades, they're silent. Only a dripping noise. It mocks me with its freedom, telling me I'm the only endangered species in these Everglades now. Assuming I'm even in the Everglades. Because the smells filling my nose aren't those of the outdoors. They're damp, musty.

Eventually, I can't deny the sharp sound of metal clanging. The squeaking of an opening door. The sound of footsteps. They're human, absolutely. They stride with determination—down a flight of stairs, it sounds like. And soon those footsteps are near me, closer.

They stop. Something makes a ripping sound and then a sliding sound. I hear a flicking noise. *Flick, flick, flick.*

Then a tinkling sound.

The footsteps, they've started again, until I feel a hovering presence. All I can do is wait. Suddenly the air moves and I hear a loud crack, and I realize something just smashed against my leg, just above my knee. Before it fully registers, it happens again—this time on my hip.

I scream because I should. I try matching the intensity of the screams to the intensity of whatever this object is coming down on my body—over and over and over—but I have no idea how hard I'm being hit or with what. All I know is that this is a sick sadist above me, one who stole Logan's life and identity and has kidnapped a little girl.

The force of the object connects with my chest, and it hinders my breathing slightly, but I still holler like a banshee because whoever this is either doesn't know me or has bought the lie that I've been cured of CIPA. I wrack my brain as I wrack my lungs, trying to make sense of these new cards dealt, these new puzzle pieces.

After about twenty blows to all areas of my body, they stop. But I continue screaming until a hand clamps over my mouth. And then a whisper: "Shut up."

I do.

The footsteps retreat to my right, back to where all the flicking and tinkling happened. They return. I feel breath against my ear, and then, barely audible, four chilling words: "*You're a damn liar.*"

It's gravelly, whispered, like a demon. My mind scrambles trying to place the voice, but it was too quiet, muffled. Was it a man? I don't know. There is something familiar about it, but in all my terror, I cannot place it. A tiny pin-sized pressure happens somewhere on my arm, and I feel a liquid surging through my veins.

And just like that, my body is on fire. Each blow delivered manifests in this diabolical agony I've never felt before, and now my screams are real.

This. This is what pain feels like—bones groaning in anguish, marrow weeping, skin split open. My skull throbs like it's going to explode. My soul cries out. Muscle fibers stinging, nerve endings singing, snapping at everything I am, scorching everything I ever was, igniting everything I will become.

Pure, unadulterated torture. I'm writhing as what was once my framework is now a mass of fire and ice and pain so loud it cuts through my teeth. I feel the color red, taste the color black; I am every murder since Cain killed Abel.

And then slowly it ebbs away, the pain. Dulls, lessens, shrinks, until my shrieks are whimpers and my senses return to their respective lanes. Until I feel nothing but my tortured mind screaming that it will never be the same, I'll never be the same.

I inhale a deep breath and hold it, listening for this monster, anticipating another onslaught of torture. But it's quiet. My body is quiet.

The ratio of rationality to irrationality dances about, trading partners like a hoedown.

This person knows of my condition.

This person beat me with I don't know what.

This person called me a liar and injected me with naloxone.

It's the same person who interrogated me about the naloxone at his mother's breakfast table, and then, ten years after breaking my heart, took me out on an airboat in the middle of nowhere and asked me to tell him something true.

CHAPTER

24

MY MIND IS buzzing as I lie here, splayed on this table or whatever it is I'm strapped to. But my body feels nothing. My eyes see nothing. I'm remembering something I learned in psychology class about repressed memories.

Some specialists believe that people tend to push traumatic events from their minds, only to have that trauma manifest in some other way. These manifestations may land them in therapy, where they can be guided to recall those memories and work through them. Suddenly, these people are finding themselves victims of abuses their conscious brains had refused to remember.

It's controversial, as other specialists believe therapists can cause their patients to create memories that never actually happened. Mixing wavering emotions with factual events can alter their mindsets, shedding potentially false light on innocent situations.

And so, as I lie here and wait, I wonder—could I have suffered at the hands of an abuser and replaced those memories with fake, fond ones? I'm sorting through every memory with Zack—all four and a half years—scrutinizing each word, every action, to see if I missed or overlooked his hidden persona.

Zack would get angry, but never violent. Not that violence would affect me anyway. Maybe that's why I never saw this side of him. I think back to when Vinny Mason touched me inappropriately—the event I so craftily threw in his mother's face during the search party meeting at City Hall when I first arrived.

Vinny was the stereotypical class creep. Every class had one; he was ours. Constantly trying to cop a feel on all the girls, always whispering dirty remarks in our ears, forever eyeing us up and down whenever we were in his sights. I wasn't all that exposed to his not-so-subtleties, since Zack never left my side. It was during Zack's basketball games that I was left wide open to Vinny's pursuit.

Once during our sophomore year, Vinny followed me to the bathroom at halftime of a home game. When I came out, he was leaning against the wall. "Hey, baby."

I passed by him without acknowledgment.

He must not have been happy I ignored him, because he called me a bitch and slid his hand up the back of my skirt and squeezed. "Whore. You're a fucking tease."

I froze, my facial muscles slack as my eyes locked with Zack's. He'd witnessed the entire thing from the doorway of the locker room. With the grace of a gazelle and the subtlety of a scorpion, he cantered over and grabbed Vinny by the shirt, dragging him out of the gym.

Zack didn't return until halfway through the third quarter. He waltzed into the gym with purpose, nostrils flared. No sign of Vinny.

When the game was over, we walked hand in hand to his car and I asked him what happened.

"I took care of it," he replied.

"Zack, you're—"

He pushed me up against his car and dipped until we were eye level. "You are dead to Vinny, got it? That's all you need to know."

Zack was right. I was dead to Vinny Mason. He never acknowledged my presence again for the rest of high school.

All these years, I assumed Zack was defending what was his. Defending my honor. Putting a skeevy little scumbag in his place. And maybe he was, but what exactly happened when they left the gym? What sort of physical or psychological torture did Zack put him through?

I shiver against my restraints, dredging up more memories that may or may not have had something sinister underneath. But I'm driving myself crazy. I move on to interrogating every single second I spent in Zack's presence since my return to Everglades City, and so many more things are making sense.

The bruise Taylor lied to me about, that he didn't want to talk about.

That cryptic phone call of hers I heard in the bathroom: *She asked about the bruise . . . I just want my daughter back.* And the call logs I saw shortly after, indicating she spoke with either Zack or Logan. A simple—albeit horrific—deduction proves Logan was *not* on the other end of that call. It may have still been Logan's phone, but everything points to Zack having killed his father, faking Logan's life through his stolen phone for the past year. Both of those calls were Zack.

I think back on the Facebook messages I read between the two of them. Zack said he'd unblock Logan from his phone for Skye's sake, but now I know the real reason. It had nothing to do with Skye; he wanted to kill his father for leaving Maggie. They probably began texting, scheduling meetups. At least Logan thought they were meetups. For Zack, they were death plots. *Yeah, let's go have lunch. Some place quiet and secluded*, Zack probably said while sharpening his hunting knife.

My father is dead to me. Zack's words.

Great job pulling off that little charade while you were here. The whole, "I've been cured of CIPA" bit. Also Zack's words.

I'll see you soon. His final words to me on FaceTime, including an awkward, misplaced wink.

It's almost always the parents. Hector's words.

It's been right in my face the entire time. The evidence is clear, gift-wrapped, and hand delivered with a pretty bow. But the reason behind it all—why he's doing this—is as chained up and blindfolded as I am.

I ask myself if I can make an assumption, and myself says go for it. Taylor is probably involved as well, I say. Myself (or maybe it's Millie, for all I know) says to keep this between us, but Taylor's words on that phone call, their alleged marital problems, her obvious hesitancy to discuss Logan at the potluck are all reasonable elements leading to that conclusion. Those and the simple fact that there's no possible way she couldn't know that her husband is harboring their daughter.

I've no idea what time of day it is, another reason I believe I'm inside somewhere. Unlike the first abduction when I could see snippets of light through the blindfold, I'm now in eternal darkness. But I hear something, those same determined footsteps from before. He's coming back. My heart pounds, because for the first time in my life, I fear pain. And this man is able to cause an immense amount of it.

I lie still, my breaths erratic. A moment of silence before footsteps go from left to right, and then the ripping of paper and something sliding against it.

Flick, flick, flick.

"Oh, my god. Nooooo . . ."

It's another syringe of naloxone. I know it now.

"Please, no! Please!" I'm whimpering and crying, pulling against the restraints, scraping my head against the hard surface trying to remove the blindfold. I want to call him out, *It's you, Zack. I know it!* but then he might kill me.

I feel the pin-sized pressure on my arm, and I jerk harder, my voice escalating—"No! God, no! Please! Don't!"

A gush surges through my veins and ignites fire again. I scream—this is my life now. Each of the previous blows he laid on my body comes to life and shouts at me, eats me alive. My head pounds and my stomach lurches with hunger. The broken bones are like sirens that refuse to be quieted. Every wound calls out to me—a roll call, and all are present.

And then it fades. My body is back to its comfortable numbness, but my brain is bleeding and deformed. I'm going to die here.

* * *

The footsteps awaken me this time; I must've slept through the door clanking and the stair stomping. I freeze, knowing what's coming. Soon I'll be writhing in pain again. But the footsteps, they're different. They're not hard and determined. They're soft, sneaking.

I wonder what he's doing, if he is purposely avoiding making noise. Perhaps he's trying to surprise me with the naloxone injection. I've heard how captors never allow their victims any sort of schedule, because even schedules can be comforting.

But then I hear a soft sound—the humming of a song, only for a moment. I hold my breath.

Drip, drip, drip . . .

"Hello?" My voice is scratchy and dry.

A shuffling sound, light breathing. I wonder if it's some sort of animal. But then the humming happens again—it's "Happy" by Pharrell Williams—and hair pricks the back of my neck. "Skye?" I whisper.

It stops.

Perhaps I'm hearing things. There's nothing here but me and my despair. And the constant dripping. I exhale a long, loud sigh.

"How do you know my name, Noa?"

I know beyond anything I heard that. I heard that voice, a child's. This child knows my name. "Skye, is that really you?" I ask.

No answer.

I think that maybe if I answer her question, she'll answer mine. "I—I've been looking for you for a while now. I'm friends with your mom and dad."

"My mommy and daddy?"

Oh, my god. It's like hearing a baby speak its first words. I'm smiling, and that smile has upgraded to giggling. I want her to talk more. "Yes! How do you know *my* name?"

"I just do."

Bubbles of laughter expel from my throat. *More! More! Give me more words!*

"Where are we?" I ask, my voice on eggshells.

Again, no answer. I tell myself not to ask direct questions. She doesn't like those, Noa. I'll learn the rules to her game. Kids like games.

Kids like games.

"Skye, I'm bored. Would you like to play a game?"

Rustling sounds, then the padding of small feet across the floor. She's walking toward me. *She's walking toward me!*

"Let's play I Spy. Do you like that game?" I ask.

"Uh-huh." I hear the smile in her voice, and it's the sweetest, most beautiful silver lining in this nightmare.

"Okay! Okay, great. Umm . . . oh, but I can't see. Do you think you can take this blindfold off me so we can play I Spy?"

She hesitates. "I already did."

I can't wrap my head around that. "Skye, you—"

A clicking sound, and light explodes around me. My pupils contract. I blink rapidly until they see a single bulb—*they see it!*—hanging from the ceiling, swaying now after being tampered with by this girl standing in front of me.

The weight of this moment is overpowering—the tiny little essence that has single-handedly upended an entire town and beyond is right here. She doesn't understand the significance of this, but I do. I see nothing else, only her. She's frail, dirty, but a thousand times more beautiful in the flesh than in any of the pictures. Freckles scatter across her nose, spilling onto her cheeks—cheeks that are punctuated with dimples, even without smiling lips. The shape of her face, the short hairs, the fly-aways sprouting from her forehead and temples. Her height, stature . . . I stare at her in awe, her face alight with the anticipation of a child about to partake in I Spy. And I wonder—how can she be so happy right now? She doesn't look like she's shed a tear a day in her life. I see it now.

Then she speaks. "I took it off of you after Father put me down here yesterday." Her hands slap over her mouth, her eyes widen—she wasn't supposed to say that.

"It's okay, I already know your father is the one doing all this."

Her hands drop and she cocks her head. "You do?"

I nod, give a reassuring smile. Then she whispers, "Don't tell him I told you."

And I whisper back, "It'll be our little secret."

She continues whispering, which makes me giggle. "You didn't look comfy while you were sleeping. I couldn't move these big things, but I could take off that thing on your head."

I turn my eyes to the big things of which she speaks—the thick metal clamps encircling my wrists and screwed into a crude, wooden table. I realize that I am, in fact, shirtless—wearing only my bra. I swallow a bout of bile and force a grin. "Well, that was very thoughtful of you. Thank you."

"You're welcome. I spy with my little eye . . . something . . ."

Her eyes move around the area, and so do mine. We are in some sort of room, windowless. Tiny. Smaller than the cabin from before, and the walls are made entirely of cinder block. Besides the single hanging bulb, I see a set of wooden stairs ascending the far wall, but I'm unable to see what it leads to. A long counter is built into the wall on my right, remnants of naloxone wrappers on it. My breath catches when, next to it, I see a thick, wooden plank wrapped up with chains. Nails have been hammered into it, spikes sticking out through the links like thorns. It sits upright against the counter, and I shiver.

"Black!"

I'm jarred back to Skye, sweet, innocent Skye, who is not at all concerned about playing a game in a dungeon with deadly weapons and a shirtless woman who is tied to a table. I raise my head to observe the rest of my body, which is clad only in underwear, but that's not what nearly makes me scream. My body is a mural of black, blue, and red. Imprints of those chains scale every inch of me, punctuated with bright red dots trickling from each wound. I shut my eyes.

Skye pokes my arm. "Hey. I said, I spy with my little eye something black."

I force my eyes open and back on her. "Ummm, my body?" I ask with a quiver.

She giggles and drags a single finger down my abdomen. "Nope. Not your scary makeup."

Puzzled, I look down again, eyeing the bloody mess and the fresh, tiny, horizontal finger swipe running through it. "Makeup?"

"Father said you're in a Halloween costume. He said you're a sexy zombie."

I blink. Register that. A giggle crawls up my throat and through my lips. "What else did he tell you?"

"He said that was part of your costume, but he put it over there so it wouldn't hurt anybody." She points to the nailed and chained plank across the room, and now I don't know whether to laugh or cry.

"Did he tell you why I'm chained to this table?"

She shakes her head thoughtfully. "No, he told me not to talk to you. And I didn't, but you talked to me first. He made me come down here because I was bad last night." Her chin tucks bashfully into her shoulder.

My lungs hesitate to inflate. They're trying, they just seem to be paralyzed. I'm putting pieces together, pieces that are good—all things considering. Skye wasn't here when he beat me or injected me. He lied to her about my wounds; he didn't want to scare her, which is good, but he also put her in a dark basement overnight. I want to probe her about this, but I need to tread carefully. Can't ask too many questions and scare her into silence again. I have to play the game.

"Okay, something black. And it's not my Halloween costume." I gaze around again and realize this game will be over soon because there aren't that many colors down here. "These metal clamps on my arms and legs?"

"No."

I spot a pile of blankets in the corner to my left, assume that's where Skye's been sleeping during her punishment, push that horrible thought from my head, and divert my eyes because they're brown and white anyway. They land on another pile of some sort of fabric in the other corner. I nod my head toward them. "Those. Those clothes."

"Yes!"

I do a double take. "Are those my clothes? Those are my clothes!"

She turns to look at them and sneezes.

"God bless you."

Wiping her nose, she faces me again. "Your turn."

My gaze lands on something interesting—a rope coiled on the floor. I'd be willing to bet anything it's the rope that Skye untied from my hands. Anger keeps me from incorporating it into our game, that and the fact that it's beige—not really a color a six-year-old could identify easily. I scan the room and notice a dark, wooden door in the ceiling. "Red."

She frowns. "That's not how you say it."

"Oh! I'm sorry. I spy with my little eye something red."

She taps a finger on her chin, her tiny eyebrows scrunched in concentration. "Hmmm . . . Hmmm . . . The makeup on your legs?"

I shake my head and stifle a smile, and the weight of this situation, the irony, overwhelms me. Here we are, two girls without tears even after we've lost everything, playing a game.

A loud bang from above shakes the light bulb, and Skye looks at me with large eyes. "He's home! He can't know we—" She runs to her nest of blankets and retrieves a thick, black strip of cloth from under her pillow. Her little face is frantic as she comes at me with it, wrapping it around my eyes and tying it clumsily. The pull of a light string, and I'm back in utter darkness as I hear her scampering over to her nest.

CHAPTER 25

I LIE HERE, COMPLETELY exposed, my heart pounding. Skye is scared of her father—rightfully so—and I fear what he would do to her if he knew we were talking, playing the most bizarre game of I Spy imaginable. I listen for the telltale signs that he's coming down: doors unlocking, metal clanking, footsteps descending. But none of those things happen.

And where are we? She said *he's home*, but it wouldn't make sense for Zack to keep her hidden in his own house. Or perhaps wherever we are is where Skye has been held all this time, and she's just been conditioned to call it "home."

All options stir bile in my stomach, then I hear another loud boom from above. Skye gasps, and I clench my teeth. But after a grueling moment, I feel her little fingers peeling back my blindfold. The swift zip of the light being pulled, and I'm staring at her face again. "He's gone," she whispers.

"Are you sure?"

A head bob.

I swallow. "Skye? What happens next?"

Her little lip quivers; she's retreating. Her expression is the same haunted shadow as the picture Zack sent me from Logan's phone. I asked the wrong question. She's stepping away, curling into herself. She's either scared of the answer or scared of the consequences of giving me the answer.

My gaze lands on my clothes in the corner, my boots sitting in a tidy row next to them. My unanswered question looms above me, buzzing around the bare bulb like a fly. *What happenzzz nexzzt?*

I fear anything I say will set her off; it's like trying to approach a seagull on the beach. "I mean, when do we eat? Aren't you hungry?"

She stops, considers this. "We eat when Father lets us out of here. I'm super hungry. So hungry."

"Do you know when he'll let us out?"

A head shake.

I am not a mother, not yet. But there is this instinct manifesting inside me, a righteous anger that Skye is so hungry. That Logan has been dead for a year, that I've been kidnapped twice now, beaten and injected with naloxone, none of those things matter right now. They're blips on a radar. What's setting off my alarms, sending an inferno of fury rolling through my body, is that this little girl is fucking *hungry.*

"Skye, sweetie? Do you like magic tricks?"

"Uh-huh."

My brain is spinning like a merry-go-round full of screaming children. An idea is forming in my mind—a horrible idea that I'd never fathom attempting if it weren't for Skye. "I have another game. I'm going to ask you something, and if you answer me honestly, I will do the best magic trick you've ever seen."

A pause. "Okay."

Relief puffs through my nose on an exhale. "Why are we here?"

She audibly gulps. "Father . . . didn't want us to move."

My eyes dart around the ceiling as her words register. "Of course," I whisper. Why hadn't I thought of this before? Zack never wanted to leave Everglades City. Taylor nagged him into it. Obviously she wouldn't leave if her kid were missing.

"Okay, next question. Where are we?"

"My new house. When do I get to see the magic trick?"

Where were Zack and Taylor moving? They said they'd already found a house there. I can't remember; somewhere near Tampa, maybe. Has Zack dragged us all the way to Tampa to keep us hidden? We must be someplace far from the Everglades, because this house has a basement, and homes in South Florida don't have basements. Skye is done answering questions, and I can't blame her. She's told me plenty. And it's all I need to hear to decide that this wicked, awful idea is my last resort if Skye and I are going to survive.

"Skye, I need you to turn around for just a second, close your eyes. No peeking, okay?"

Her tiny head tilts, sending straggly brown strands of hair at an angle. "It's magic trick time?"

I nod. "Yes, are you ready?"

Excitement exaggerates her facial expressions, and she nods a single large nod.

"Okay! Abra cadabra, close your eyes!" I say as gallantly as I can through a voice I've screamed hoarse. She squeals and spins around, her hands slapping over her eyes.

I start with my right hand. Solidifying my shoulder socket, I bend my elbow as my hand strains against the restraints. Nothing gives. I pull harder. Something in my wrist pops, but the restraints give about an inch. I huff and keep pulling. More popping and snapping. My hand feels dislocated, but I keep tugging with all my strength. There's a slick sound, like the peeling of a banana, but still I pull. Miraculously, my right hand slides free of the restraint.

"Are you all done?" she asks.

"Not yet! Just hang on!" I look at the hand I've just freed. It's scraped and bloody, especially my knuckles, and I think it might be broken. I try making a fist, but something in the anatomy of my hand malfunctions, doesn't allow the movement.

I can't focus on what I've just done to myself. I swing over to the left one and immediately begin pulling.

Snap!

Crunch!

Pop!

Scrape!

"What's that noise?" she asks.

"It's all part of the surprise!" I say excitedly, but the whole while I'm apologizing to my body for the trauma I'm putting it through. I'm purposely being reckless, taking advantage of my condition, but it's life or death at this point—mine *and* Skye's. With two mangled hands free, I begin working on my feet. But with the angle of my foot and the location of the shackles around my ankle, it's impossible to slide my foot out without skinning it entirely. Instead, I rotate my foot down until I look like a ballerina and dislocate it from my ankle completely.

Crack!

It slides out and flops to the side. I bite my lip as I feebly pop it back into place. I don't know if I've done it successfully, but it's back to a ninety-degree angle, despite the immediate bruising and swelling, and I do the same for the other foot.

"Don't look yet, Skye. I'm almost done!"

When I'm finally able to swing both legs over the side of the table, I pause before jumping down. I don't know the damage I've done to my feet, and I need to make sure I'm even able to walk.

I tentatively plant my left foot first. There are some crunching sounds and I'm a bit unbalanced, but I'm able to put pressure on it. I bring the right one down. It sits at a strange angle and the skin is bunched oddly, but I'm free!

I hobble to the corner where my clothes lie in disarray, and I'm not surprised to see what's missing—my vest, my gun, my knife, my tracker, and my phone. But I delicately slide one foot into my black jeans, then the other. My hands are stiff and nearly immobile, but I power through until I'm able to button and zip my pants. I stuff my mangled feet into my boots—which fit snugly with all the swelling—and tie them tight, like a walking cast. My sweatshirt is the last thing to go on, and I arrange it over my abdomen, my arms, and now none of my injuries are visible.

Except my hands.

"Can I open them?"

I pull my hands into my sleeves. "Yes. Open them."

She does, and gasps when she doesn't see me on the table. She spins to behold my fully clothed form, my arms jutted in the air. "Ta-da!"

Her little jaw drops, her eyes darting from the table to me and back again. “How’d you do that?”

“Magic!”

But she doesn’t look impressed; she looks mortified. “He can’t know!”

I try running to her, but my ankles, they aren’t cooperating. I stumble to my knees and scoot the rest of the way, grab her tiny fingers with only my fingertips—they are colder than they should be. How cold, I don’t know. But it’s not a healthy temperature if I’m able to feel it. “Skye? Listen. Do you want to get out of here?”

She doesn’t answer, just glances between me and the staircase.

“Honey, I know more magic tricks. I can make us disappear! Your father won’t even know we’ve gone.”

“We’ll get in so much trouble.”

“We won’t, I promise. Where do you want to go? Who would you like to see first?”

She doesn’t answer. She’s backing away from me. I’m saying all the wrong things.

“Skye, what did you do last night? What did you do that was bad and made your father put you down here with me?”

Her tiny fingers worry over each other, her eyebrows tilting this way and that. “I looked out the window. Father caught me when he pulled in the driveway. Then he said this is where the bad girls go. ’Cause you’re a bad girl too.”

I shake my head. “No, I’m not a bad girl. And neither are you. So we don’t deserve to be down here. Let’s go get something to eat, okay?”

Finally, she bobs her head.

“Great.” I stand, faltering, and limp toward the stairs.

“It’s locked,” she says as my boot hits the first step.

I stop and look up the staircase at the heavy wooden door bolted with three thick locks. I want to test it anyway, but my legs aren't working properly and I'm not sure I could get back down these steps. "Will you check it, just to be sure?" I ask her.

She scampers toward me and quietly ascends the staircase. An attempted twist of the knob proves we're locked down here. But I haven't forgotten that I spied something red—a hatch door on the other side of this basement.

I point to it. "What about that?"

She balks. "It's too high!"

I thrust my arms out. "But I do magic tricks! Remember?" After a quick survey, I determine the ceiling is only seven feet high, then look around for something long enough to prod at the door. My eyes land on the chained plank—the *prop* for my *Halloween costume*.

It's heavy when I lift it, and my recently dislocated wrists struggle with the weight. I stagger toward the hatch and grit my teeth as I thrust the plank upward with both hands. The door gives at the hinges, ascending a few inches and revealing a sliver of daylight before dropping back down.

My nerves on edge, I scan the room for something to hoist us up, but find only the massive table which is screwed into the floor. I want to cry. We are so close to being free, and if Zack comes back and sees that I've escaped the shackles, I don't know what he'll do to me or to Skye.

A loud noise turns my head toward Skye's little nest, and she's dragging a large, empty oil drum from an alcove I failed to see from the table. "How 'bout this?"

I clap my sleeved hands. "You see? You're such a good girl!" I scurry to help her, and soon we have the drum directly beneath the hatch. “Okay, you hold it steady while I climb on it first, okay?” Skye’s tiny frame will do nothing to steady the bulbous barrel, but I want her to feel useful.

She obliges—her little arms hug it, barely covering a quarter of the circumference. My wrists pop as I brace them on top of the steel drum, and I force my knees to bend. My ankles grind and shift as I hop, my shins landing on the surface. I smile down at her. “You did it! You held it for me!”

She beams and sets her shoulders as I slowly adjust my squat. I point to the plank. “Very carefully hand me my Halloween prop. Don’t hurt yourself on those nails!”

“Oh, boy,” she says as she heaves it up by the handle.

I take it from her, and punch it upward and knock the hatch door clean open.

I stand up straight, thrusting my head through the square of fresh, beautiful atmosphere with tips of palm branches waving at me. My heart races as I strain to keep my thoughts straight. “Okay, you need to climb up here with me. But you have to be very careful so we don’t fall, Skye.”

But she’s frozen, hesitant. She’s changing her mind. No. No, no, no.

“What’s wrong?” I ask as my hands begin trembling.

She’s backing away from me, shaking her head. “He’s gonna get mad. So mad. He said I’m not allowed to leave.”

Sweet, obedient little Skye. I want to jump off the drum and hug her. “We can’t stay here. Sweetheart, I can’t leave you behind.”

Her tiny pink lip quivers, and a tear slides down her cherub cheek. “Please don’t go.”

Skye is crying. Of all the reasons she should be crying, of all the people who should have made her cry . . . She's crying because of me. Now I'm crying too. We're beholding each other, the two girls who never cry, both broken to tears in our own personal pit of hell.

"Skye, what is it you want? I know you don't want to be here with your father. Where do you want to go? I'll take you wherever you want. Please, we have to go. And I don't want to leave without you."

A door slams above us, and loud footsteps walk with determination. I nearly tumble off the drum, and Skye cries even harder, her fleshy little hands cupping her mouth. "He's here!" And she begins jumping in place.

This is now or never. And if I stay here and he sees I've escaped the restraints, I'll die. But it will kill me to leave her, and there's no time for both of us to climb out.

"Just promise you'll come back, okay?" Her tears have stopped just as suddenly as they appeared, having been replaced by resolution. Like she's the alpha now. She jerks on the string light and plunges us into darkness, but with the open hatch door, we're still able to see each other.

I set my jaw. "I promise you. Now quick! Go lie down and pretend you're sleeping! When he comes down, tell him you don't know where I went. Act shocked that I'm not here, act scared. Tell him you never spoke to me and that I never saw you." I grab onto the lip of the open hatch door as Skye darts back to her nest and curls up in a ball.

I hate leaving her here. I hate this more than anything. But I cannot stay. Zack will break me. I've destroyed myself escaping that table, and if he shoots me up with more naloxone, I won't be able to handle that pain. I turn to her one last time, tears streaming down my face. "I'm coming back for you, okay?"

She smiles and gives me the cutest thumbs-up I've ever seen. "You got this."

I nod. I got this. Then, knowing this is my one shot, I jump.

The drum wobbles in a circle, and my left elbow is planted firmly on the ground, my right wrist anchored on the lip of the opening. One slip and I'll fall back into this torture chamber. I push up, forcing my left shoulder into the ground. It's sheer survival-mode adrenaline that rocks my body forward until I'm able to roll onto my back and draw my legs up, and I'm officially outside.

I drop the door closed, stand, and back away. It's a cellar. My eyes scan across the property as I stumble backward—there's a house on top of this cellar, and I'm in the backyard. It's small, this house, and I try memorizing as much as I can while tripping toward the woods behind it, steering clear of any windows. "Black shingled roof, gray stucco, wooden deck," I chant, running as best I can. It's all the detail I'm able to perceive of where Skye Flynn is being held captive.

I trip and fall more often than not, but I close my eyes and burn the image of this place in my mind. When I see the cops, I want to give them a thorough description. No hallucinations, no theories.

Black shingled roof, gray stucco, wooden deck.

Once again, I'm running aimlessly. I'm a speck of flesh in an endless world, no idea where I am. The sun is high in the sky, unwilling to hint at which direction I'm heading. I just run on legs that feel like puzzle pieces forced into the wrong fit. My gait is so awkward, it's hard to stay upright.

My pace slows after a while. Not because I think I'm safe now, but because my body is shutting down. There's no doubt I've been running on severely broken ankles, catching my falls on transparently broken hands. My body has suffered serious trauma with no food or sustenance since yesterday. My energy is nearly depleted. The only thing keeping me going is the knowledge that I can't feel any of these things—and the fact that I found Skye. Again. And this time I know where she is.

Black shingled roof, gray stucco, wooden deck.

I slosh through marshes, pushing through silver saw palmettos and sabal palms until I feel like that bulky, empty oil drum—useless, unable to move—and I fall to the earth. I'm going to die out here, in this place with flora and fauna that still manage to look like the Everglades.

CHAPTER

26

I'VE COLLAPSED NEXT to a fallen branch, rotted, but the ground is dry. A breeze rattles through palm trees and slash pines, and I try to sit up, but my wrists offer no support. Pushing up my sleeves, I observe the horror that is my hands. Swollen, bloody, and jagged, and a bone poking through the skin just below the knuckle of my right ring finger.

I fear if I remove my boots, I won't be able to get them back on. But I imagine my feet look nearly the same. My mouth feels like cotton; I'm dizzy.

A rumbling engine, I hear it. I can barely walk anymore, but I hear a car, or I did, so I must be close to a road. And where there are roads, there is eventually civilization.

I swing up into a sitting position, break a stick off the fallen branch, and use it to hoist myself up. I break off another and use them as crutches, following the sound of the engine.

I've hobbled about a hundred feet when I see the road. It glimmers like a mirage, and I pray that it's not.

But then my makeshift crutch hits the pavement, and I know I'm on the home stretch. I don't know which way to go, but all roads lead somewhere.

I'm too weak to be excited.

* * *

The branches help immensely. Since they handle the brunt of my weight, I'm able to take note of my surroundings as I stagger down the road. I think I recognize various landmarks, but there's no way. Zack and Taylor were moving away from the Everglades, but I swear I'm in them now.

I see a crossroad ahead, and I quicken my pace until I'm able to read the signs: *Hannover Drive* and *Papaya Avenue.*

"Well, I'll be damned." I'm in Everglades City. Skye must've been mistaken or confused when she said we were in their new house. But that doesn't matter now, because this means Skye is in Everglades City too, and soon all this will be over.

I'm grinning now, because I know exactly where I am—Jamie lives just down the street on Papaya. I can see his house now.

"Jamie!" My branches haul me closer and closer to his delightfully ugly, disproportioned Smurf-blue ranch. "Jamie!"

I nearly laugh when I see his truck in the driveway.

"Jamie!"

I'm in his front yard now; his door swings open and there's Jamie. He beholds me, and I watch him register all this through his facial expressions—confusion, recognition, then horror—and I burst into tears.

"Noa?" He flies down his porch steps, his eyes darting this way and that, and catches me just as I'm collapsing.

"Oh, my god! What are you doing out here? What did you—shit! What happened?"

I'm sobbing. I can't speak. He carries me into his house and deposits me on his couch. "Noa, talk to me. What were you doing out there?" he demands as he closes and locks the door, then moves to the windows and pulls the curtains shut. He hustles to stand over me, his arms akimbo. His shirt is covered in my blood. I'm feeling light-headed.

"I found her. It's Zack. Zack's had her all this time!"

Jamie steps closer and lowers slowly onto the couch. He rubs his forehead. "What?"

I try sitting up. "Jamie, listen to me. Zack. Has. Skye."

He leans away from me, a confused grin on his face. "Wh—I'm sorry. What? Zack? Why do you think Zack has Skye?"

My tongue is sticky, swollen. "I need water."

He leaps from the couch and disappears into what I assume is the kitchen, returning with a bottle of Evian and a bag of Hormel pepperoni. I drink deeply and devour handfuls of the processed meat. I feel the energy blooming throughout my body, the water nourishing my parched soul. "Thank you."

He doesn't reply. He seats himself, his knee bobbing rapidly and his folded hands shaking in front of his mouth.

I toss the empty bag on the coffee table, having pulled the silicone packet that I nearly swallowed from my mouth. "Jamie, you need to listen to me. Logan Flynn is dead. Zack killed him a long time ago. I saw his body out somewhere in the Ten Thousand Islands."

Outside of his wild knee, Jamie is a stone, his eyes glued to the floor.

"Zack has Skye in a cellar in some house. I don't know where, but it's not far from here. Probably his; he lives right down the street, right? It's got a black shingled roof, gray stucco, and a wooden deck in the backyard."

Now both knees are bouncing, trembling limbs independent of the rest of his body. ADHD at its finest.

"I was kidnapped again. Jamie! Zack kidnapped me, and he beat the hell out of me with a plank full of nails and chains." My voice breaks and tears swell to the surface as I recount what I just survived. "He injected me with naloxone—Jamie, he's dangerous! Look at me!" Unable to push my sleeves up, I grab the hem and raise it, revealing my bra and my black and blue torso. "And he's got Skye! Call the cops!"

Jamie's face is blank as he surveys my nearly naked upper half. His mouth is open, his eyes glazed. Finally, he shuts his eyes and rubs his hands down his face. "Noa. I—I can't. I don't know. I don't—I don't know what you've done, but they found Skye's body yesterday."

And all the energy I just fed myself evaporates as I drop my shirt and collapse back onto the couch.

"She'd been dead for a while. You imagined seeing her. You imagined seeing her in this cellar, and you imagined seeing her last week in that warehouse."

"Cabin."

He looks at me sternly. "Warehouse."

My mind is exploding. It's burst into a million pieces inside my skull, skittering about like maggots and eating at itself. "It's not true," I manage.

"It is true!" He stands and paces, grinding his knuckles into the opposite palm. "I went with Zack and Taylor to identify the body. You've gone crazy, Noa. You're seeing things. And you always have. You need to go to a hospital. And not just for the ridiculous number of injuries you have. You need psychiatric treatment."

Tears stream down my face. Is this true? Have I had a history of hallucinating? Is there more wrong with me than just an insensitivity to pain? I gaze down at my injured hands, the exposed anatomy. And no, I don't feel it, but it's there. Even Jamie sees it. I'm not imagining this.

"Jamie, I was kidnapped and tortured. I saw Skye. I had conversations with her, I touched her. She told me her father is the one holding her hostage. He locked her in a cellar. The same cellar he locked me in. He chained me to a table and beat me." I gesture to my wounds, because I'm not hallucinating those.

Jamie surveys me again, his face red and contorted. "Did you see him?"

"No. But I saw her. Jamie, I know I saw her. You have to call the cops, now!"

He slaps his hands over his head. "Noa, listen to what you're saying. You saw Logan's dead body? Do you hear yourself?"

I stare at him.

"Skye is dead, Noa. My goddaughter is dead."

I don't believe it. There's no way she's dead. I saw her. We played I Spy. She told me her father is keeping her there. I don't have a history of seeing people. I'm not delusional. I don't have schizophrenia. The only reason I've been questioning my sanity these last few days is because it seems to be the consensus.

I know what I saw, and I have proof. My hand slowly moves to the hem of my shirt and lifts it. It's there, just as I remembered—a tiny fingerprint swiped through the blood.

I look up at Jamie, who has seated himself on the coffee table and is scrubbing his face with frustrated hands. I force myself into a sitting position and glance around the room as I fight this battle with vertigo. I scrutinize the place once the room stops spinning, the house Jamie wouldn't let me in before because he said it was messy. It's a typical bachelor pad. Minimal everything. Furniture he tolerates because he has to. A massive TV against the wall. A gaming console and all its paraphernalia. A recliner. A big picture window, a coffee table with empty beer cans.

I try peering into the kitchen, but this is no open floor plan. This house is old, and the kitchen minds its own business. Then there's the hallway—dark, unbecoming. But my eyes stop on a door at the end of the hall. A door with three locks.

It's as if he heard my gaze land on the door, because suddenly Jamie's eyes are on me. Observing me observing the door.

My heart is in my throat as I heave off the couch and propel myself past Jamie and down the hall. He sighs heavily the moment I stop in front of the door, but he doesn't stop me.

It looks like it's a door to a garage, but Jamie doesn't have a garage.

My left hand, of its own accord, reaches to unlock each deadbolt.

Click.

Click.

Click.

There's a hook and eye lock, too. Also a door chain. Both in place. And my hand, it just removes all barriers and I find myself turning the handle and pushing the door open.

It's horrifying, the wooden staircase leading down. It's déjà vu in the flesh. The cinder block walls. The corner of that counter protruding, the one holding all the naloxone paraphernalia. The corner of a raw, wooden table . . .

I just escaped this place. Then came right back.

Skye is down there—alive—and I feel my knees giving out, my lungs no longer functioning. I back away from the basement, trying to do berserk math. Jamie's house that was strangely raised. A blue front with a back I'd never seen, but the same black shingled roof as the place I escaped. My parents' house—the front is yellow, but the back. It's white paneling. Fronts don't always match backs.

A hand appears from behind me and slams the door shut. I spin, pinned now between the door and Jamie as he relocks the dead bolts, replaces the chain, inserts the hook into the eye.

My brain glitches as the door pulses against my back and Jamie props both hands upon it on either side of my head. He leans down until our eyes are inches apart. "Now what am I supposed to do with you?"

CHAPTER

27

WE CONTINUE TO stare into each other's souls. I'm trapped here against this door, trying to calculate every moment spent with Jamie since I've been here, just like I did with Zack. But none of it makes sense. I searched the Big Cypress Preserve with him, saved his life when Morgan Higgins was killing him. And most importantly, Skye *told* me it was her father.

Jamie thinks I've been healed from CIPA. He wouldn't know to inject me with naloxone in order for me to feel pain.

He's not even blinking; I'm not sure if I am or not. He seemed so genuine whenever he spoke of Skye, mentioning more than once that he was the godfather.

The god . . . father.

What sort of six-year-old calls her dad *Father*? No, it would be daddy or the like. But she repeatedly referred to her captor as Father, and the word rolls over in my head until it's no longer a word and I think I'm spelling it wrong. *Father didn't want us to move . . .*

The stare-down continues until I'm wondering why he hasn't killed me yet, or at least why he hasn't thrown me back in the basement.

My heart pounds. Skye is still down there.

I whisper, "You're a liar. She's alive. She's in the cellar under your house. Does Zack know? Is he in on this too?"

A shadow falls over his face, and suddenly I'm scooped off the door and thrown over his shoulder, being marched down the hallway. "Zack knows nothing. And he won't know. And you're the goddamned liar," he bites out when he tosses me on the couch.

And now I can't breathe. That sentence, the exact one that was whispered in my ear just before the first injection that I thought came from Zack. My teeth chatter as he steps toward me. "What have I lied to you about?"

"About being healed of CIPA. You're not, and I've known since the day after you arrived here."

"Zack told you, didn't he?"

He steps back and places both hands behind his neck. "Nope. Zack didn't share any of your secrets with me, ever. Although I figured you told him the truth, since, you know"—he smirks—"you love him and he loves you."

My head sways side to side. I have to get Skye.

He seats himself on the other end of the couch, his hardened features lifting just an inch. "Noer, you did a great performance. Wearing your big ol' steel boots during the search party, complaining of being hungry. I really did believe you. For about fifteen minutes, until we got to that wacky restaurant for lunch."

I drop my gaze to the floor, trying to recall that day. We'd had a good time, laughing and recollecting memories, making jokes with the waitress, tossing peanuts, and eating the hot peppers. I even had him convinced with the coughing attack after he made me eat one. I turn questioning eyes back to him.

He clicks his tongue. "You mocked me for having to go to the bathroom a second time, remember? You were right, I didn't have to go. I went to tell the waitress to give me the mildest peppers they have."

Shock grips my facial muscles, contorting, and he stares with a somber expression. "You thought you were so smooth, choking and crying and making a scene. The peppers weren't even hot. And you've been lying to me ever since." He tsks and drapes his arm across the back of the sofa.

"Oh, I'm the liar?" I spit out. "You've got this entire town in a frenzy because a little girl is in your basement. And now you're trying to tell me she's dead. Why?" Tears fill my eyes as I stare at this man sitting next to me. I've loved him like a brother. But something has happened to him. Something went severely wrong somewhere.

His jaw ticks. "Tell me why you lied to me first."

I need to play this safely. I'm dying—literally, I need to get to a hospital—and I'm stuck on a sofa next to a monster who's got his best friend's daughter locked downstairs. My voice softens, my head tilts. "I'm sorry I lied to you. But this . . . Tell me the truth, Jamie. Tell me everything. I've never done anything to you. We were best friends. What's going on? What happened to you? Let me help you. Please."

His eyes narrow; he licks his lips.

"Jamie, I saved your life. How could you do this to me?" I gesture to my torn-up body. I don't need to feel pain to know that it can't hold out much longer.

He rubs at his face. "You did save my life," he says, muffled, then drops his hands. "Which is the only reason

I haven't killed you. You've really put me in a pickle now. I kidnapped you after the vigil because you were suspecting Logan. You got his number somehow and were blowing his phone up. During a fucking vigil, Noer. What's wrong with you?"

"So you do have his phone. You've been the one updating his Facebook, texting me, luring me to his dead body. You killed him."

Jamie lifts his hip and pulls a pack of cigarettes and a lighter from his pocket. He slips one between his lips and ignites the lighter. "Yup."

I curl my legs into my chest, trying to get as far away from him as possible. I can't run. My ankles are broken—even more so after all the running—and he'll catch me in a heartbeat. I thought I was so clever, thinking it was Zack. But Logan was wearing his wedding ring. He never left Maggie. Jamie killed him and made the whole affair up, keeping him very much alive through Facebook and texts. "Why?" I whisper.

He tips his head back and exhales a cloud of smoke, speaking into it like it's a word bubble. "Nothing you need to worry about."

My breaths are forced, each one manually executed as I figure out what to do next. If ever I had to think rationally, it's now. Even in this situation that is anything but rational. He won't tell me why he killed Logan, but if I keep throwing down the best friend card, he may give me more information on why he took Skye and what he plans on doing with her. "I—I got Logan's number from Taylor's phone. I was leery of him because he blocked me on Facebook. Well, *you* blocked me on Facebook."

He nods and drags on his cigarette again. "Yeah. It's called risk management. I didn't want you suspecting

Logan or even bringing his name up. Everyone thinks he's a sleazeball who lives in Connecticut. I thought you'd leave him alone if he blocked you. But, of course, you didn't, because you don't understand that there are consequences to your actions. You never have. So I lured you to his body to scare the shit out of you, teach you to mind your own business. The other option was killing you too. Which you know I can't do. Too bad you can't feel pain, Noa. I hated having to go to this extreme." He gestures to my body. "You think I wanted to kidnap you? Twice? You were the one who saved me from that psycho Higgins dude, so trust me when I say that smacking you around with that plank hurt me worse than it hurt you."

My mind goes to a dark place, trying to make sense of his mentality. Jamie somehow believes it's his responsibility to correct my behavior, but I don't know why, or how Skye fits into that.

He butts his cigarette out in an ashtray. "And how the hell did you escape this time? I didn't even know you were gone. I gave you the benefit of the doubt. Thought you were finally realizing what the rest of us already know—sticking your hand in a fire fucking burns. But no. You ripped your hands and feet off instead. You've no concept of right and wrong, and now look at you. It's impossible trying to deal with someone you can't hurt and can't bring yourself to kill."

My heart pounds as I wrestle with his "logic," trying to contort my mentality to his. The cellar is manifesting with the hidden child, glowing like an amulet. I can feel her down there. I sense her directly under me. I need to get her out, both of us out. I decide to answer his question, hoping he'll return the favor. "I did exactly what it looks like. I forced them out. Broke a lot of bones in the process. But I thought it was because Zack was doing all this . . ." I pause, and when he doesn't react, I say, "Why was Morgan Higgins attacking you?"

I catch a hint of sympathy in his cold, hard face. Like the Jamie I used to know. "You asked for the truth, and now you're going to get it. Morgan knew that I had Skye and that I'd killed Logan. He was trying to kill me, and you killed him first."

Time freezes, pulses, glitches throughout the universe and every realm therein. I killed an innocent man. My mind feels like the embodiment of every sin, sins too heinous for any human to commit.

One word falls from my lips—"No."

He sighs, both sad and angry. "Skye had been in those shacks. The ones they found her DNA in. Not long, Noa. I brought her to my house the day I picked her up from school. But during the canvassing and all the interrogations, I couldn't have her here."

"She just got in the car with you?"

"Of course, I'm her godfather. Anyway, for those first twenty-four hours, I had to move her around a lot. Stay on top of where the search parties were going. So after that meeting at City Hall—the one where you first showed up—I memorized the grid and made sure to put her wherever I was going to be searching that next day."

"But I was with you."

Jamie huffs. "Yeah. Always ruining my life, you." And he playfully shoves my foot. It cracks loudly. "Oh, sorry. Not like you felt it, though. That's why I made us stick together that first day. I didn't want you wandering off and finding her. Then the next day we split up and I sent you to search north of the shacks. I didn't want you near them. She wasn't there anymore, I'd moved her to a different one far enough away. But I'd left a mess there that I had to clean up—the chicken nuggets and the food I'd brought her the night before. But Morgan, the vagrant, he apparently saw us leaving. He went in and found the food. So when I went back that day to clean up, he was there." Jamie's hands go over his face. "He called me out on Logan, Noa. I don't know how he knew. And you killed him before I could find out."

My body heaves and I retch on the floor. Morgan Higgins was innocent, and I killed him. He knew the whole story. He was bringing justice to Logan and to Skye. And I killed him before he could.

Another round of vomit splatters on Jamie's rug, and he leans over to pat my back. "Look, I get that you feel guilty, but Morgan shouldn't have gone all vigilante on me. What he was doing was illegal. You did the right thing."

"Don't touch me." I spit the last of the sour acid into the puddle and reach for the water bottle on the coffee table.

Jamie stands and meanders to the bathroom, exiting with a couple of towels. He unfolds them and tosses them onto my vomit, then returns to his place on the sofa. "You're gross, Noer. You kiss Hector with that mouth?"

Tears spill down my cheeks. "I killed Morgan because I wanted to protect you. I didn't know you were a murderer and a child abductor. I thought you were my friend!"

His eyes widen. "We are friends. Look, Noa, I never wanted you to know all this. I didn't want you involved. You involved yourself, and if Morgan had killed me, Skye would have died. She was in some random shack in the middle of nowhere, no one would have found her in time. It was bad enough that I was stuck in the hospital. She ran out of food and was scared shitless by the time I got back. If she'd gone any longer without water, she would have died of dehydration. You saved her life when you saved mine."

I feel that transformation again, the rational to irrational, as I try to take comfort in his words. But I can't get the image of little Skye out of my head, stuck out in a cabin in the middle of nowhere, all by herself, for days. I can't imagine how scared she was, how scarred she must be now, and probably will be for the rest of her life.

Jamie must read the horror on my face because he says, "Stop it, Noa. She was fine. We made a game out of it. Besides, she's been here at the house most of the time. I told you, I just had to move her around a bit near the beginning while the search party was going on."

But I shake my head. "Jamie, that spooky little group of cabins you kept me in after the vigil . . . How can you justify leaving a little girl there by herself?"

"You mean the 'warehouse'?" He grins.

"Stop trying to make me think I'm crazy! I was never in a warehouse and you know it. She was there, I saw her. She untied my hands . . ."

His face is contorting—it's slow, but I recognize it. It's shiningly angry. "So you're saying for a fact that Skye untied you? Because she told me she didn't. And if she lied to me, I'll punish her." He stands, his hands clenched at his sides. "She's already in deep shit for talking to you when I told her not to."

I try sitting up, but I've lost all energy. Too much trauma and blood loss. Jamie knows she untied me—the rope with her DNA is downstairs. He purposely planted the one he knew she didn't touch in that warehouse. This is another game of his, but I'll tell him whatever he wants to hear to keep him from hurting her. "Okay! It was a warehouse, and I lied about Skye. Hallucinated it all. She didn't untie me. Her DNA wasn't found on the ropes, remember?" I debate whether to tell him that she didn't speak to me while I was down there, but I already confessed that she had called him Father. I don't want him to catch me in any more lies.

He looks at me, considers me as he sits on the edge of the coffee table just two feet from my face. "You really are delusional if you think you can trick me with my own staged setup. I moved the chair and the rope and your shoes, Noa. I put them in that warehouse to make everyone think you were crazy."

I nod slowly. "And they do." Jamie has been gaslighting me all along, trying to make me look crazy about the location of my abduction so no one would believe me.

And using poor Howard Zilnich as a scapegoat—the random owner of a random rope Jamie stole from a random warehouse. The name Jamie told me before authorities had even released it. Detective Lawson would only say, "We're investigating it." How devilishly clever.

I shut my eyes, I have to. Sensory overload, and I can't handle it. Other things are falling into place, things I should have seen before. Jamie was the one who informed me that I was hit in the head with a plank after the vigil; no one else mentioned that or even knew about it. What was it that Zack had said on the FaceTime call? *A plank, huh? I must've missed that part.*

I think back to after that abduction, when Jamie asked me why I had wandered off toward the docks. He knew I had done it intentionally, while Taylor thought that was just where the abductor had thrown our purses. Then there was his irrational fear that someone was at his house when I was on the phone with him after Hector left for Vegas—*Oh, shit,* he'd said. *Someone's here.* His demeanor had almost given me a heart attack.

It was Zack. I FaceTimed with Zack while his daughter was locked in the basement below him, and he had no idea.

"Why did you take her? Why are you doing all this, Jamie? Tell me, please."

The coffee table groans as he stands, and he paces around it. "Stop making this harder than it has to be, Noa. I'm stuck between a rock and a hard place, because I don't know what to do with you now that you know. I killed Logan when he found out."

I turn my head toward him. "When Logan found out what? You didn't have Skye when you killed him."

He stops pacing and turns to me, the coffee table between us. "What Logan found out is what set this whole thing in motion."

"Jamie . . . I'm so confused." I have to close my eyes again.

His footsteps start back up, and the coffee table creaks again; I assume he's reseated himself on it. "You and me both. I don't know what to do. I can't kill you. You saved my life."

At this, my eyes pop open dauntlessly. "Oh, you won't kill me, but you'll strap me down and beat the hell out of me? Me, of all people. Me, who doesn't feel pain. But then you *inject* me with something so that I would? That's sadistic. You're sick, Jamie."

"You don't know shit about pain, Noa!" He leaps from the coffee table and is standing over me now with fists. "You don't know shit about anything. You never have. You can't properly live in this world without pain. Without pain, you have no boundaries, no consequences. You don't understand phrases like 'no pain, no gain,' which is a cliché for a reason. Success is pointless without the pain from the hard work it takes to achieve it. You shouldn't get to experience pleasure if you're not acquainted with its opposite. Pain is the thorn to your rose-colored glasses, and without it you're a simple-minded, shallow, entitled child."

I watch him pacing the length of the sofa, back and forth. "You've no idea what my life is like."

He swings a finger in my face. "No, you have no idea what *life* is like! Everything has always been so perfect for you. Nothing to hurt you, a perfect relationship all through middle and high school. And when Zack broke up with you, you acted like it was the worst thing in the world. Like no one had ever gone through a breakup before. 'Boohoo, poor Noa. The girl who never feels pain just got her first dose of being butt-hurt and thinks she's gonna die.' See what that *pain* did to you? You left here and moved to Miami and continued your perfect life over there. Not a hair out of place."

"You don't know what breakups are like because you've never been in love, Jamie. No, I can't hurt physically, but I hurt emotionally. You're the exact opposite. You can cry over all your physical pain, but you couldn't hurt your emotions if you beat them with a nail-studded plank."

He squats down in front of me, seething. "Bullshit. I wish my father took his fists to *my emotions*. You think getting smacked around by my dad was the worst thing? No. It was mental and emotional torture—being betrayed by my body every day in school, when all I wanted was to sit at my desk like everyone else, and my body said no. 'No, Jamie. We're going to stand for a while, maybe distract other kids. And the harder you try to concentrate and behave, the more fidgety we're going to become until you're riddled with anxiety.' I was mentally exhausted by the time I got home, defeated. But there was my dad, who had already gotten the phone calls from the school. And he didn't believe in ADHD. So if you want to tell me that I'm emotionless, then you're goddamn right. I turned that shit off a long time ago to stay alive. Physical pain was the only punishment I feared, and you needed a good dose of it."

I blink erratically as something dawns on me. Jamie was conditioned to believe that pain is the only way to establish boundaries. That's why he's harboring such anger toward me, saying I can't understand there are consequences to my actions, that I know nothing about life. I'd pity him if that mentality hadn't almost killed me. I grit my teeth as anger bubbles through my veins. "So you thought you needed to . . . what? Punish me? I did nothing wrong. You're the one who murdered Logan and abducted Skye, and you think I needed to be punished. You really are sadistic. You still know nothing about me, Jamie. You're just as ignorant of my condition as you were when we were kids. At least I'm trying to understand your mentality. Here's one of those clichés that you don't understand at all—you hurt the ones you love. Case in point." I gesture between the two of us.

He scoffs. "Please. Something that resonated with you when Zack broke your little heart? He's another one who doesn't know shit about life. He's always gotten everything he's ever wanted. You, then Taylor. He easily started on every sports team in high school, and his parents just handed him the airboat company after college. I don't think he's ever felt physical pain in his life either, and he doesn't even have any shitty conditions! I have struggled with everything I've ever attempted in life, Noa. I've worked a hundred times harder at everything and still have never seen the fruits of my labors. So Zack needed to be taught a lesson too." His face goes from hard to inquisitive before asking, "When did you fall back in love with him, by the way? Before or after you came back?"

My jaw drops open at this, and I turn my head toward him. "Jamie? Will you stop with that, please? I don't love—"

Popping gravel beneath tires and the low hum of a vehicle whip our heads toward the covered window, and the curtains illuminate with headlights. The engine stops; a car door slams.

Jamie tenses. "Shit."

"Who's here?" I whisper.

His eyes turn from the window to me, dark and threatening. "Stay quiet."

A pair of footsteps moves up his porch, then five loud knocks.

CHAPTER

28

JAMIE PUTS A menacing finger to his lips and mouths—*don't make a sound.*

But I want to scream, call out to whoever is out there to run! Get help! Skye is trapped in the cellar! Logan is dead and Jamie is a monster! Another series of knocks barrage the door, and then a voice that changes everything—

"Jamie? Open up."

It's Taylor.

I turn shocked eyes to Jamie, unable to speak even if I wanted to. He shakes his head at me, glowering, not a muscle moving otherwise.

"Jamie! Let me in, please? We need to talk."

She's here, the mother of the infamous missing child—the child in the cellar. The girl she's been looking for over two weeks now, and she's so close. This ends now. I sit up straight, attempt to stand. "Tay—"

Jamie bounds off the coffee table and tackles me back onto the couch, slapping a hand over my mouth and restraining my arms. "Shut up," he growls in my ear. I'm lying against his chest, his heart beating into my back. I can't move.

"I hear you moving in there! Come on, Jamie. I'm sorry. I . . . I love you."

I gasp into his suffocating hand, squirm, try to rotate my head to look at him because I can't believe what I'm hearing. But he tightens his grip over my mouth, around my waist. One arm is pinned under our bodies and the other he's captured by the wrist.

"It's over between Zack and me. For real this time."

I can't breathe. I no longer have the strength to fight Jamie's hold. My muscles, lungs, everything deflates until my body is ragged, simply draped over his. I marvel at his even breathing, the slow cadence of practiced inhales and exhales, while my entire world continues to jolt upside down.

Jamie and Taylor.

For how long? How did this escalate to Skye being held captive in his cellar?

Taylor begins pacing the length of Jamie's porch, her frustration manifesting through her swift steps. I follow her silhouette through the curtains—back and forth—hands on her head.

She finally halts in front of the door. "Jamie, if you don't open up, I'm calling the cops."

Jamie's strength ebbs just slightly—enough for me to turn my head and catch his gaze. I widen my eyes, nod my head, toss it toward the door as much as his grip allows.

"Oh, you'd love that, wouldn't you?" he whispers against my ear. "She's gonna leave soon. She's not calling any cops."

Taylor stamps her foot. "I'll call them right now, Jamie! I'll tell them everything."

A whimper escapes my throat; I don't mean to do it. It only forces Jamie to tighten his grip again—his hand over my mouth, the other across my body and securing my wrist. My entire body is pressed against his, head to toe.

With a disgruntled sigh, Taylor pounds down the stairs.

"See? Told you she'd leave soon. She'd never call the cops," Jamie says as I'm frantically shaking my head. Taylor cannot be bluffing. I need her to call the cops.

I groan—a nonverbal plea to release me now that she's left.

He squeezes me tighter. "So you can scream before she gets to her car? I'm not—"

An explosion.

We jump as shards of glass hurl through the room, rain across the rug like diamonds, among them a melon-sized rock that shakes the floor as it crashes against it. Taylor's arm is shoved through the frosted pane of the front door—or where the pane used to be—groping around for the lock and knocking out the remaining jagged teeth of the window.

Jamie loosens his grip enough for me to jerk my head free, but he still has my wrist, and I can't escape him fast enough because she twists the lock and throws the door open. She halts the moment she beholds Jamie and me lying on the couch, his arms wrapped around me, our bodies spooning.

"What the—what is this?"

"Taylor, I—"

Jamie shoves me off him and catapults from the couch, grabbing her wrist as she's accosting him.

"Taylor! Calm down," he says. "We aren't doing anything."

She punches his shoulder. Again.

"Stop," he warns.

But she keeps throwing punches, her other hand confined in his grasp, until Jamie leans back and slaps her across the face—hard.

My gasp is authentic. No pretenses, no acting.

Her head whips to the side, her hair scattering across her face and sticking to her tear-streaked cheeks. Slowly she straightens her head until she's staring him in the face—a cold, emotionless glare.

This has happened before—I can tell by the familiarity of their dynamics; the intimacy speaks of a dark history. I remember the bruise on her back, wonder now how Jamie put it there.

Jamie throws a hand in my direction. "Look at her, Taylor. She's a mess. And why are you here?" He shifts his eyes between us, then turns to her and says through gritted teeth, "And watch your mouth."

"Oh, like you haven't told her already." Her eyes flick to me and scan my body. My injuries are covered for the most part, but I'm clearly not in good shape. "What did he do to you?" The quiver in her voice and chin betrays her angry façade.

"Taylor, he—"

"Why do you even care?" Jamie interrupts me, shaking her by the wrist. "You're married to Zack."

In a flash, Taylor jerks free of Jamie's hold. "Then why am I here? It's you, Jamie! I choose you. And you're—" She throws a hand in my direction, tears filling her eyes.

"Oh, shut up, Taylor." Jamie spins a circle, his hands on his head in exasperation. "No one is buying your bullshit. You've been saying for years that you're going to leave Zack for me, and you never do. This is no different.

And look at what you've done to my front door. And now Noa fucking knows. Goddammit, you're making everything so much worse."

My head is exploding. They've been having an affair for years. She's been sleeping with both Zack and Jamie, and Zack seems none the wiser. I don't know the details, but other things are falling into place. If Taylor and Zack were moving away, that means she was serious about breaking things off with Jamie and choosing Zack for good.

Which gives Jamie a motive for kidnapping Skye.

Father didn't want us to move.

Taylor could be involved in Skye's kidnapping too, since she and Jamie have years and years worth of secrets together. But what if she isn't? I fear what Jamie would do if I were to blurt it out—I have to think strategically. Did he really think he could keep her in his basement forever? Perhaps he wasn't thinking, was simply acting on his psychotic instinct when he took Skye, desperate and willing to do anything to keep Taylor from moving away.

Unless I'm underestimating him, and he plans on doing to Skye what he did to Logan.

Every muscle in my throat clenches at that thought. *What is his ultimate goal?*

"What is she doing here?" Taylor asks.

"No, what are *you* doing here?" Jamie returns through bared teeth. "What's your reason for showing up here, breaking my door, and telling me you want me after pushing me away for months? For acting like a crazy psycho, like I'm cheating on you, because Noa is here?"

Her indomitable stare falters, tears fill her eyes. "I want the truth, Jamie. And I thought you'd give it to me if I got back together with you. Maybe you gave her the truth." She turns to me and says, "What has he told you about Zack's dad, Logan?"

My jaw drops and I look to Jamie. I don't know what to say. I can't have him killing me too. Jamie gives me a sardonic smile and sweeps his hand toward Taylor—*be my guest.*

"Um . . ." I take a shaky breath. "That Logan is dead? That Logan is dead."

Taylor covers her mouth. "Oh, my gosh. I knew it." She fights back a sob and wipes at the tears in her eyes. "You lied, Jamie. You murdered my father-in-law. Admit it." She plops into the recliner as if her legs can no longer hold her up.

Jamie stares at Taylor, considers her, but I can't read his expression. Taylor speaks to me but is staring daggers at Jamie. "Last year, Logan caught Jamie and me at a restaurant over in Naples. I never saw him again after that night. He apparently 'left his wife and moved to Connecticut.'" She flutters air quotes around her face.

What Logan found out is what set this whole thing in motion. Jamie's cryptic message suddenly bursts with clarity.

Jamie runs his thumb along an eyebrow bent in frustration. "Taylor, why are you telling her this?"

Taylor's eyes finally break away from Jamie and turn to me. "I believed him, once Zack started getting texts and Facebook messages from Logan. I let it go." Her tears fall freely now, draining down her bright pink cheek. "Until the day of the vigil. Remember when we were putting the candles together? I got the first phone call in over a year from Logan's phone."

"The one you took in the bathroom at City Hall?" I manage.

She nods. "Big surprise—it was Jamie. Threatening me."

"I didn't threaten you."

"Yeah, okay. 'So what's your decision?' That's what you said. You call me from my father-in-law's phone, who's been MIA for a year, and you say that. If that's not a threat, I don't know what is."

"Why didn't you go to the cops, Taylor?" I blurt.

She looks at me like I'm crazy, and Jamie starts laughing. "Yeah, Taylor. Tell her why you didn't go to the cops." He perches on the edge of the sofa and leans toward her in anticipation.

Taylor looks between the two of us. "You saw the bruise, Noa. You saw him hit me just now. You asked how I got that bruise—well, here's the truth. I came here the morning of the vigil and asked Jamie if he had taken Skye."

Reality shifts like a kaleidoscope again, pieces and facts tumbling all over each other. Taylor doesn't know that Skye is in the basement. She's not involved. Jamie is acting solo on this entire mission; no one is helping him. Not Zack, not Taylor. I don't know how to tell her without getting us killed.

"He shoved me down the porch steps and I landed on that rock." She points to it lying among the sea of glass.

I open my mouth, but Jamie scoffs loudly. "Don't make yourself out to be a victim, Taylor. You love being manhandled. She asked why you didn't go to the cops, and that has nothing to do with me or what I'd do to you. You didn't go to the cops because then everyone would have found out you've been cheating on your husband for the better part of ten years. It's the same reason you never probed about Logan disappearing. You were happy to assume he never told Zack you were cheating on him because Logan was cheating too. And that he moved to Connecticut—all so you wouldn't have to confess your infidelity. And now you would rather your daughter go missing than to look bad in the public eye. You're a selfish person and a horrible wife and mother."

Taylor begins sobbing. "I'm so sorry."

Jamie amusedly watches her breaking down, chewing on his thumbnail from the sofa. "Then why don't you tell Zack the truth? Tell him how I'm a much better lay than he is. How you tried to break it off with me after Skye was born because all of a sudden you had a conscience and wanted Skye to have her dad. That we didn't fuck again until you heard I started dating Jenysis and got jealous. Tell him how you fucked the both of us for years until your cold, dead heart decided to be wholesome and monogamous—again—and you talked him into moving away so you'd never have to see me again."

Taylor slams a palm on the arm of the recliner. "I wanted to leave because I was scared that you did something to Logan. And then Skye goes missing," she whispers through her tears. "I just want my daughter back."

It's the day of the vigil all over again—the underlying demand for her child. I'm unable to fully comprehend the level of evil Taylor and Jamie have committed that has led to this, but Skye is innocent. She shouldn't be the pawn in their melodramatic affair. And neither should I, or Zack, or the rest of the town. I'm done hesitating. This ends now.

"Taylor, Skye is in the basement!"

She freezes, looks at me. "She's alive?"

I nod.

Her breath catches and she looks at Jamie. They're in a stare-off, each waiting for the other to react, ready to pounce. Then, without any question, any confirmation, she leaps from the chair and bolts toward the basement door. Jamie is right behind her, grabbing her by the hair, and she spins around to swing at him. He catches her arm and restrains her, and she jerks and flails in unsuccessful attempts to escape. "Skye!" she wails. "Let go of me, I want my baby! Skye!"

I'm yelling at Jamie to stop, trying to stand, but my ankles have officially given out and I keep falling back on the couch.

Jamie wrestles Taylor to the floor and straddles her, his hands pinning her wrists down. He's yelling at her to shut up, but she is screaming incoherently, the decibel level enough to shatter glass. He releases one wrist to cover her mouth, and she begins punching him, gouging at his eyes.

"Jamie, stop! Taylor! Please!" I've rolled to the floor and am scrambling toward them, crawling through the piles of glass, and I grab onto Jamie's arm and try to pull him off her.

His face is so calm, it's scarier than Taylor's screaming one. I don't know what he's going to do, how this is going to end. His strength is uncanny—I'm not hindering him in the least. Finally, Taylor somehow bites his hand. Jamie hollers and bolts upright, throwing me off him, and Taylor continues screaming for Skye so loudly that someone is bound to hear. He lunges toward me, and I cower until I realize he's not coming at me, but is reaching for the big rock lying among the glass.

My mind twists in awe when his hand locks onto the rock. Taylor's screams are suddenly underwater, an echo, and I barely hear my own as my peripheral vision dissipates, and the only thing I'm left seeing is Jamie raising the rock and bringing it down on Taylor's head.

And the Everglades are quiet once again.

CHAPTER

29

NEVER IN MY life have I shed such despairing tears. Jamie dismounts Taylor's body and kneels in front of her, staring.

I can't move, yet my entire body is trembling. He couldn't have killed her. There's no way she's dead. None of this happened, I'm inside the worst nightmare ever. I lie in the shattered glass and stare at the ceiling because I can't look at Taylor. I can't see the blood or her bashed-in head. I just wait for him to kill me too.

I roll my head toward Jamie. He's running his fingers tenderly over her face, through her hair that I refuse to behold. He stands and retrieves a blanket from the back of the sofa and drapes it over her body.

Finally, I sit up. "Jamie, why?" I weep.

He sighs, rubs his forehead.

"You got what you wanted! You kidnapped Skye so Taylor would come back to you, and it worked. You had her back! You loved her. The three of you could've run away together. Isn't that what you wanted?"

"I don't love her anymore."

"But why did you kill her?"

"I didn't mean to. I was trying to shut her up. She wouldn't shut up." This helplessness I feel, the events that have just transpired before my eyes, it's too much. My resolution is cracking, and I shut my eyes, weeping, as he retreats from her dead body and approaches my severely injured one. He kneels in front of me now, just as he did with her.

"Are you going to kill me?"

"I told you, I can't. You saved my life." My heart hammers when he performs the same absurd actions—brushing my hair with his fingers, stroking my face.

My eyes stay locked on him, unblinking. It's like he's fantasizing my death—the icing on the cake for him, his escape from this alleged rock and hard place.

"What happens next?" I whisper.

"I don't know," he whispers back. "It was never, ever supposed to come to this."

"Where . . . where is my phone?"

He sighs. "It's all back on the island with Logan's body. Along with your gun, your knife, and that tracker thing on your ankle."

"The email. It will be sent soon . . ."

"What email?" he asks. But I don't respond because it doesn't matter. The cops will be sent to some random island in the Everglades if Janna does her job. An island where I am not. I'll die here on the floor, right next to Taylor, and Jamie will dispose of our bodies just like he did Logan's. No one will ever find us.

Or Skye.

Jamie scoops me off the floor and returns me to the sofa. "Stay here," he mutters and disappears into the kitchen.

I couldn't escape if I tried. All this is thundering through my head like an avalanche. I must be going into shock because of everything that's happened, the loudest thought of all is Jamie's statement—*I don't love her anymore.*

So flippant, so matter of fact, after all he went through to get her. Of all the things I should be pondering while in this physical and mental state, it's this. But epiphanies can happen during psychological shock. Things fall into place. Jamie confessed that he loved me in high school—after he was released from the hospital and I was driving him home. It flustered me when he said it, threw me off. I blamed myself, didn't stop to think that it was completely inappropriate for him to be in love with his best friend's girlfriend. But those thoughts—the logistics, the dynamics—they're all sorting themselves out now.

Jamie's always wanted what Zack has. He was always one step behind him. Zack was a starter on the football team; Jamie was second string. Zack made the basketball team; Jamie didn't. Zack easily made straight As; Jamie struggled just to make Cs. Zack should have been homecoming king; Jamie capitalized on our breakup and sabotaged it—because the one thing Jamie had going for him was his looks and personality. He couldn't get Zack's grades or athleticism, but he could get his girls.

Jamie's been harassing me about Zack since I came back. I don't know if Zack has feelings for me or not, but I guarantee that my saving Jamie isn't the only reason he's keeping me alive. If Zack loves me, then Jamie loves me.

I am the new object of his affection.

I thought I was Jamie's pawn, but I'm not. I'm the queen.

Jamie continues moving about in the kitchen. I feel Taylor's body so close to me—dead. Skye's body below me—alive. My eyes move everywhere except to Taylor. I can't look at her. They dart from his ceiling to the window, then over to the busted door, and finally down to my body. My black jeans, black sweatshirt. I can feel my swollen feet pulsing in my black hiking boots, and there's something else I feel poking into my side—annoying.

It's all back on the island with Logan's body. Along with your gun, your knife, and that tracker thing on your ankle.

There's something missing from that list, though—a tiny detail. One that's only five inches—three when folded—and shaped like a claw.

Jamie appears in the doorway, fiddling with something. Paper rips. Sliding sounds.

Flick, flick, flick.

This can't be happening. I have too many broken bones and open wounds. If he injects me right now, if I feel the repercussions of what I've done to my body to save Skye—I'd rather die than experience that. My heart is in my throat. "No, Jamie, please!"

He strides toward me with his syringe. His mouth is a line, sober and grim. "You told Taylor that Skye was in the basement. You made me kill her. You're the reason she's dead." He sits on the coffee table and grabs my arm.

"Jamie! No! Please, just kill me instead!" I try pulling away before he can push up the sleeve of my sweatshirt, but his grip is impenetrable.

"I told you I can't kill you because you saved my life. But you can't get away with this. You told her Skye was in the basement. I've tried twice now to restrain you, and that doesn't work. This is the only way I can get you to cooperate." He slides my sleeve up to my elbow.

"Jamie-Jamie-*Jamie*! It's what you wanted! Why else would you tell her about Logan unless you planned to kill her?"

He pauses and looks in my eyes, the syringe hovering inches above my arm.

I swallow and search his face frantically for what he wants to hear. "You called her from his phone and gave her an ultimatum. You admitted to her just now that you killed him. You wouldn't have told her those things if you weren't going to kill her anyway." I swear his eyes darken, his jaw ticks slightly, so I alter my approach. "I—I knew what you were doing! Don't you think I know you by now? Don't punish me for knowing you so well—I was trying to do you a favor."

With my arm in one hand and his syringe in the other, he narrows his eyes in a manner that says, *choose a hand.*

I place my fingers on his hand gripping my arm—the hand I choose. "You've never deserved any of this, Jamie. I am so sorry for all the ways I hurt you, for Zack and Taylor and everyone hurting you. I'm sorry for what your dad did to you. You have always been such a good person and friend, and I'm so, so sorry."

His jaw tightens, nostrils flared. I may be saying all the wrong things, I don't know. But I've never been more desperate in my entire life. I have never, ever feared anything like I fear pain in this moment. But that needle isn't in my arm yet, and I need to stay on this path.

"Jamie . . . I love you, and I know you love me. I know that deep down, you don't want to hurt me. I need you, Jamie—I'm so scared and confused. Please, just hold me right now. Just forgive me . . ."

Ever so slowly, the space between my arm and the syringe grows. His grip on my arm relents.

"I love you, Jamie. You've got such a mess here, but I'm going to help you clean it up. We need to get rid of her body and her car out front. We're going to make it. And Skye—she'll be fine! She already calls you father."

He releases my arm. "I told her to call me that. Made her drop the god part. I could be her dad, but Taylor would never get a paternity test."

I have to manually keep my face neutral so he can't read my thoughts. Skye is Zack's child; she looks just like him. But regardless, Jamie wants Skye to be his child—so much so that he's keeping her alive in his basement instead of killing her. Could a paternity test be another reason Jamie is holding on to her? Is that his end game in all this? What will he do when he finds out she's not his? I smile encouragingly and whisper, "Now we can get her tested. We can order one online, no one will ever have to know. Jamie, there is a way to fix all this."

The syringe tinkles against the coffee table as it leaves his hand, but he makes no other movements. I don't blame him for not trusting me; it's all so dangerous, so fragile. There are many things I don't know. But there's one thing Jamie doesn't know.

"Hug me," I plead.

He kneels on the floor and studies me with both hands on my face. There's ambition in his expression, a cloaked passion. He's going to do something right now—either squeeze my skull until it pops and splinters, or kiss me. It could go either way. Seconds tick by—four, five—then slowly, he wraps his arms around my body in a gentle embrace. I squirm beneath him—he thinks I'm uncomfortable, and I am. But I'm also reaching into my pocket to remove that tiny detail, the one that pokes me over and over.

Jamie took everything from me. Not only my health and my life, but also my phone and my weapons. But there was one thing he missed. My karambit knife.

Smart, clever Jamie didn't check my pockets. And now his body is on top of mine, his mind distracted because he finally has something that Zack wants. I moan in time with my fidgeting, because if he discovers what I'm doing, it's all over.

"I need to be able to trust you," he whispers into my neck, his embrace tightening.

"Trust me," I say as I extend my hand over his back and flip the blade open. And before he can reply, I plunge the knife into his back.

He howls and slips from my body to the floor. But the knife, I'm still holding it, and it slices through his ribs, tearing into everything as he falls. His lungs. His organs. His kidneys. Because my knife, it's sharp. My father made sure of that.

His back hits the floor, and I hear the air escaping his lungs. He's grabbing for the syringe on the table, but I stab him in the neck before he grips it. His fingers splay and his throat gurgles, and I grab the syringe and bury it in the couch cushions behind me.

His hands continue reaching for me, and I scoot as far back into the couch as I can, gripping the knife at my chest in case he gets some renewed, vengeful energy. I'm trying to out-scream him—I can't listen to him dying, the air wheezing from his lungs, his labored cries growing weaker and weaker.

Soon his hands are no longer grabbing. Silence now, just the sound of my labored breathing, my heart pounding. It's the only breath in the room, the only heartbeat despite all the bodies. Tentatively, I look down on the face of my high school best friend. His beautiful blue eyes are open, but they see nothing. His mouth—those full lips—also open, speaking nothing. His dimples are absent, his blond hair unhampered. Jamie, who's always been so full of life, is dead.

My vision fades for a moment, and every move is laborious. I can't cry or fall apart; I'm not done. Now it's me versus death, because I came here to save Skye, and I can't if I die in the process.

I have no choice but to roll onto his blood-soaked body. I grimace at the whooshing sound of the lingering air in his lungs when I land on him. With my elbows, I drag myself off him, leaving a trail of blood like a snail as I crawl to his phone lying a few feet away on the rug. Cell phone creators knew what they were doing when they made emergency calls possible without needing a passcode.

"Nine-one-one, what's your emergency?"

"I found Skye Flynn. And I'm about to die. We're at Jamie Camden's house in Everglades City, at Hanover and Papaya." I end the call and toss the phone on the couch. If I'm going to die now, I want to be able to see Skye one last time. I can't do that if I continue answering the dispatcher's questions.

I move to the recliner to retrieve a throw and cover his body, then I walk on my knees to Taylor. A puddle of blood seeps from under her blanket. Gazing at the ceiling and fumbling with the blanket at her hips, I reach into her pocket and pull out her phone. Slip it into my own back pocket. I've done what I can with Jamie's phone; I know Taylor's password so Skye can call her dad. Then I crawl toward that basement door, the one house in all of South Florida with a basement.

I trekked the Everglades for miles—with broken ankles, with healthy ankles—and yet the ten feet to that basement door is the hardest thing I've ever done.

Until I'm there, and I realize it will be even harder to stand up to reach the locks. I have nothing to brace myself on, nothing to help me up. I smash my face into the small crack at the bottom of the door. "Skye!"

Nothing. I hear nothing.

My lips press into the crevice. "Skyyyyyeeee!"

I force my body into a sitting position and grab onto the door handle, hoisting myself up onto broken, black, swollen ankles. I don't know a lock from a chicken coop right now, a basement from a hallucination, but I let my warped motor skills take over.

Click.

Click.

Click.

There's a hook stuck in an eye . . . *Cast the beam out of thine own eye; and then shalt thou see clearly to cast out the mote of thy brother's eye.* I remove it.

There's a chain in a slit. *Suddenly there was such a violent earthquake . . . and everyone's chains came loose.* I slide it until it falls.

I turn the knob and throw the door open. *If anyone hears My voice and opens the door, I will come in to him . . .*

I stare down the wooden staircase. Pan past the cinder block walls, the counter, the naloxone wrappings, the table with its shackles. "Skye?"

My knees are giving, my ankles unable to support me. I'm falling. Everything is going black.

"Noa? You came back."

"Come," I say, and she does. So obedient, Skye. So perfect.

"Skye, take this phone and call your daddy." I slide Taylor's phone from my back pocket and hand it to her. "Stay here on the landing, though, okay? Don't go in the living room. It's your mom's phone, do you know the passcode?"

She cocks her head and takes the phone, eyes it. "I spy with my little eye, something red."

"I give up, Skye, what is it?"

She turns the phone toward me, a large, red button displayed in the middle of the screen, and above it one word that makes me drop onto my back—RECORDING.

CHAPTER

30

TAYLOR SPELLS WAS on a suicide mission. And, like most of her ventures, it was elaborate, pretentious, designed to glorify herself.

Not that she planned for Jamie to kill her. It seems she wanted to get his confession to killing Logan recorded before killing herself, but we may have skipped a few steps.

Of course, these are speculations—conclusions we came to once everything came out in the open. We'll never know for sure because I keep killing the people with the answers.

Once Skye obediently called Zack, he flew to Jamie's house. The reunion, from what I remember, was an emotional one. Newsworthy. The photo was front page and the top hit on every news media outlet—Zack and Skye embracing. She never shed a tear, but he shed many.

It wasn't the only thing that was newsworthy. The secret love life of Taylor and Jamie is the top trending story across all platforms, nationwide.

Sherriff Muncie and the gang listened to the entire conversation between her and Jamie, which she'd recorded on her phone, just like she wanted. A suicide note was found in her purse—two, actually. The first one was dated the day of the vigil. According to the contents of the note, her plan was to jump from the roof of City Hall during the event designed to honor her daughter because as a mother, she could no longer bear the pain and sadness. (God forbid she not be the center of attention, Zack had said.)

Perhaps it's why she decided to give me her purse and claim frantically that she was going to the bathroom. I don't know if I should be flattered or disturbed that she wanted me to find the note. Regardless, she must have lost her nerve because she didn't go through with it, and I never found it.

But Taylor went on to make bigger and better plans. It was impossible, she realized, to rescue Skye without tarnishing her own reputation, so she drafted another suicide letter that painted her just as much a victim as her daughter. This second one was dated the same day she and Jamie died and consisted of three words written on a Post-it: *They are right.* It was stuck to a four-page printout of hate comments people had written about her on internet articles about Skye's disappearance. On the last page was her handwriting again:

None of this would have happened if it weren't for Jamie. Check my phone recordings. If Skye is found, tell her I love her, but I hope she forgets about me. She deserves better.

In the front seat of her car, next to her purse with the notes, they found large quantities of various medications she stole from the hospital where she was employed, leading authorities to believe she was going to overdose after she got Jamie's confession on record. Another medication she allegedly stole—ten syringes of naloxone. I constantly wonder if she knew why Jamie had asked her for those syringes, and how he got her to do it. There are many things I find myself wondering about.

If we are right that Taylor's plan was to die heroically and send Jamie to prison, she failed. Zack and the media continue dragging her name through the mud—and Jamie's—posthumously.

She cared more about her own image than the safety of her child!

She would rather have died than expose her infidelity!

So gallant of her, to sacrifice her life in order to finally confess to her husband her ten-year affair with his best friend—the murderer of his father!

But in my heart, I feel sorry for her. In the little time I'd gotten to know Taylor these last two weeks, I felt like she was just a girl—a selfish one, yes—who had gotten in over her head. She eventually grew out of her high school snobbery but could never adjust to this small-town life. I truly believe she wanted to be a good wife and mother to Zack and Skye, but she was so deep into her lies and deception, so wrapped up in herself, that she was beyond the point of no return. And having to deal with Jamie? No woman could handle him. Jenysis's words, not mine.

* * *

The one thing everyone agrees on? Skye Flynn is a beautiful little miracle. She's captured the heart of the nation—unbeknownst to herself, as she is simply a happy-go-lucky child who loves wearing pigtails. Her first day back at school was televised, and when a reporter asked her if she was happy to be back, she said, "Yes, my dad packed me unicorn cupcakes for lunch. Wanna see?"

Zack shut down the media inquiries shortly after, refusing to exploit his daughter. He said he wanted to preserve her innocence for as long as possible, and if she still had it after what she went through with Jamie, then he sure as hell wasn't going to allow the media a stab at it.

I was unable to attend Logan's memorial service because I was in recovery. But I'm still mourning this tragic loss of a great man. I'm being released today, a solid week later, with strict orders not to even attempt to walk for four months. Both ankles needed extensive surgery and are currently covered in plaster casts. It's possible I'll need supplemental surgeries in the future, the doctor told me. She jokingly said I wouldn't need anesthesia, that I'm a living, breathing epidural. I hadn't heard that one before.

My left hand fared better than my right, a simple bandage placed over the skinned knuckles. My right hand, though—it needed surgery too, to fix the splintered bone. Another bulky cast renders that hand useless, and I'll be ambidextrous by the time this is all over.

Thankfully, the puncture wounds and bruises from Jamie's plank are all superficial and healing nicely. I'm as useless as a sack of potatoes, but I'm alive.

I'm on extended sick leave from work, obviously. Janna came to visit and droned on and on about how Shelby continues to ruin everything, and she said to please get well soon so she can fire her. And I just nodded and smiled, because I'm picking my battles now, prioritizing my own dynamics and logistics, and dealing with her screwup isn't one of them. Who knows? I might quit when all this is said and done.

My parents left nearly an hour ago. I made them leave, actually, because they just wanted to argue with me about being in Miami by myself. "You shouldn't be alone, Noa. You should stay with us for a while," my mother said.

"I won't be alone. I have Hector," I replied, at which my mother huffed and my father rolled his eyes. But I'm not fighting this one right now, either. I'll see them at Christmas. And that's what I told them as I sent them away.

Hector is driving me home now, and I use my cast to punch the automatic button on the door. The window glides down until it disappears, letting the briny humidity infiltrate his vehicle. I close my eyes as the thick air whips against my face, and I breathe it in.

He chuckles. "Uh, you don't realize this, but it's really hot out there."

"I realize it. I can taste it and smell it. I've just missed Miami." I roll the window back up before Hector suffocates.

"Miami has missed you, too, beautiful." He winks. "Welcome home."

SIX MONTHS LATER

SKYE GASPS AND grabs my hand as we enter the opulent lobby of the Ritz-Carlton Orlando. She tips her head to gaze up at the massive chandeliers, causing her Minnie Mouse hat to topple off.

I reach down to retrieve it for her, balancing precariously on the heavy walking casts.

"Thanks, Noa. This place is like a castle! Can we stay here the next time we come?"

I laugh and straighten the lopsided ears she replaced on her head. "Sure! Three nights at the Disney Polynesian Hotel didn't do it for you?"

She halts in the middle of the lobby, her jaw dropped. "I *loved* the Polynesian. I want to stay at all the places." She throws her hands up and spins, then retrieves her own hat when it inevitably falls again. She grabs my hand and leads me toward the lounge, dodging the throngs of families and suitcases.

"We can stay at all the places. Don't worry. Your dad will be here soon to pick you up."

She plops in an overstuffed armchair. "Why is he picking me up here? I thought you were taking me home."

"I offered to," I answer as I lower into the chair next to hers. "But he said it would be ridiculous for me to drive all the way from Orlando to Everglades City, then all the way back over to Miami." I shrug.

Our gazes drift toward the automatic doors as an older couple in Hawaiian shirts glide by, followed by Zack.

She grins as he meanders toward us and stops at the edge of the oriental rug under our chairs. "How was girls' weekend in Orlando?" he asks as Skye leaps from the chair and throws herself into his arms.

"So fun! Me and Noa got to go to the front of all the lines for the rides. We didn't have to wait one time!"

Zack swings her up onto his hip and leans down to hug me. "Really? Noa, did you pay for fast passes?"

"No, I rode around the park in an electric wheelchair. I just started walking again a couple weeks ago, and look at me." I gesture to the giant boots. "I look like an astronaut."

Skye places her Minnie ears on Zack's head. "Because Noa is . . . *disabled*. And people in wheelchairs don't have to wait in lines," she says matter-of-factly before removing them.

"Well, well, well. I guess there's a silver lining to everything," Zack says as Skye shimmies down his leg. He glances around the foyer, clicks his tongue. "Well, I did just drive all this way. Care to have a drink, Noa?"

I follow his tilting head toward a mahogany bar with LED lights illuminating the perimeter. With a glance at my watch, I say, "Sure. I have a few minutes."

"Can I go over there?" Skye points toward the patio, where a woman dressed in Victorian clothing and a top hat along with a man wearing a fanciful robot costume have just started a skit.

Zack crinkles his face. "What's that?"

"The steampunk characters from that restaurant down in City Walk. Probably an advertisement," I reply. The woman flails her hands animatedly, speaking in a high-pitched British accent—a magnet to all the awe-struck children.

"Okay," Zack relents, and Skye runs toward the gathering crowd.

She stops about halfway and makes an about face, careening toward me and throwing her arms around my shoulders. "Thank you for taking me to Disney, Noa. I love you."

I snuggle into her hug. "I love you more. I'll see you soon, I promise. Maybe next weekend?"

Her head bobs and she scurries off.

Zack and I stare at her as she retreats. "God, I love that girl," I say.

He chuckles. "You and me both." Then he turns to me. "Should we head over to the bar? Or do you want to stay here and I'll bring you a drink? Since you're, you know—*disabled*."

I wave him off and heave myself up. "It's ten feet away, I can walk. Besides, it's closer to where Skye is. We can keep an eye on her."

My phone alarm goes off just as we arrive at the bar. Restroom break. "I'll be right back," I say as he's getting situated on a barstool.

When I've finished, I exit the bathroom to see a tumbler of brown liquid sitting on the counter with a pink bendy straw. "One Noa cocktail," he says, gesturing to it with his own glass, sans straw.

I laugh. "Dr. Pepper on the rocks? I'm surprised you remember."

"It's your favorite. Oh, only this time it's loaded. With rum. Cheers." He clinks our glasses.

He points to the stool next to him, and I sit. "How'd Skye do this weekend?" he asks.

I nod. "Very well. She talked a lot about her mom. Which is normal. Healthy, even. But she had fun. I think this was good for her. I even got her to cry a couple of times."

Zack grins, his knuckles drumming the countertop. It annoys me, but this is what he does to avoid addressing his feelings. "You're good for her," he says.

I beam. "Thanks."

I can't take it anymore. I reach over to rest a hand on his constantly thrumming knuckles.

He chuckles and rakes his hands through his hair instead. "Sorry."

"How have you been?" I ask.

He sighs. "Oh, you know. How you'd expect a guy to be after his daughter was kidnapped, his wife and best friend die, and then he finds out they'd been sleeping together all along. Oh, and that his dad never did have an affair, but was actually dead all this time . . . My life is a bowl of cherries."

"I'm sorry, Zack. This whole thing. I still can't wrap my head around it."

His knuckles, they're thrumming again. "But I gotta stay strong, you know. For Skye. For my mom. No rest for the weary."

"Stop punctuating your rants with clichés. And please, for the love of God, stop drumming the counter."

He leans back and releases the most pleasant, cathartic laugh. "Noa, this is why I love you. You don't put up with my shit."

I groan theatrically to hide my discomfort. "Please. You don't love me."

He's silent, which makes me more uncomfortable. Then he clears his throat. "Can I ask you something?"

"S—sure . . ."

"Would you have married me? If Taylor had never come to our school?"

The chaos around us—the chattering people, the rolling luggage, the whimsical performance—they fade into white noise. "In a heartbeat."

His elbows go to the counter, his head in his hands. "God, I fucked up so bad."

The sound of melodious children's laughter brings our surroundings back to the forefront, and we turn toward the jovial skit that's captivated Skye and many of the other patrons. She waves at us, and we wave back.

I sip the last of my Noa cocktail until the straw makes loud sucking noises around the melting ice. When he puts his fingers on my wrist, I jump and look at him. His eyes are boring into mine.

"Can we try again, Noa?"

I nearly drop my glass. "What?"

"I told you before, Taylor was a mistake. And look. Look what happened to us. But Jamie was right. I never stopped loving you. I was a dumb, foolish child back then. I lost the best thing that ever happened to me." He's inching closer, having nearly scooted off his stool. "And sitting here with you now, in this place . . . Skye over there, so happy. You did that, and—I am completely and utterly in love with you."

I stare at him, frozen, as Skye's laughter floats above everyone else's.

"You're it for me, Noa. You always have been."

I blink because it's the only thing I'm capable of.

"You love Skye, and she loves you. You're a better mother to her than Taylor ever was. You're the only reason she's come this far. I see the love in your eyes, every time you look at her. It just makes me fall in love with you even more. Please, Noa."

Somewhere inside me is a young girl flipping for joy, crying, rejoicing in this day she never thought would come. And I let her; she deserves it. She's been through enough.

I set my glass on the counter. "Zack, when you broke up with me for her . . . a part of me died inside. The part that loved you unconditionally. You killed it."

He leans back, drops his eyes to the floor.

"You were the love of my life, Zack. You broke me so severely that for years I craved nightmares because they were better than reality. You made your decision that night."

His hands grip his hair, tears pricking along his eyelids. He swallows hard. "I know. It was wrong. But we have a second chance. We're still young! We—"

"Zack, I will never stop loving you. But I'm no longer *in* love with you. I will be your family, Skye's family, and I will cherish the memories we made while we were dating for as long as I live." I stand, and so does he.

It hurts me to behold the pain on his face. So much so that I apologize.

He shakes his head. "No, don't. I am where I am today because of the decisions I made. None of this would have happened if I'd stayed with you."

I frown. "Don't give me that much credit. Jamie would have pursued me, just like he did Taylor. He wanted whatever you had. You know that."

He smirks and shoves his hands in his pockets. "No, he wouldn't. He would have wanted you, but he would've never acted on it. You're way stronger than Taylor ever was. She was easy prey. He respected you more than that."

His hand comes up, and I tense when he caresses my cheek. "I made my bed, and now I'm lying in it." Both hands are on my face now, and he's standing inches away.

"Seriously, with the clichés, Zack."

He chuckles, then grows serious. "Can I kiss you?"

The young girl inside me faints. I ignore her, because that's all she is—a child. I'm the adult. "No. I'm sorry. I'm dating Hector." I place my hands over his and slowly lower them from my face.

He drops them to his sides, his face falls. "Can we talk about that?"

I wave to the bartender for the check. "Uh, sure. What is there to talk about?"

"It's just that . . ." He rubs his jaw and gazes around, avoiding eye contact with me. "Well . . . I looked him up, Noa. This Hector from Miami, attorney at law." He waves air quotes around, and I puzzle my face.

"I can't find him anywhere."

I laugh as I grab the check from the bartender. "Well, then you didn't look very hard."

He snatches it from me. "Sometimes people tend to . . . create people in their minds for whatever reason. To keep them from being lonely, I don't know."

I halt in the middle of trying to grab it back. "What are you saying?" My hand falls to my lap.

"What is Hector's last name?"

"You know, you truly can't google someone if you don't know their last name. Seriously, you didn't look very hard." I dig through my purse for dollar bills, but I don't know the total because the check is crumpled in his fist.

He presses his open hand on my frantically searching wrist. "Okay. Why has no one ever met him?"

I blink. "They have. My mother met him the first time I was kidnapped. He said she was lovely."

"Yeah? And what did she say about him?"

I shake my head. "She didn't say anything."

He gives me a look—*I told you so.*

I dart my eyes up to his. "Jamie met him! Jamie stayed at my place, they talked. They hated each other."

Now he looks at me with sympathy. "Jamie's dead."

I roll my eyes. "So you think I've dreamed Hector up?"

He shrugs a single shoulder. "Like Millie?"

"C'mon, Zack. Millie wasn't real, and I knew she wasn't. She just . . . helped. Gave me really good advice." I wave my hand dismissively and reach for the bill.

He pulls it away. "Like Hector does?"

I double over, cackling like a crazy person. "I've never had delusions in my life, Zack. I don't know what you're talking about. This is ridiculous. Give me the bill so I can pay and get out of here. I have plans. With Hector, actually."

Resigned, he sits back on the stool. "At what time?"

"He's meeting me here at twelve thirty."

He nods. "And what time is it now, Noa? What's the time?"

I glance at my phone. Then stare at it is as a realization sinks in. "Twelve fifty-five," I whisper.

"Noa . . ."

I swallow the lump in my throat. He's not here. Something's wrong—he's never been late.

He uncrumples the check and reaches for his wallet. "I'll pay. The drink was my idea," he says patronizingly.

I shake my head. "No. No, I—" I choke on the lump. Numb, I reach for the check anyway, but before I can grab it, before he can pull it away, a third hand comes into the mix and plucks it from Zack's grasp.

"This one's on me. Sorry I'm late, Noa. Traffic."

There's a kiss on my cheek, a hand around my waist, and I'm staring at Zack's horrified face. My soul sighs in relief as I throw my arms around Hector's neck. "You scared me, I thought something had happened. It's twelve fifty-five, Hector!" And I playfully shove his shoulder.

He laughs. "You thought I stood you up?"

"No, I thought you got in a car accident. I didn't even realize the time until Zack—oh!" I gallantly swing a hand toward Zack's pale face and slack jaw. "Hector, it's with greatest pleasure that I introduce you to Zack." I smirk.

"Zack, it's a pleasure to finally meet you. Hector Morales. I've heard wonderful things from Noa. And for what it's worth, you're in our thoughts and prayers."

Zack's head bobs as he stands to shake his hand. He clears his throat. "Thank you. I've heard a lot"—a swallow—"a lot about you too."

Skye approaches, the steampunk skit having ended. "Hi, Hector," she cries. "Noa and me had so much fun. Come with us next time, okay?"

Hector gives her a high-five, assures her he will, then turns back to Zack.

I lean down to Skye and whisper in her ear. "Your daddy didn't think Hector was real."

She jerks back, looks at me, then bursts out laughing. Soon I'm laughing too, and we laugh and laugh until we have tears rolling down our cheeks.

ACKNOWLEDGMENTS

PLEASE NOTE THAT the information in this book about CIPA is solely derived from my research, and in no way do I claim to be an expert on the subject. Noa's experiences are simply a work of fiction, so please forgive any liberties I may have taken regarding the condition or any experiences with this condition. Thank you for understanding!

To my agent, Maria Napolitano, and the Bookcase Literary Agency team—Flavia Viotti and Meire Dias—this 1,000% would not have happened if you hadn't taken a leap of faith on this sad, indecisive girl who likes to write. Thank you for believing in me and fighting for me, and for always, always being kind.

To the Crooked Lane team—Rebecca Nelson, Melissa Rechter, Madeline Rathle, Dulce Botello, and Kate McManus. You all are a powerhouse! Your support and enthusiasm have taken this debut to a level I never thought possible. If ever there was a group of professionals I want on my side, it's this one. I'm keeping you all.

To my editor, James Bock, and your uncanny ability to crawl into my brain and interpret flawlessly what I'm trying to communicate. I'm going to need you to tap into that power now, because I can't conjure up words to describe what a gem you are. Thank you for polishing this manuscript to a level I never could've done in a million years.

To my husband, Robert, who is my biggest supporter and would move mountains just to make me smile. You are my soulmate, monkey. I love you. LOML is ours and no one else's.

To my sons, Robbie and Andrew, for being the best sons a mother could ask for. I am so proud of both of you, and I love you beyond time, space, dimensions, and all the things.

To Tarryn, who has been there from the beginning. You're my lifeline in more ways than you'll ever know. Whatever thick, evil substances our souls are made of, they're the same thing.

To Joyce Sweeney and Jamie Morris, my writing coaches for over a decade now. Thank you for imparting your wisdom and knowledge to this eager sponge.

To Claire Contreras for your amazing friendship! I'm so happy for you that you escaped Miami, but I really love it when you come back and play with me.

To my beta readers—Melissa Carpenter, Stephanie Drewry, and Jennifer Evans. Your excitement toward this manuscript was like pouring gasoline on my tiny, pathetic flame. Thank you, thank you!

To Kirk Weiss, for your excellent friendship, your mad attorney skills, and for providing me with alcohol at all times. Your people are my people until the end of time. And even then, your zombies will be my zombies.